ROSEWATER

ROSEWATER

LIV LITTLE

DIALOGUE BOOKS

First published in Great Britain in 2023 by Dialogue Books

10 9 8 7 6 5 4 3 2 1

A CIP catalogue record for this book is available from the British Library.

Hardback ISBN 978-0-349-70295-7
C-format ISBN 978-1-408-71705-9

Typeset in Garamond by M Rules
Printed and bound in Great Britain by Clays Ltd, Elcograf S.p.A

Papers used by Dialogue Books are from well-managed forests and other
responsible sources.

Dialogue Books
Carmelite House
50 Victoria Embankment
London EC4Y 0DZ

www.dialoguebooks.co.uk

Dialogue Books, part of Little Brown, Book Group Limited,
an Hachette UK company.

For Suhaiyla

1

Several loud thuds ricochet from my front door and reverberate through my little space. My flat is a collection of plywood walls that have been haphazardly installed to give the illusion of being an apartment, rather than a tiny studio. Even a quiet hum in the sitting room can be heard from the kitchen. And so the doorbell's piercing ring, followed by three frenzied bangs, makes my head sting. The blind still being down makes it hard to tell what time it is. Stretching over the body in my bed, I grab my phone, and through squinted eyes see that it's 4 p.m. I'm not ready to get up.

Last night was a heady mixture of sweat, tangled bodies and the synthesised melodies of funky house. The club, ordinarily begging for attention, had been wedged full. A collective of DJs took it over for the night. They had thrown a party which, despite initial hesitation from our manager, was strictly no boys and no straights. After my shift and more shots of sambuca than one person should ever consume if they want to maintain a functioning liver, Bea had come back to mine. It was our routine. Her soft, naked body was now sprawled out next to me in bed, her heavy breathing evidence of deep sleep. She has a remarkable talent for sleeping through a ruckus.

I put my phone back down and my eyes involuntarily start to close. But then the bangs and rings restart, creating a hysterical cacophony that sends sharp electrical currents through my head and forces me awake.

It must be Jim from downstairs. He's the only person who would call on me with such vim. I try sending a telepathic message telling him to shut the hell up, but the bangs keep coming. I'm gearing up to stand and open the door, to be overwhelmed by the foul stench of a man who smokes forty fags a day. There's a bitter nausea now bubbling in my tummy. I know that only a cup of sugary tea can make me human again. Saliva gathers in my stale mouth in anticipation.

A T-shirt with Ms Lauryn Hill's face on it and a pair of chequered boxer shorts are the only clothing options in my immediate vicinity. My legs, which have been left fragile and shaking from last night's antics, do their best to haul my tender torso out of bed and into the hallway. Next to a small, square, glass award I won for my self-published poetry collection, I see a pair of rectangular sunglasses in my basket of miscellaneous items. I put them on in an attempt to settle my surroundings, which won't stop spinning.

Walking slowly towards the door, the impatient nature of Jim's bangs is beginning to test me. He is fucking miserable and I'm not in the mood to have him lose his shit at me because the delivery driver has got our flat numbers mixed up yet again. One time, he made a poor attempt to disguise the fact that he'd nosed around in a package of dildos clearly labelled with my name.

I manage to repeat the motion of placing one foot in front of the other, steadying myself on the wall as I move along the hallway. But as I near the front of the flat, it isn't Jim's voice I can hear. It's someone with an unfamiliar accent. I can't place it.

'Miss, we know you are in there. We can see your lights are on and we have a warrant.'

I hold my breath and quickly shuffle into the kitchen to the left of me, doing my best to avoid being spotted through the sliver of glass in the front door. Sneaking a look, I part the raggedy net curtain above the sink in front of me, still half expecting – hoping – to see Jim's bony, yellow-tinted frame leaning on the balcony. But standing outside, I see part of a stocky, olive-skinned man with a freshly trimmed head. He's clutching an envelope with uncomfortable ease.

'Darlin', if you let us in, we can make this whole process go a lot faster and with a lot less drama.' Another voice chimes in from behind him.

Looking around, the bald guy clocks my eyes through the gap in the curtain and, without hesitation, attempts to lodge his chubby arm in through my open kitchen window. I'm faster than him though and manage to clamp the window shut before he gets his arm inside. There's a faint knock as his fingers meet the plastic trim of the window frame.

I panic slightly. 'I'm not your "darlin'". There's nothing for you here.' My voice cracks.

'You're not doing yourself any favours with that attitude,' the first man replies. There is clear and deliberate discontent in his voice.

'Are you Elsie Macintosh? Is this your property?' the second voice says. I don't answer, but it continues. 'Like Derrick said, you can make this as hard or easy as you like. We have a job to do and if you are Miss Macintosh, we have the right to repossess this property under Section 21 and Section 8 of The Housing Act of England and Wales. You failed to show up to your court hearing on not one, but two occasions.'

There is a deafening silence as I think back to the stacks of warning letters that filled me with dread. Letters that are now stuffed in a drawer in the kitchen. Letters so overwhelming that I didn't know what do with them at the time. The amount of debt I've been repaying for the past few years has exceeded my income. And though a handful of companies allowed me to extend my payment plan once, there were no second chances. The ever-looming threat of debt collectors has been debilitating, like being eaten alive from the inside. Every moment of potential joy has been overshadowed by the possibility of having my security pulled out from under me. Now, at this moment, this nightmare has finally become a reality.

'We're going to need you to show us some ID.'

I don't move.

'Miss, we're not going to leave. We can do this all day. We have a warrant, so we do have the right to enter the property. But we are offering you the opportunity to leave without us having to enter forcefully and damage your belongings in the process. This is your last chance though.'

I take shallow, disjointed breaths as my chest stiffens. I want to hurry back to the bedroom, close my eyes and wish it all away. I move slowly into the hallway, my hands and feet growing in heat and stickiness. I think back to the YouTube video series on pranayama and anxiety that I watched a couple of weeks ago.

Take long, deep breaths and focus on how your body feels.

Remember, you've got this, sis, a woman with purple sister-locs had said.

My heart is beating too fast. I sit on the floor and lean back against the peeling green wallpaper in the claustrophobic corridor. I close my eyes and imagine the woman from the video guiding me breath by breath. Despite her disclaimer that her sessions shouldn't be used as an alternative to therapy, this is what they have become. Mum used to say that only self-important people would waste money paying people to listen to their problems, which probably weren't even problems to begin with. They were just the realities of life. I used to think she was right but now I'm not too sure.

My mind is in a loop, jumping between the intermittent loud bangs at the front door and the texture of my syrupy palms, and despairing at the fact that I have no backup plan. Here, in this moment, I think I might die. My heart feels as though it's going to erupt.

Breathe in deeply and feel your body. Let out all the tension and stress of Babylon as you exhale.

I piece together soundbites from the woman's videos and try to breathe. Almost a year ago, when I first moved into this flat, I had breathed a sigh of relief to finally have a home, and now look at me, barely staving off a panic attack on the hallway floor.

'Oi buffting, what's that noise? Are you coming back to bed?' Bea calls out from the bedroom. Of all the times she chooses to wake up. How am I supposed to explain to her that there will be nowhere for me or my things or her to go in approximately five minutes? Humiliation takes hold of me.

Hi, I know we just fuck and that this isn't serious, but I'm now homeless, and it would be great if I could stay with you.

'One sec,' I manage to respond in between shallow breaths. Focusing on the words from the anxiety video, I continue to breathe in and out for what feels like several minutes, attempting to block out the bangs at the door. None of the anxiety articles, posts, books, videos or podcasts speak about what to do in the middle of an eviction. They never talked about what to do when the walls around you are *literally* caving in.

My breathing slows just slightly and I pick myself up off the floor and practically crawl back to the bedroom. I consider joining the boxes of journals nesting safely underneath the bed.

'Drama with that neighbour of yours?' Bea asks. She looks cute and sleepy and a bit messy, still recovering from yesterday.

'I wish.' I struggle to enunciate. The inside of my mouth feels numb.

Bea notices. 'What's going on?' she asks, unsure of how to approach a situation that is clearly unfolding fast.

I drown out her voice and look over her head to a shelf in the corner of the room and a scattering of well-loved books sitting on the record player. I spent years convincing my nan to let me have it, so I could play my own vinyls. She hadn't played a record on it for at least ten years, instead favouring a selection of YouTube playlists of jazz, soul and R&B that she'd discovered after Mum bought her a computer for Christmas. Nan's record player was the first thing I'd unpacked. I'm still working on her passing her vinyls on to me.

I suddenly grab a Kelela album from the trunk of records that lives at the end of my bed, move across the room and place it on the turntable, turning the volume dial up to its limit.

'Listen, there's a situation outside,' I splutter, struggling to find space to breathe.

'Okay!' Bea shouts over the music. 'Be specific.'

'Bailiffs,' I yell back.

'Oh shit.' Her face drops with concern. 'What did you do?'

I feel my brow furrow involuntarily.

'I mean, what's going on?' she corrects herself.

'What's going on is that I have to leave, and they can apparently force entry. But I think all the doors are locked, so I have a little bit of time to figure out whatever the fuck I'm supposed to do.' I'm trying to convince myself, as well as Bea.

'Lucky I don't need to be anywhere this morning,' she jests. She's trying to lighten the mood but my facial expression shuts her down. This isn't funny. And I don't want her to talk, I want her to disappear.

I want to disappear.

'Last night was fun …' she continues as the bedroom fills with the haunting melody of 'A Message'. Appropriate. I sit on the edge of my bed and close my eyes, hoping that I'll magically be somewhere else by the time they open again.

The bangs from the door are only audible between song changes. Bea moves the corner of the duvet, which has been covering her right thigh. This is her way of inviting me to take its place, to get me out of my trance. She can't tell, but my breathing is still a bit stilted, though my palms are no longer as sweaty. Maybe those wellness videos really can help. I decide I can ride this anxiety out. I lie back on the bed next to Bea, comatose, and think about Crocker House.

Even though it was years ago, I still remember the elation I felt when I was offered a studio in a block in Walworth. This was after two-and-a-half years at the Hub, the youth hostel I'd been living in after I left home. It didn't matter how unloved the studio looked; Crocker House was all mine. I was there for five years until the council sold off the building to a developer. There were demonstrations, a small amount of media coverage and a standoff between residents, supporters and the community, but we all knew the outcome. Families who had lived in Crocker House for years were forced to relocate. I was one of the lucky ones because the flat I was moved into, the flat I'm in now, was nearby and not everyone was allocated something in the same area. I heard rumours that some people ended up outside of London, families forced to completely reconfigure their lives away from the communities that they had been a part of for so long. Social fucking cleansing. I never saw the majority of my neighbours again. Every time I think about that place, my stomach drops. It was like the heart of the area had been ripped out and replaced with something soulless. And here I am again, thinking about what home should feel like, about to lose another one.

My reflections are interrupted by the scratching of the Kelela album as it jumps where it always does, on the third song, and reveals that the bangs have passed. For a moment, I consider the possibility that it might be over, that I've bought myself a little more time to figure my life out. I jump up and replace the album with *Baduizm*, which is next on the pile. My eyes move across the room, taking it all in, from my books, half-open cardboard boxes, records resting against the trunk, to the few pieces of art mounted on the walls. There is one image I particularly love, a print of an oil painting filled with hues of yellow and brown by an artist called Sola Olulode. In the picture, two people lie on the grass, their heads adjoining. It's a peaceful image, full of rest. I was so happy the day I bought it at an exhibition in Camberwell. It was the first thing that had gone up in the flat. I crave that peace now.

'Want some?' I turn around to face Bea, who is gesturing to a half-smoked spliff from last night.

I accept and inhale, sitting back down on the bed. My thoughts quieten. Bea straddles me, pursing her lips over mine, inhaling directly from me. Ignoring the fact that she hasn't brushed her teeth, we sort of half-kiss. I force myself to focus on the music, but every time there is a pause, I listen out in anticipation for the return of the bailiffs. The repetitive words of 'On & On' circulate as I inhale again and again. Warmth fills my chest as we reposition our bodies so that Bea is resting on me. Her boobs press gently against my side and one of her long, thick twists tickles my thigh.

'Your heart is pumping mad quick,' she says. 'What do you want to do?'

There's no way to answer her question, so I don't. I focus instead on my heart rate, breathing in the spliff for five and exhaling without making a sound. 'Otherside of the Game' now plays and Erykah Badu's soothing questioning mirrors my current situation. I don't know what I'm gonna do.

Suddenly, there is a loud crash at the front door and before I can react, I hear the pattering of footsteps making their way down the hallway. I'm light-headed from smoking and the only weapon vaguely within reach is a broom in the corner of the room, which I get up and grab. As I open the bedroom door, the two bailiffs are standing in front of me.

'Get out! Get the FUCK out!' I shout.

Bea is now standing up. I don't know how, but she's managed to get dressed quickly, ready to back me if required. Both of us are frozen, waiting for someone to make the first move.

'Now, there's no need to use that sort of language,' the one in front says, scolding me as a reminder that I'm now in his classroom, his space. He's wearing a name badge that says 'Derrick'.

'You can't force yourselves into people's homes like this. I didn't let you in,' I say, feeling equal parts embarrassed by and angry at the situation.

'You are being evicted today. We have the right to execute this on behalf of the J&P Housing Association, who require the property back this evening. I'll need your keys.' Derrick reaches out his hand.

I start to shake my head. I want to say that I need to be left the fuck alone. But instead:

'How do you even know that it's me you're looking for?'

'Well can we see some ID?'

'I don't have any, so you'll have to leave.'

'Is that weed we can smell in there?' Derrick leers further into the bedroom. 'And what's that purse over there? Does that not have any ID in it?' He gestures to my beaten-up leather wallet resting on the wooden corner unit. I say nothing.

'Listen, we can call the police if you'd prefer. But I'm not sure you really want that. Whose side do you think they'll take? Us or the person who failed to keep up with rent and show up to their court hearing?'

'Twice,' the accomplice adds.

'See, Miss Macintosh, you've lost all rights to remain in this property. We are simply doing our job.'

'Bea, record these goons.' I don't have any plans to share the footage, but I hope it might make them reconsider.

'Please don't film us,' Derrick says.

'I have the right to film you, scum of the earth. You're in my flat.'

'I'll remind you that this isn't your property anymore. It's the property of J&P Housing. And like I said, we are here to execute a warrant. Here you go.'

'I don't know how you sleep at night,' Bea shouts from behind me.

The sidekick hands me a piece of paper. It reads:

Under Section 21 The Housing Act of England and Wales,
You were made aware on 12 April that due to a signifi-
cant amount of rent arrears you would be served with three
months' notice to vacate the property unless the outstand-
ing debts were recompensed by 12 May.
As you failed to attend your court hearings on 5 May and
12 May, or settle what was owed, J&P Housing Association
retains the right to repossess your property.
J&P has tried to contact you several times. However, we
are yet to receive a response.
If you would like to dispute this case, we recommend that
you seek legal counsel.

I read over the letter slowly and digesting each word feels as though I'm being force-fed a spoilt piece of food.

Bea puts on the hoodie of my Adidas tracksuit and, with the neck drawstring and hood all the way up, stands next to me in the doorway. She keeps filming the men in my hallway, still telling me to leave.

'We've placed an eviction notice outside your house. This is completely lawful. You can make this easy, or you can make it harder than it needs to be. We don't want any trouble.' The sidekick accompanies this with a smile so sensitive and out of place it's like he's playing dress-up, only pretending to be the baddie who throws people out of their own homes. I feel my chest tightening again.

'Does this make you feel like big men? Forcing entry into people's flats for a living?' I kiss my teeth, which surprises everyone, myself included, as the only people I know who still do this are my Guyanese elders. There is nothing more for me to say. My stomach gurgles. I push past the men, leaving Bea in the hallway to defend my flat, as I run into the bathroom just in time for a vicious eruption of bile. I sit there in the silence for a moment, my heart thumping in my ears. I splash my face with cold water afterwards and swig a healthy amount of mouthwash.

'Everything all right?' one of the men calls from the other side of the door.

'Listen ... are you really telling me there's nothing I can do? This was supposed to be a place for me to settle,' I say helplessly to myself with my back against the bathroom door. I feel pathetic.

'Miss, our hands are tied. If you'd attended either one of the court hearings, you might have been able to come to some sort of arrangement. But you're out now. Look, we can give you ...' he stops speaking, it seems, to check the time.

'What do you think?' he asks his friend.

'One hour. We've already been waiting outside for a while.'

'Yeah, one hour should be enough to get your things

together. Looks like you're what they call a minimalist anyway.' The casual cruelty stings.

'We're going to wait right here though. So don't try and pull any stunts.'

'Like I have much choice,' I murmur. There's no point begging these two foreign creatures to recognise my humanity. Even if they could do anything to remedy the situation, I know they wouldn't.

I hear the men make their way into the kitchen and turn on the kettle, and I'm left with sixty minutes to pack up my worldly belongings and figure out whatever the fuck I'm supposed to do next.

I take a deep breath, stand up slowly and exit the bathroom. I find Bea where I left her, standing guard in the hallway and still filming.

'Look, I don't need people at the club finding out about this mess. Okay?' I say bluntly.

'I'm not trying to get involved with your business like that,' Bea replies, part indifference, part concern. 'But I'm here if you need me.'

'Cool, well thanks for recording,' I say as she hands me back my phone. 'You can go you know, you don't have to stay. I'll see you later.'

Bea delivers a piercing look and offers to help me pack, but I don't let her. Bea and I fuck a lot, and yes, she's jokes to go out with, but it's not like we're *real* friends. We never talk about our feelings.

As she makes her way out of my flat, I look around at the place I've called home for the past year. The bailiff is right. It is minimally decorated. Moving into this flat was the first time in a long time I'd had more than just one room to myself and so, despite how small it is, I didn't have furniture to fill it out. I'd had big plans though: seeds I wanted to plant; original pieces of art I wanted to hang.

Putting the remainder of my things into boxes won't take long. I have more books and journals than anything else. I've been collecting them since I was fourteen. My earliest finds were from the school library and then the rest came from charity shops, New Beacon and gifts from my nan. I'm easy to buy for. All possessions so treasured that I can't even bring myself to make notes in them. I'm sure this is part of the inherited DNA that comes with growing up around first-generation West Indians. Every time I'd visit my nan's, she'd have a story to tell about a serving dish or glassware set that would only come out on special occasions. *This pot is older than you*, she'd say.

I pick up my phone then and scroll through my contacts, wondering who to call. Mum and Dad are a no go, and they're probably busy with the twins anyway. Nan will do nothing but worry if I call her, and besides, there's no way I'm moving back to Bristol. Even though my nan's house was my sanctuary growing up, my brain's natural response to that city is still to avoid, avoid, run. I know she'll suggest I come back. I'm not sure I have the energy for that conversation right now.

I only have a handful of other saved numbers in my phone, and, sandwiched between the names of girls I've met through work or dating apps, there's Juliet. My best friend. We've been tight since school, and even though we haven't spoken for a couple of months, she's the one person I know I can always call. Before I have a chance to think about any outstanding awkwardness or what I'll say, she answers the phone.

'Elsie?'

'Um, hi J.'

'What's wrong?' Her intonation flutters with worry. She knows me too well.

'Are you busy?' I sniffle.

'Elsie, where are you?' Her voice grows in seriousness and concern. She lowers the music playing in the background. Sounds like she's with a client.

'I'm sorry to have to ask but there's been a bit of a situation ... Can I please stay with you? Just for a little bit and—'

'Of course, you can.' She cuts me off. 'Always.'

I can't respond.

'Elsie are you okay? Are you at your place?' she continues.

'Yes.' My voice breaks.

'I'll be there soon, okay? I promise everything will be fine. Just try to breathe.'

And for the first time in the last hour, my body really listens.

2

I pack my belongings into boxes with urgency. Twelve to be precise: one for kitchen utensils; three for clothes; another three for books and records; two for shoes; one for artwork; one for bedding; and a final smaller box for my journals. Even though I'm rushing, I treat each item with respect – remembering the moment they found their way to me and into this home. But then there's no time left so I leave the curtains as they are and take a final orbit around the place that I thought was mine, trying to ignore the impenetrable gaze of the bailiffs who have been delivering their thirty . . . twenty . . . ten-minute countdowns as promised. My rotation is interrupted by a faint and familiar tap at the front door. It's Juliet.

The first thing she does is squeeze me tight. My eyes glaze with a thin layer of water. She's here, for the first time in months. Juliet looks past me into the flat to one of the men, who upon hearing the door, reinstated his initial position in my hallway. Her eyes move then to the boxes on the floor, all without letting go of me. I want to stay in her arms, but we first have to manoeuvre all my belongings into her bedraggled green Mini. It's about to be written off, but her grandma left the car to her after she died, so Juliet refuses to get rid of it.

'Who are they?' Juliet whispers into my ear, her curly hair sticking momentarily to my warm, damp cheeks, a combination of sweat and tears.

'Bailiffs.' I gulp down the shame. 'We have ten minutes to get everything into your car. Then they're locking the door.'

I can see Juliet's brain kicking into gear, just like it used to when we were twelve and she'd concoct some witty comeback that would disarm wannabe bullies in the playground. Though the look on her face is serious now, more brutal than usual.

'I'll put the back seat down and we'll get everything in. Don't you worry, Els.'

Releasing me from her tender, perfumed squeeze, she picks up the heaviest box with her thin but capable arms, and without complaint walks it out the door and towards the lift. I follow with a lighter box, disregarding the bailiffs who are looking from us to their watches and back again. After six efficient laps, everything is inside the lift, which Juliet has wedged open with the biggest box. We're both sticky with sweat from the end-of-summer heat. Juliet's pulled her hair back and there is a sheen covering her nose, cheekbones and forehead. Her honeyed skin is glowing, and I realise how much I've missed her. Even after everything, she's here.

When I return to the flat to finally hand over the keys, the men are barricading the front door.

'I just want to make sure there isn't anything else still inside.'

'We checked. Nothing is there, and you've had more than enough time now anyway.' Derrick opens out his palm. Reluctantly I strip my bunch of keys of their miniature clog keyring and bottle opener and drop what's left into his hand.

I do not want our skin to touch. I feel Juliet's comforting hand on my shoulder.

'Let's go, my love. We'll be back at mine before you know it.'

I let Juliet turn me around, taking in the block for the last time as I join my things in the lift. There isn't much air in the small space, and I hold my breath until we make it to the ground floor. My body feels weak, and we still have to load up the car.

After another thirty minutes of manoeuvring and strategically lifting boxes into the tiny car, we're on our way. I stare out of the window. I feel numb. When we stop at a traffic light, Juliet places her hand on my lap.

'It will all be all right Els, I promise.'

I don't respond. There is too much anger and sadness inside for me to know what to say. Then there's a release brought on by the safety of Juliet and this bashed-up Mini. She plays the one album she has, the self-titled *Tracy Chapman*, and the tears start to fall. I sob loudly. I don't remember the journey back to hers.

Once we finish unloading my things from the car and into Juliet's eclectic two-bedroom flat in Peckham, I pause at the purple-framed mirror by the front door. The person staring back at me looks faint. Washed out and tired. I don't want to look at her. I move into the sitting room.

I flop onto the sofa, exhausted and drained. Juliet sits across from me in her favourite yellow velvet chair. Patchwork quilts hang on the walls and wine bottles take the place of candle holders. Even though she graduated a few years ago, Juliet's flat resembles her room in Leeds university halls. Surprising, because this is a home she actually owns. It seems to be a rite of passage for Juliet and her friends to be set up in their own flats once they graduate. Imagine.

She lights some incense and a hypnotising cloud of nag champa rises, dancing in circles across the room. The knots are still tight in my stomach. I can't tell if they are a product of anxiety or the remnants of my hangover, though last night now feels a very long time ago. It's probably both. This isn't where I envisioned myself being at twenty-eight. It's probably not how most people envision finding themselves at any age.

Juliet breaks the lengthy silence.

'So, what happened?'

'I got evicted, J.' Grumbling is my only means of communication. I have no energy left to feel anything outside of dejection.

'I should've known this was going to happen. They pay me cash in hand at the bar, and even though I make half-decent tips on the weekend and I get a little bit from the odd gig, I'm still fucked and in debt. It's exhausting. I'm exhausted.' I pause to catch my breath, then notice Juliet's worried face. 'But this isn't going to be a permanent thing J, I swear. And I know the way we left things was a bit tekki, I just ... I just don't have many options right now.'

'None of that matters anymore, Els. You know you can stay here as long as you like.'

'I'm so pissed off at myself, at everyone, at everything. It's not like I've just been sitting around not trying to make things work. That place was the first flat that felt like it could be a forever home, with a permanent lease on the table.' I shake my head wearily and blot my eyes with my fingertips, willing my face not to crumple and allow more tears to flow.

'I know. It's the first place you let me see.'

Oh Lord, I hope Juliet doesn't start to cry too.

'Trust me, you wouldn't have liked the other places.' I avoid her eyes by staring down into her colourful woven rug.

'I love you, Els. I'd love anywhere that you call home.'

'Well, even I didn't love those places. They were grim. This was my chance to make a real home for myself. We aren't the same, you know. This is yours.' I use my hand to gesture at the walls that envelop us. 'No offence but I don't expect you to get it . . .'

'No, Elsie, don't do that. I'm right here listening. And I'm so sure your poetry is gonna blow! It's going to happen for you so soon.' She tries to reassure me in the familiar way she always does. I usually love her unwavering optimism but not tonight.

I've been writing poetry since I was eight years old and the consensus is that my writing bangs. I even won junior poet laureate a couple of years back and people printed one of my poems (about an imagined utopia in which straight things didn't exist) on totes and T-shirts. Every show, someone would request I read the poem itself, and begrudgingly I'd perform it. But my poetry and these giggs don't pay the bills. No matter how hard I try.

'I need to figure out what to do next,' I proclaim, my eyes moving over Juliet's outfit, which is so bright and distracting I'm surprised I didn't notice it earlier. I wonder if she wore it to teach in. Juliet has an eclectic sense of style, which sits somewhere between 'Put Your Records On' Corinne Bailey Rae and 2007 Solange. Her clothes either come from charity shops or a hundred per cent sustainable graduate designers who use waste material to make their collections. There's no in-between.

She pulls out a pre-rolled fag from her baccy tin and moves over to the sofa next to me – a sofa found on one of her Free-cycle raids some time last year, despite being able to afford an entirely new one. When I pointed this out, she told me that she was learning how to upholster online, but the chair is still wearing its tattered brown slip. I guess she hasn't found the time yet.

'Why don't you finally give yourself the space and time to figure out what it is you want to do? I can stop Airbnb-ing the other bedroom. I know it's only small and I usually use it for work, but you can have it for now. And I'll be chanting for you every day. Maybe we can chant together?' Juliet's mum, Helen, has been practising Buddhism for ever, and when I used to go to hers as a kid, the sounds of *Nam Myōhō Renge Kyō* would echo throughout the house. I smile at the memory.

'I appreciate you but mi tiyad.'

She giggles.

'You're lucky that your mum let you figure out what it is that you wanted to do. That "find yourself" stuff is some white girl shit.' Juliet's dad is Jamaican but her mum, who was a single parent in all but name is mixed-race (British-Ghanaian).

Juliet smiles and I smile then too. It feels good and it keeps me from crying.

'Maybe we should unpack your need for things to be black and white,' Juliet retorts, pretending to adjust a pair of invisible glasses and assuming the pose of the concerned therapist.

I roll my eyes dramatically. 'You grew up different.'

Juliet's dad was high up in a big law firm, which meant they'd often bounce between cities, as he'd be tasked with launching new branches. During their longest stint in one place, her mum had a job teaching at Colston's Girls' School in Bristol, a job she took so that she'd have something to do. My mum had pushed hard for me to get into the school on a bursary. Unlike my genius younger brothers, I didn't scholarship my way in. I was assigned to be Juliet's buddy on the first day, and despite being polar opposites, we stuck.

'Let's leave that conversation for another time then,' Juliet replies. 'How are you feeling, Els? Today was a lot. Has your anxiety been playing up? Are you still doing those breathing exercises I sent you?'

'I don't need you to therapise me today.' I try to muster up a playful tone but all I can get across is the exhaustion I feel. I see hurt flash across Juliet's face.

'I'm on the same side as you, you know. There's no need to snap at me.' She says this in the way a parent would after their teenage daughter screams, *I hate you!*

The last thing I want is for Juliet and I to have another argument so soon after being back together.

'I'm sorry, J. I'm just stressed. You should probably ignore everything that comes out of my mouth for the next hour.'

'What kind of debt are we talking anyway, Els? I can lend you some money. Or get you some therapy sessions. Whatever you need.'

I immediately shake my head. 'No, you're doing more than enough having me stay here. Plus, we're not talking about a couple of hundred quid.' I deliberately ignore her comment about therapy.

'Have you been borrowing money? Who from?'

'I don't wanna go into it.'

She folds her arms in protest.

'Fine. I've been taking out payday loans … I had a credit card at one point, and I don't know, there was some other shit.'

Juliet says nothing, stunned.

'You know, there have been a lot of times when I really needed the money and didn't have anyone who could lend it to me. Not everyone goes to university, J, and not everyone has a flat to fill with trinkets and little elephants from their travels to India.'

I pick up a miniature sculpture resting on the mantelpiece and roll it around my palm. I can see Juliet in the corner of my eye deciding not to rise to the bait.

'Elsie, I'm so sorry that this is happening to you.'

'It's not your fault, but thanks.'

'You'll get through it. We'll get you through it. I'm sure you can get some sort of payment plan going or something?'

I've already tried these, but I don't feel like walking Juliet through my financial chronicles right now.

'Maybe.'

'And if you need some extra money to get you where you need to be, why don't you do some work with me?'

Juliet isn't referring to her day job as a primary school teacher, surrounded from 8 a.m. to 3 p.m. by snotty four-year-olds. Instead, she is referring to her second job: working as a cam girl. I accidentally let out a snort at the suggestion. She looks offended.

'Sorry, J. I'm just laughing at the thought of veiny

appendages and the creepy men that they belong to hiding behind their computer screens. You know that shit isn't for me. I'm not as free-spirited as you ... Plus, they'll probably be able to tell it's a dyke talking dirty to them!'

In spite of herself, Juliet slithers onto the floor and starts cackling uncontrollably at the thought of me in front of the camera. The room fills with deep belly laughs.

'There are loads of ways to do it though, Els. Sometimes I just do it over the phone. And do you really think that the rest of us aren't pretending most of the time? I'm telling you, they aren't discerning enough to know whether they're talking to a girl who loves dick or you know, you. There are loads of queer women who do sex work. Plus, you are a poet, so you've got bars for days.' She catches her breath, her laughter starting to peter out, and looks me in the eyes.

'I can be smooth, I can't lie,' I say, feeling around in my back pocket. I find a baggy with crumbs of weed in it. I crumble it up in the ball of my right thumb and index finger and pinch some of Juliet's tobacco. I roll and light it off the candle on her coffee table.

'I'll think about it,' I say, exhaling.

'Okay, good.' She smiles at me and the dimple in her right cheek surfaces.

'You know the one thing I have thought about?' I say, exhaling perfectly round Os that imitate the shape of my shaved head. 'I've always been curious about the idea of fucking straight guys with a strap. I like the idea of having them in a vulnerable position. Is that fucked up?'

Juliet shakes her head and smiles. I continue.

'That or being paid to be really mean to them. A girl I used to work with was a dominatrix. I never understood how she kept a straight face.'

'I'm here for it,' Juliet replies. 'I think there is something feminist as fuck about a queer woman being paid to make straight men squirm.'

We turn quiet, unsure of what should come next. Juliet suddenly stands.

'Let me grab some bedding and take my things out of your room so you have space. I want you to feel at home. And know that if you need to talk about anything, I'm here.' She looks at me, and I know that every word she says is sincere. There is something naturally maternal about Juliet. She wants me to know that she loves me unconditionally and will always show up, no questions asked. I feel a pang of guilt for not speaking to her these past few months.

'I've got a shift at the club tonight as well, so I better get cracking,' I say with a sigh.

After pulling my room together for me, Juliet retreats to her bedroom and I'm alone for the first time in hours. From the freshly plumped pillows on the bed, the smells of lavender and other essential oils I can't decipher engulf the room. I lie on top of the mattress in the foetal position and think about what I would be able to do if life wasn't preventing me from doing more than just surviving.

My eyes sag involuntarily, along with the rest of my body, still and tired and ready to sleep. I have nothing left in me, but I can't afford to be late or miss a shift. Especially not now. And I don't want to give the bar owners any ammunition to suggest that my heart isn't absolutely invested in the job, even though we all know that it isn't that deep. Plus, Bea can be a chatty patty, and I'm worried that she'll tell someone about today if I'm not there. My phone beeps, reminding me that work starts in an hour and fifteen, and my thoughts resume their frantic, uncoordinated dance routine.

3

I arrive at the club twenty minutes late for work. Only a handful of misplaced stragglers would dare to arrive before 10 p.m., so it's fine. Based just off Streatham High Road, Boom is one of few surviving Black-owned local businesses around. Well, technically coBlack-owned by Jamie and his boyfriend, Antonio, who is Italian and loves to snap his fingers and call you 'sis'. The bar is a disjointed but comfortable mash-up of different genres and hasn't had a proper facelift in years. Instead, Jamie and Antonio continue to buy mismatched decorations to hide the ageing walls. Leopard-print lamps and matching throws live on every table, rainbow stickers decorate the bar and glow-in-the-dark stars sprawl across the ceiling. Even though the pay is whack, the staff remain. We like it here.

I drop my stuff off in the staff room (a tiny area in the back of the club that also operates as a storage cupboard), and in an attempt to bring me back to life, splash my face with cold water in the metal sink in the corner. And it works; considering that I feel like shit, my face isn't giving away as much as it could. I've been blessed with the ability to avoid bags piling up under my eyes, regardless of how little sleep I've had the night before, and this means that right now, I can pretend to be a relatively normal, sentient human being. I grab the cleaning products and start wiping the tables, putting minimal effort into reversing the years' worth of drink and bodily fluid build-up that engulfs the booths at the side of the dance floor.

As I manoeuvre around to the bar and begin peeling cling film off the spout of a bottle of Jameson's, she walks in. After everything this afternoon, I'd forgotten that it's just Bea and me tonight on shift. Sunday is always a quiet night at the club.

'All right?' My head nods like a bobbing dog as she walks towards the bar. We have been sleeping together – on and off – for the past year. It's a casual thing, so the fact that she's been given an accidental window into my life makes me feel unprotected. But no one else is here, so my worry eases a little.

'I mean, are *you* all right?' Bea replies. 'I didn't think you would come in after what happened earlier.'

'I'm cool, I have options. Don't worry about me, babes.' I exaggerate a wink, feign normality, change the subject. I'm not sure if Bea is buying it. 'You *really* enjoyed yourself last night, which is the main thing.'

'Um, *we* enjoyed ourselves,' Bea responds in a playful tone.

'It's true, you are mad bendy.' I weave my fingers together, close my eyes and shift my head from side to side in an imitation of Bea dancing. That's what she does for a living (outside of working at the bar). She's done some pretty cool shit, including starring in a video for Kelis. Mostly she dances for independent artists in the UK.

I notice that Bea looks even hotter than usual, which distracts me from my own self-consciousness. Even though last night was incredibly messy, her hair is now the product of a fresh twist-out and her signature purple lipstick is perfectly lined. I look at her fitted green T-shirt, with no bra underneath, for a second too long. She notices, but before she can joke, we are interrupted by Jamie.

'Okay girls, remember we have that sambuca that's about to go out of date. So, make sure to use that up first. It's about a week away from turning,' Jamie instructs.

My stomach almost regurgitates at the thought of its liquorice flavour, coating the inside of my mouth without mercy.

'Also, it's Antonio's birthday and I'm taking him to Sexy Fish. So, you can close at 1 a.m. if it isn't busy. Do not forget to take out the bins like last time,' Jamie continues, with an emphasis on the second part of his sentence.

As he heads out the door, Bea shouts, 'Have fun!' behind him.

'Thank God it's just us,' I say, letting out a sigh. 'I couldn't manage another evening of chat about him and Antonio's future wedding plans.'

'Are you sure you don't want to go home? I can manage on my own. Like only two people will probably come in.'

'Like I said, I'm cool, Bea.'

'Also, turns out my friend has a spare room going in Camberwell. It's like seven hundred a month plus bills.' Bea looks at me expectantly.

'We make, what? Seven-fifty an hour here?'

'Yeah, I know. It's why I moved back into my mum's. It's impossible to save. But don't worry about it. Just thought you might need something for the short-term.'

I nod in a way that says *I'll think about it*. Juliet and Bea's extended parenting couldn't be more different to my experience. My childhood was cut short when Mum and Dad had the twins and I was suddenly expected to cook, clean and care for them. And go to school. My parents couldn't afford a childminder, and because Mum always seemed to hate Nan, and Dad's parents were all the way in Manchester, everything became my job. They both worked sixty-hour weeks and were constantly exhausted. I was tired too and my grades started to slip at a time when it mattered. But Mum was unsympathetic. Dad was complicit. It wasn't a house where any of us spoke about how we felt. Everyone just kept things bottled up. On the rare occasion that I had time to breathe, I'd go to my nan's house for respite. I wish I could have lived with her. I resented Mum so much growing up and Dad even more so for being mute. Soon as I could leave that house, I did. And without their support.

Fortunately, a group of people walk into the bar and jolt me from my thoughts. And even though they're loud and massively overdressed for where we are, I'm grateful for their disruption. People who aren't from the area only tend to pass through on weekends, as the selection of restaurants and wine bars around is limited. I turn away from Bea towards the group.

'Can we see a wine menu?' asks the blonde in the group, as her friends make themselves comfortable in a booth.

'We don't have one, but if you tell me what you're after, I'll let you know if we have it,' says Bea.

'What sort of reds do you have? I usually enjoy a Syrah. Something like that would be great.'

'I think we have one red. A Malbec,' I chime in.

'Just a Malbec?' the woman scoffs.

'Yes. Just a Malbec,' I reply, keeping my voice level.

'Can I taste it?' I don't know where this woman thinks we are, but I pull out the bottle of wine as requested. Under her watchful gaze, I open the bottle and start to pour some out into a glass.

'That's enough,' she says bluntly. 'I asked for a taste, not the whole glass.' I turn in the direction of Bea as the woman smells the wine.

'You see, this is how you try wine. Watch me,' she continues. I wait a few seconds before turning to face her, unsure as to whether she's really demanding that I watch her sample the wine. Bea interjects.

'Do you want it then?' she asks, her right eyebrow raised.

'It will do,' the woman says before also whispering, 'You two could learn a thing or two,' under her breath. It's loud enough for us to hear.

'Are you done?' I have to bite my tongue, because what I really want to do is tell her to move from in front of me.

Bea steps in. 'We'll bring the wine over, so you can go sit down with your friends. Just a moment.'

After delivering the red wine to the table (which I realise is the first bottle I've ever sold), Bea pours me a shot of tequila and grabs a slice of pre-chopped lime. We don't usually do shots so brazenly at work, but we need a release. The alcohol stings the back of my throat and clears my mind.

'What are you doing tonight?' I ask Bea.

'I'm supposed to be staying at Karma's later.'

I pause. 'Karma?'

'It's his artist name.'

I roll my eyes. 'Oh my God, Bea! That's worse than the last one. What was it? Nicey Boo, Icy Boo ...'

'Icy Blu,' Bea corrects me.

'I'm dead. I'm actually dead.' Laughter pours out of me, and

I feel lighter. Bea's forever dating the same-looking mixed-race boys with dreads who make heavily instrumental music. Her current boyfriend is clearly no different.

'I can't stand you,' Bea says, trying to conceal her laughter. 'Anyway, it isn't like you have a place for us to go right now.' The sting of her words causes my face to drop.

'I didn't mean ...' Bea's voice trails off as she clocks the weight of her words. I say nothing.

An hour passes and just as we are lining up our next shot, the blonde woman shouts out at us from the booth.

'Um, excuse me, we're ready to pay.' She clicks her fingers.

I've spent time working on my temper but can see that Bea, a couple of shots deep, is ready to go off. I wave back at the woman sarcastically.

'You can pay up here.'

'How was the wine?' I ask as the group approaches the counter.

'Below average,' the woman responds proudly, as though it is her duty to leave us with a poor review. Her friends shuffle awkwardly.

I print out the bill.

'Twenty-nine ninety-nine for that?! The cheek!' She rolls her eyes and sighs before getting out her card to pay. I wish I'd charged her more.

I smile and wave theatrically as the group finally leaves the bar. As they're on their way out, Maggie enters. I'm unsure how long she's been standing at the door. I'm glad to see her.

'They were bloody awful, weren't they?' she says, walking over to us. She orders a bottle of Sol – the same as always.

Maggie's one of the few people at the club whose energy I love. She doesn't have any children and has spent her life travelling the world playing in darts tournaments. She could be a griot; her stories are deep, rich and full of flavour. She's always wearing men's shirts and baggy trousers, usually accompanied by a black beanie, worn at a slight angle. She has a very specific swag. I can picture Maggie in the rave back in the day, getting pure gyal. She loves to tell me about the underground parties she used to attend and how they were filthier than anything our generation could possibly imagine. She also tells me stories about the harassment she had to deal with from all angles. Those are less fun. She loves a good 'back in my day', something I'm in need of tonight, so I'm disappointed when she says:

'I'm only stopping for one tonight, girls. Oh and Elsie, I wanted to give you this.' She hands me a first edition copy of *I Wonder as I Wander*, Langston Hughes' autobiography. It has a faded grey cover and multiple pages are folded over. A loved copy. I'll enjoy sifting through the annotations she's left behind.

'Maggie, you always come through with the gems. Are you sure?'

'Yeah, take it, enjoy it. I've read this one cover to cover.'

'Thank you, Aunty,' I say, testing out the title.

She doesn't respond, just smiles, content with her Sol in hand as she plops a fiver on the table. She notices the empty shot glasses lined up behind the bar, and through a smile and raised eyebrows says,

'Drinking on the job?'

'Well . . .' I feel like a teenager caught drinking illegally.

She shrugs playfully. 'I'm not here to judge, just don't get yourselves into any trouble.' She settles down on one of the bar stools opposite us, bottle in hand.

Under her watchful gaze, I refrain from grabbing another shot.

Just then, the blonde woman comes stomping back in.

'I left my purse in here, on the counter. Where is it?' She looks back and forth from me to Bea and back again.

'What does your purse look like?' Bea asks.

'It's a black cardholder. Ralph Lauren. Small.' The woman says these words with the brevity of someone ready to explode. Her lips and teeth are stained from the red wine, and her cheeks redden to match. She's clearly already decided that we're the enemy.

'Nothing like that has turned up, but you are welcome to look around,' Bea replies, doing her best to conjure up charm for a woman whose attitude she can't stand.

The woman scurries around the booth where she had been sitting and then finds her way back to the bar. She looks Bea straight in the face.

'I know I left it here. On the bar.'

Keeping her voice steady, Bea says, 'Well, it's been a quiet night, so it's likely we would have found it already.'

'I'd like to speak to your manager.'

'Our manager isn't here, but feel free to leave a message and we'll pass it on.'

'I know one of you two has it.'

Bea's had enough. 'Listen, your friends really ought to check you. You didn't leave your purse here and don't ever get it twisted and think that because I'm on the other side of the bar that you can speak to me anyhow.'

'What about the CCTV camera over there? I'd like to see the footage,' the woman demands.

'It's broken,' I say.

'So, you should probably leave now,' scoffs Bea.

Maggie, who is watching this all unfold, pipes up.

'Look, why don't you come back tomorrow with a clear head and when you're able to speak to these girls like they are real people. They wouldn't take your things. I've been coming in here for a long time.'

The woman stares at Maggie for a second, and then 'ugh' is the only sound she makes. She shrinks in a way I've seen happen around Maggie before. And out of nowhere she starts crying. Unmoved, the three of us look at each other, unsure as to what we're supposed to do next. The woman can't really be crying. Sensing she's not going to get a reaction, she eventually turns and makes her way out of the club.

'Nah,' says Bea in Maggie's direction. 'It's a good thing you're here because that could've ended a whole lot differently.'

'I think you two should go home. You aren't gonna get very many more people coming in now. Are you all right?'

'Yeah,' says Bea, who is shaking her head.

'We were going to close up soon anyway. Thanks for the book, Maggie. The second drink is on the house!' I hand Maggie a bottle of Sol for the road.

Maggie looks at me with concern. I worry that I'm wearing the stress of the day all over my face, or maybe I'm just visibly drunk. I've managed to keep my feelings in check all shift but the way that woman just spoke to us has stirred things up. I quickly check myself in the bathroom and a single, salty tear streams involuntarily out of each eye and down my face. I know if I let any more stray there will be too many for me to avoid crumpling into a mound on the floor. I wash my face with cold water and decide to resume flirting with Bea. Sex and poetry are my safe places, and right now I only have access to one. I don't think now is the time to confront how I'm really feeling deep down.

A handful of customers trickle in and out for the next hour. As the last person leaves, Bea and I start to wrap up bottles in anticipation of the end of the shift. Just the tequila is now left out on the counter.

Bea looks up and grins. 'Shall we finish it off?'

She pours out four shots each of tequila. Each one tickles my throat and simultaneously loosens my muscles. Bea stops after the third, but I keep going. I drink until I can just about feel a sensation in my fingers and toes, which reassures me that I'm still alive. By the time I have my fourth, I'm slurring, and Bea tells me it's time to stop.

'Where are you staying? What's the address? It's time to get you in a cab.'

'Juuuuliet's,' I sing merrily.

Bea tries to hold my thumb over my phone and on the third attempt, it unlocks. I can hear her having a conversation with someone but I'm unable to decipher who it is.

Everything is pretty hazy by the time we pull up outside Juliet's. My limbs are weighing me down. It's an effort to get them to move. Juliet makes her way towards the car and Bea opens the door on my side of the vehicle. The driver asks us to hurry up but it takes several attempts to steady myself before I'm up, only able to stand by leaning on the side of the car.

'I can take it from here,' Juliet says. She thanks Bea, who turns to get back into the taxi, and offers me her bony shoulder to lean on.

My two girls.

4

I wake up in a daze, not dissimilar to the night before. This time it isn't knocks at my door but my phone vibrating non-stop. Sandwiched between conspiracy theory re-shares from my nan and a reminder that it's time to get my coil removed and replaced, there are several missed calls from Jamie. I wince at the memory of the periods I battled with before having my Mirena fitted, which fuses into panic at the oddity of Jamie calling out of hours. What if didn't lock up properly and the bar was broken into in the middle of the night? I can't remember how we left it . . . But I ignore my phone as I hear footsteps shuffling down the hall.

'All right in there?' Juliet knocks gently on my bedroom door to deliver what I know is a sugary cup of tea.

'Mmmm,' I groan.

'I've got to run out,' she says, pushing the door slightly ajar. 'But take it easy today. I'm worried about you.' Juliet's face is full of concern.

'Ugh, fuck's sake,' I mutter to myself, snippets of the night coming back to me. 'You were a mess last night.' I pull the duvet over my head.

'And it's bloody cold in here, Els. Don't be funny about

using the heater I put in over there. This is the coldest room in the house. I still don't understand how my room is like a sauna in August but in here its icy regardless of the temperature outside.'

I'm cautious about running up Juliet's electricity bill so have opted for wearing extra layers in bed instead, something I've not done since I first left home and would have to decide between buying food or topping up the electricity.

Juliet sits down at the bottom of the bed. She has a serious look on her face.

'What is it?' I ask.

'I just thought that maybe at some point we should talk? Maybe it's a good time?' Oh God, not now.

'Talk about what? We talked a lot yesterday.'

'If you call one conversation a lot, then sure.' Her eyes widen and she sucks the air into her cheeks disapprovingly. I consider disappearing entirely under the duvet.

'Els, if you want to continue to act like you have no idea what I'm going on about, then that is fine. But we both know you aren't being entirely honest. I can't force you to talk, but I am here when you're ready.' She says this without breaking eye contact and her words penetrate my core. Why does she always want to talk everything through? There are some things that are better left unsaid, untouched, unbothered.

My phone resumes buzzing aggressively. It's Jamie calling again, and I welcome the interruption, so I answer and smile at Juliet apologetically. Her eyebrows shoot up in response. But before I can even say 'Hello,' Jamie goes:

'You and Beatrice need to come in right now. Did you get my email? We've had a serious complaint.'

'No, I haven't seen it yet. Everything okay?' I say, attempting to avoid sounding too croaky.

'No, it isn't okay.' Jamie sounds particularly pissed. 'You need to come over to the club now and make sure your friend is there too. She's not answering my calls.'

'I'll be there as soon as I can,' I say reluctantly, before hanging up the phone. I know that he wouldn't call me out of hours unless absolutely necessary.

'What happened?' Juliet's looking at me like I'm some sort of sick chicken.

'I'm not sure,' I reply, at the same time opening my inbox to find Jamie's email.

Beneath online shopping and Just Eat discount codes, there is one unread email in my inbox with the subject header, 'URGENT'. I open it to see Jamie has forwarded a Google review of the club, dated this morning. I read it aloud.

1 day ago

AVOID AT ALL COSTS

This has to be one of the most horrific places I have ever been. My purse was stolen last night by the two members of staff on shift, and on top of this they were exceptionally rude all evening. They did not know the products sold and despite the venue being empty all night, they hardly acknowledged our existence. Their CCTV cameras are FAKE. I have no idea how they expect their business to survive. I suggest they re-evaluate the shoddy service and most importantly, unreliable and untrustworthy staff.

I will never step foot in this business ever again and strongly advise others against it too.

'That bitch.' The words leave my mouth involuntarily. 'If I don't take a minute to breathe, J ...' I'm pissed but also relieved she didn't see us doing shots.

Juliet's jaw is on the floor, her sympathetic pose turned to outrage.

'What the actual fuck? I'm so sorry, Els. I have teacher training today, ahead of the new school year. But I'll call you when I'm on a break. Probably around eleven, okay? I love you. Call me if you need anything.' She strokes my arm and runs out the door.

Several WhatsApps from Bea pop up on my phone.

Bea: Have you seen the email???

Bea: I CANNOT

Bea: Who does she think she is?

Bea: I'm honestly so angry

Bea: dfgndgbdfsxa`cszvdsc!!!

Bea: I'm getting ready to head in now. Meet at the entrance for Streatham Common station?

Bea: 1 hour?

Bea: Fuck's sake

Bea: I just can't believe it

Bea: I'm PISSED

Bea: Okay, I'm getting ready to leave. 1 hour? Is that ok?

I reply: KMT Yeah. See you in an hr.

I move to the kitchen and gulp down the remnants of black coffee from the percolator that Juliet's left on the stove. The fact that she takes her coffee consumption seriously is a definite perk of living here. Right now, I need all the caffeine

I can get. I inhale the restorative scent of the rich coffee beans.

After a quick wash, I throw on a pair of loose-fitting low-rise jeans, black platform Dr. Martens and an oversized green denim jacket. As I look in the mirror there are a few dry patches on my cheeks. These usually flare up when I'm stressed. I douse my face in a healthy amount of almond oil and get some on the gold hoops that line my ears. As I wipe the remnants of oil away, tired brown eyes stare back at me.

I open the door and cool air blows gently against my scalp. There is a damp cloud of grey hanging over Peckham, but I chance going out without an umbrella. It's only spitting, which is sort of refreshing. It's Monday morning rush hour and Peckham Rye station is packed – people push through the barriers like their lives depend on it. As my Oyster card beeps, it informs me that I'm now in the red. Classic.

There's one available seat on the train, next to an older Black man. He could be sixty or eighty-five. It's hard to tell. He looks up and down at me disapprovingly, just like the way my dad's dad did when I walked into his house after a two-year-long hiatus. I half expect him to cuss me out: *I'm surprised you even remember that you have a grandparent* and *Is this what the kids are wearing these days?* But this man beside me is properly fly. He is wearing a full suit, pinky ring and hat cocked to one side with perfectly polished shoes. I smile at him and he goes back to flicking through his paper.

As I pull up at Streatham Common station, I see Bea standing by a signpost. She is less dressed up than usual, softer, but just as beautiful.

She looks relived to see me. 'That woman.'

'Don't get me started. I'm just gonna keep breathing because otherwise . . .'

Bea links her arm into mine and steers us in the direction of the club. She smells good, her perfume a mix of vanilla and brown sugar. Approaching the entrance of the bar, we sigh in harmony.

'Well, if it isn't the trouble-making couple,' Jamie says in greeting. Antonio stands next to him. His lips are pursed tightly together like he's ready to insert himself into the conversation. He always perks up when given the opportunity to tell someone off.

'Do you seriously believe anything in that horrific review?' Bea asks.

'Do I think you would steal from a customer? No.'

'Well, why are we here then?' I snap.

'You are here because of *that*! Honestly, your attitude needs work. You can't scare off the limited number of customers we have. That on top of your consistent lateness is just . . .' Jamie gestures at the air.

'Look, we didn't give that woman anything more than she gave us. Are you saying that it's okay for customers to talk to your team like shit?'

'If they are paying, you need to be nice to them. And there is no need to swear. This is still work.' Jamie tuts at me and shakes his head dramatically.

Bea backs me up. 'This woman was rude. Properly rude. Next level rude. Plus, Elsie has had enough of a tough time recently. Don't take it all out on her.' I shoot Bea a look. I don't want her to tell anyone about what happened yesterday.

'Oh, is this your girlfriend now? Is that why you're speaking on her behalf? Anything you'd like to say for yourself, princess?' Jamie interjects. He enjoys dousing everything he says with a healthy amount of sarcasm. Bea and I shuffle so that there is a greater space between us.

I say nothing and Antonio chimes in. 'We have a business to run and bad customer reviews don't help. Just because we are nice and friendly bosses doesn't mean that you girls can act however you want.'

Bea gives me a look to say, *Yeah fucking right you are.*

'You don't pay enough for us to be trampled on in order to satisfy the needs of a woman who has no respect and assumes that all Black people should, by birthright, be there to serve her.' I can't help myself.

Jamie's voice is calm. 'You know, if you don't like it, you can always leave. I can think of a number of other people who will be happy to take your job if you can't comply.'

Tears prickle at the back of my throat. I try to keep it together, but Bea seems to notice. 'Look, Jamie, she's already lost her flat. Don't do anything rash over some random white bitc— I mean woman.' Antonio and I flinch at Bea's remark, but for different reasons. The one thing I asked her not to mention . . . she never could listen.

'Elsie!' Jamie and Antonio turn concerned. 'Why didn't you tell us that you're going through a rough time? I can see if anyone I know has a spare room. What happened?'

'I'm not a charity case, Jamie, I'm fine. Bea shouldn't have mentioned anything.' I can't help but be sharp. Bea's eyes move to the floor. 'Listen, point heard about trying to be nice to everyone, even asshole – sorry, *difficult* – customers.'

'Just start showing up to work on time and with a little less attitude,' Antonio says.

'Is that all?' I ask, willing him to go no further.

Jamie sighs. 'You can both go. We'll deal with this woman and her review, although I'm sure she won't be coming back any time soon. We don't want to develop a reputation for terrible customer service. Things are tough enough.' He looks wistfully at Antonio. I sense there's more they're not saying, but I take the opportunity to leave.

As Bea and I leave the club, there is a discernible silence between us.

'That was close,' she says.

'Yeah.' I'm short with my response and don't look at her when I speak.

'Elsie, I . . .'

'I specifically asked you not to say anything to anyone about what happened.'

Bea's face falls. 'Sorry, I just thought they might go gentler on you if they knew.'

'I didn't need you to defend me like that, Bea.'

The truth is, Bea has seen and heard too much already. I want to say that at this moment I'm pissed off and don't need sympathy or saving, and that I feel like we're about to cross the line where casual and committed seep into one another. But breaking it off with Bea entirely feels like the best way to protect myself at this moment. So, instead I say:

'I think we should stop seeing each other'.

She looks shocked, but quickly turns angry.

'All right, Romeo. But maybe you should realise that not everything is that deep,' Bea snaps.

'Just because it's not deep to you doesn't mean it's not deep to me. But there's no point in talking anymore. We've said what needs to be said.' There's a (small) quiet part of my brain that is telling me to calm down but in the rest of my brain my emotions are large and loud and overtaking my ability to articulate anything other than anger and avoidance.

'You're fucking insufferable sometimes, you know that? Don't try to move to me when you remember that I've got something you want.'

Bea turns and storms off in the opposite direction to the station. The air is sticky and I watch for a minute as she walks across the street and past several estate agents, until she disappears into the crowd.

5

The sound of smashing glass jolts me violently out of my sleep, interrupting the chaos of my hellish dream. From the kitchen I can hear Juliet saying:

'Careful, let me get the Hoover. No, no. Don't worry. Don't move.'

Juliet's friend, Andrew, must be over for breakfast. The new school year doesn't start until next week, which he has clearly taken as an opportunity to make his *third* visit of the week. He pretends to be nice but gives me secret serial-killer energy. A week ago, while Andrew was over and Juliet was in the toilet, he asked me if I thought they were a good fit. They abso-fucking-lutely are not. Flippantly, I'd said:

'For some reason, she seems to not totally hate having you around.'

He didn't pick up on my sarcasm (proof of his murderous tendencies) and since then he's been laying it on thick with her, clearly convinced they have a future together. She's completely oblivious to this fact, even though he practically drools when she walks into the room.

There's a knock at my bedroom door.

'Els! Andrew brought you a pastry and an extra-hot almond flat white.'

Prick. It annoys me that he's remembered how I take my coffee. And that the only reason I now leave my room is because I love the soft cinnamon rolls he brings.

They're sitting around the table in the corner of the orange sitting room underneath a Frida Kahlo print.

'How's it going, Elsie?' Andrew says as I walk in. His hair is tied up into a stupid little man bun and he's wearing a huge, faded T-shirt with a picture of Frodo Baggins on it. Frodo is holding a can of Ting, and 'Lord of the Ting' is written in a serif font underneath. He's *sooooo* ironic. I feel ill.

'Fine, you?'

'Great, yeah. I was just telling Juliet that I'm thinking about organising a ski trip.'

I try not to roll my eyes. Of course, the guy who does a lot of nothing is planning a holiday, probably to the Château of Mum and Dad. 'You can come if you want . . .' he says, fiddling with his rings, knowing – hoping – I'll say no.

'I think I'll pass, but thanks for the invite. And by the way, she hates the cold.' Just like one of those party games designed to test how well a couple knows each other (which usually end in divorce), I smile because I know Juliet better than he thinks he does.

'That's true,' Juliet chuckles.

'Oh, I see. Well, maybe I can convince you to try it out anyway. I think you'll like it,' Andrew says, stretching his arm across the back of Juliet's chair and giving her shoulder a squeeze. She doesn't say anything, just finishes off her vegan pain au chocolat with a smile.

'Good luck,' I add.

Keen to change the subject, he asks, 'So, what are you two up to today then?'

Juliet had made me promise that I'd go to the housing association to try and get them to appeal their decision. I don't want to go, there are too many memories there, but Juliet is determined. She's spent the past couple of days googling and finding out more information about 'my rights', determined that the outcome of this situation will be me getting offered another flat, and for that flat to be even better than the last.

She is trying hard to share the burden, even though I've told her I can figure this thing out on my own. She never listens. We had sat down last night to discuss what my strategy should be, and I let her think it was helpful, but really, the outcome is inevitable. It's too late. Too broken. And by not showing up at court, I've already missed my chances to appeal. I'm over the momentary glitch in our relationship, but I only wish my life being upended hadn't been the thing to provide the reset we needed. She's not tried to have one of her 'talks' since the night I came home drunk from work, which means she must be over it all too.

'We're not up to much,' Juliet responds, coyly. 'But Elsie and I do have to head out in a bit. You're more than welcome to hang around here but I don't know when we'll be back.'

'No, that's fine. Enjoy your thing,' Andrew says, picking up his jacket and half-finished coffee.

'See you soon.' Juliet hugs him. He holds on a little too long.

'Byeeee,' I say enthusiastically as he closes the door.

Juliet gives me a look.

'I just don't get how you and him even became friends! Don't tell me you think he isn't pretentious as fuck?'

'Els, he's fine. He's lovely, actually.'

I sigh, deciding now isn't the time to explain to her all the reasons why Andrew is bad vibes.

Juliet drives us through Peckham and Camberwell and then into Walworth. There are several developments being built and signs shouting about their new gyms and restaurants. As we near the grey, brutalist building of my housing association, my muscles clench. The memories flood in.

I think back to the day at home in Bristol when everything exploded. I was fifteen, almost sixteen, and I had a detention at school for missing a homework deadline and was subsequently late to pick up the twins. I knew this would mean Mum would get a call at work and have to stop what she was doing to go and get them. I tried to explain this to the teacher, but she thought I was looking for an excuse to get out of my punishment, rather than questioning what was going on for me at home. I sat in detention in silence, staring at the clock and with every tick, anxiety melded with frustration. Juliet, my usual confidant, had moved to London by then, so I couldn't go to hers once I was out. I didn't want to go home either and face my mum, so I sat in a park until it got dark. Mum practically had steam coming out of her ears when I got home. She shouted at me, told me to leave if I couldn't keep up with my responsibilities and that I didn't know what it meant to *really* struggle. That I was doing the bare minimum. She said she wasn't working for fun. She was doing it so she could send my brothers to a private school just in case, like me, they weren't smart enough to get a scholarship. I think she thought she could call my bluff, scare me into submission, but I left. I went to London and moved into The Hub. Mum and I didn't speak for six years after that, and I spent all my free time coming and going from this housing association trying to find a permanent place to live.

Not much has changed.

'They might treat we like dog, but it was those hands, *her hands,* that squeezed me tight and showed me how I'm fierce, like lion,' says Juliet, quoting a line from her favourite of my poems at me as we arrive at our destination. I appreciate what she's trying to do but my nerves fail to settle. Even the most well-meaning of motivational speeches won't be able to undo the years of fear that returning to this building represents.

I leave Juliet in her car and walk in the direction of the sliding doors of the most uninspiring and uninviting building I've ever seen. My internal monologue is practically yelling, reminding me of the way this interaction will go. How it has always gone. Me being ignored, dismissed, unheard. Knots gather in my stomach and a little bit of bile rises. I'm forced to swallow. I spot a makeshift sign on the door of the lift which reads, 'out of order'. By the time I make it up the first few flights of stairs, my breaths are short, and sweat has gathered above my lip and brow.

There's a woman at the top of the stairs with a buggy and three children between the ages of one and five. She seems relatively unfazed by the huge number of stairs she's just ascended. I try to conceal my breathlessness as I pass her.

I don't have an appointment, so I go straight to the customer service desk and explain my situation. The woman at the front desk looks me up and down, her glasses resting on the edge of her nose. I mirror her position and look at her up and down in response. She takes some of my details and reads through something on the computer screen.

'I'm not sure they'll be able to help, but you can wait over there if you like,' she says finally, gesturing to the angular seating in the corner. 'And you might be here for a while. We're busy today.'

An older woman walks up close behind me and I smell her before I see her. The woman at the front desk asks her to leave. She knows her name. It looks like lots of people know her name. Seems as though she's reached a level of notoriety through following a repeated routine.

'It's time for you to go,' the receptionist says in a patronising tone. She moves away from her desk to usher the woman out of the building.

I have time to kill so I follow and walk over to the door where the receptionist has unceremoniously directed the old lady to exit. The woman is small and carries with her a retractable walking stick covered in flowers, and a tote bag overflowing with odds and ends. She's wearing a long dress with a battered jacket. She steadies herself, ready to embark on the daunting descent back down the hundreds of steps. I think of my nan.

'Are you all right? Do you need help with anything?' I ask her.

'No, darlin',' she says in a thick Jamaican accent. 'Ain't nuttin here fi mi, nuttin here fi yuh eitha.' I smile at her sadly. She's right.

So, rather than wait for the humiliation of being told that I shouldn't have defaulted on my payments because my tenancy had not yet been assured, that I really should have taken paying rent more seriously and that I'd have to apply to be put back on the housing register, that I should've opened the piles of letters and shown up to my court hearings, I offer to carry the woman's bag and follow her down the stairs. We walk together slowly, in comfortable silence, apart from the odd 'thank you' from her. I wonder whether the people who are walking past us on the stairwell, screwing up their faces at her smell, might think we're grandmother and granddaughter. A pang of guilt erupts in my chest about the length of time I haven't seen my own.

'Ignore dem,' the woman grumbles, her eyes never leaving the staircase.

We reach the bottom and I want to give her the five-pound note wedged into my back pocket, but she hasn't asked for anything and I think she might take offence at the assumption. As she slowly saunters off, I walk around the corner of the building and pause. I'm not ready for the third degree from Juliet. I spot her car, and as soon as she clocks me she smiles at me like a mother waiting to collect her child at the end of the school day.

'How'd it go?' She asks hopefully when I hop into the car. She doesn't seem to notice I've only been gone fifteen minutes.

'Yeah fine, you know. No answers for me today but I'm sure I'll have some clarity soon.' I busy myself with my seatbelt so she can't see my eyes.

'That's great.' Juliet smiles and turns the key in the ignition, and I try to level up with her optimism.

Lying in bed after tonight's shift, I decide to bite the bullet and call Bea to apologise for switching at her. Maggie had sensed that her absences at the bar all week hadn't been due to ill health. She told me to stop being stush because if Bea was what I wanted, even just for right now, I'd have to be the one to reach out. If I'm honest, I've missed her body and reckon seeing her will be the thing to pull me out of my misery.

The phone rings four times and then there's silence, even though I'm sure she's picked up.

'Hellooo?'

'Yes?' She doesn't want to make things easy for me.

'Look, I'm sorry for the way I spoke to you the other day. It wasn't cool.'

'Is that it?' Bea's not over being short with me, and I roll my eyes at her response.

'And I miss you.' I suck my lip thinking about the parts I miss most.

'Sure you do.' She pauses. 'Look, if you want to make it up to me – first do something nice for me, and second but most importantly you can make sure you'll never talk to me like that again. I'm not that girl, you know.' I imagine Bea scowling down the phone.

'Let me take you out for dinner tomorrow night. Okay?' Me and Bea have never *gone out* before, but this way our interaction won't just be about sex. It can be sex *and* dinner.

'Mmm.'

'What, are you checking your diary yeah? Sure you can make time for me.'

'Just text me where I need to be and at what time,' Bea says and then hangs up the phone.

I smile.

6

Bea comes bounding over to my table in the middle of Simply Viet, the restaurant I chose to meet in. She's completely over-dressed in a red boiler suit and black-platformed Buffalos, with bright red, ombré lips to match. I've never seen her this way before, but Bea has a way of making any outfit or hairstyle look buff. I know that she's made an effort, but it also somehow comes off as effortless.

'Wow.'

'I look good innit.' She smiles.

'Very.'

'This is the first time you've taken me out so, you know, I had to try. Just a little.'

'For a meal that can accommodate a Boom-sized budget?'

'Nah, it's cool. I've heard this place is tasty.'

'You're tasty.' I grin.

'And you're cheesy.' She tilts her head playfully.

We're back to normal.

The restaurant is full and decorated plainly with wooden chairs and tables. I order a bunch of starters for us to share: crispy seaweed, dumplings, satay chicken and a bottle of white wine.

They're cash only, and I have none, so I leave Bea pouring the wine and run out quickly to withdraw some money on the high street. Standing in front of me in the queue is a woman speaking on the phone in a faint Bajan accent. I'm sure I recognise her voice. The woman goes up to the ATM, takes out her money, and as she turns around, she notices me. It's Alison, my nan's best friend. Those two were inseparable whilst I was growing up, but I haven't seen her around for years. I heard that her and my nan grew apart, but hers is a face full of warmth that I'm happy to see. I beam back.

'Elsie?!' she exclaims, hanging up her phone call. 'Well, it's been a long, long time. How lovely to bump into you, darling.' She pushes her grey bob out of her face. 'You look well.'

'So do you! How are you?'

'Surviving, you know. Getting older. Can't believe this is little Elsie standing in front of me. I remember when you were this big.' She gestures to her knees, and I can't help but smile.

'What about you, Aunty Alison? You haven't changed, not even a little bit.'

'Ever the charmer. But don't change the subject, I want to talk about you. Are you visiting London? Or do you live here? Look at you. You look well, little Elsie. Are you still writing poetry?'

'Sort of, sort of. I still have some things to figure out.' Now's not the time to talk about my non-existent career. 'Nan didn't tell me you lived around here.'

'We're all always figuring it out. I moved a few years back. All my children are here, and some have children now. And anyway, this is where I lived when I first came over ...' She pauses, her face suddenly sad.

'Have you spoken to Nan recently? I'm sure she misses you. I miss you!' I surprise myself and give her a huge hug. Alison seems taken aback but eventually embraces me in equal measure.

'Your grandma is a funny woman.'

'I'll tell her I saw you next time we speak.'

'Oh, don't worry about that. Best you don't. You know, so much time has passed. And we . . .' She stops and I'm not sure if something has happened between them or if she's just sad that they haven't spoken.

'Anyway, sweetie, I have to go. Look after yourself, okay?' And she rushes off before I can say anything else.

When I get back to the restaurant, Bea looks a little bored.

'You were gone for a minute. Was the queue really long? I tried to save you some of these but they were too goddam delicious.' She picks up a dumpling with her chopsticks and I open my mouth.

'Mmm . . . I can't believe you only left me one! I bumped into someone I know, actually. A friend of my nan's. She was a really close family friend when I was younger but I haven't seen her in years.'

Bea seems uninterested, but she's saved by a waitress asking:

'Are you ready for mains? The duck pancakes and pho?'

We enjoy our evening together after that, devouring the bottle of wine and then ordering two more glasses. We're surprised to discover that we can chill outside the context of the bar and bed. When the bill comes, Bea offers to pay without actually wanting to, so I settle up with the last of my cash for the month. I want to laugh at myself because even when I can't afford to, I'm here, paying for food in the hope of sex. Priorities.

Outside, the air is warm. Bea rests her head on my shoulder and links her arm into mine.

'Do you want to get a drink somewhere else?' I ask.

'Or you could come back to mine?' Bea offers. 'I just moved into a new place.'

This is a relief. I have no money left. 'Sick, let's do that. You clearly don't want to waste any time.'

'Not like that. I just have a bottle of rum there. Someone bought it for us as a housewarming gift.'

She calls a cab and we start to make out on the back seat. I catch the driver gawking at us through the mirror and pull away. After ten minutes, we're outside. Bea's flat is small. It has one bedroom but there's a sofa bed – I assume that her and her flatmate take it in turns to sleep on it. She puts on Ginuwine's 'Pony'. I laugh.

'Remember the first time this started playing? The first time we were back at yours?' Bea says, laughing with me. That night, she'd commented on how rogue my sex playlist was, so when this came on, she started cracking up. We both did. It had broken the ice.

We knock back a couple of rum and Cokes until Bea guides me to the bedroom. I'm not drunk, just a bit tipsy, and I notice some guy's stuff in her room. There's a bottle of cologne sitting on the side. I take a sniff. It isn't Bea's scent.

'This isn't yours.'

'No, this is.' She points to a bottle on her bedside table. Bea's dancing around the room and undressing with haste.

'So, whose is this?'

'It's Karma's.'

I look around, suddenly understanding. 'So, this is his flat?'

'It's *our* flat but he's visiting his mum this weekend. Don't tell me you suddenly have a problem with it?'

We usually hook up at mine and I now feel a little repulsed at the thought of fucking where she sleeps with him every night. She hadn't told me they were now living together.

'I've cleaned the sheets, don't be weird. It's hardly like we're exclusive, is it? Plus, it adds a little suspense . . . someone could walk in at any time.' She pulls me into her.

I'm usually okay with being a scumbag, but today I have to tell myself, *Chill. It's fine. This is what you wanted.* I low-key thought she'd divert from the path leading to properly shacking up with a man.

I'm sitting on the edge of the bed and Bea is kneeling on the floor, and I surrender as she unbuttons my denim shirt and traces her dewy lips from my collar bone down to my stomach. Her mouth tickles the bits of fluff lining my belly button, and my whole body convulses eagerly. She stands to turn up the music and proceeds to dance, moving her body to Beyoncé's 'Dance for You'. We're still on my playlist. Every time I go to touch her, she swats my hand away, teasing me. She wants me to beg for it, and so she slowly removes her bra, one of two items of clothing she has left on. As the song comes to an end and she's fully hypnotised me, she eventually grants my wish. We're up for hours and only spend a little bit of that time talking about how this is too good to ever give up. Our communication is all physical, and tonight is enough to remind us that we'd be foolish to ever starve ourselves of each other's company.

*

There's a clock in Bea's bedroom and it reads 2 a.m.

'Want a cup of tea before we go to sleep?' Bea asks.

'Sure. Milk minus the cow please.'

From the kitchen she says, 'How many wet dreams did you have about me before you decided to take me out for dinner?'

In a pink dressing gown with a lace trim, she delivers a cup of tea to my bedside table. It has a little too much milk in it.

'Ha. Ha. Very funny.'

'For real though, you must have been extra thirsty to butter me up with dinner and dumplings.' The reason Bea knows what's up is because she's on exactly the same flex.

'So, you and Karma? You must be serious about him if you're doing up happy home,' I say, placing the focus back on her.

'I guess. But since when were you so interested in what happens between me and him?'

'I'm not.'

'Yeah, okay.'

'I mean, maybe I am a little curious.' Bea is looking at me, waiting for me to go on. 'Would he be cool if he knew I was here?'

'Obviously not.'

'Is he good in bed?'

Bea shifts uncomfortably.

'Is he better or worse than me?' I probe.

'Don't do that.'

'Just answer the question.'

'You're better,' Bea whispers reluctantly.

I smile.

'But that's not the only reason you date someone, you know? For just mind-blowing sex.'

'Bet it helps though. The mind-blowing bit.' I smile at her in acknowledgement.

'I've been meaning to tell you something ...' Bea's voice goes quiet.

'Go on ...'

'I think he could be the one.'

I'm stunned. All I can say is, 'Don't tell me you're gonna be Wifey Karma?'

Her mood shifts. 'I'm twenty-nine, you know, and I do want to have kids one day. He's not a bad option. He's a lot better than the men I've dated before.'

'You have dated worse. But real talk, you don't have to settle. Wanting kids shouldn't be a factor. You're also clearly not straight. A life of heteronormality might not be for you.'

'I am straight.'

'What do you call this then?'

'I call this "me liking what we have going on". You're the only girl I fuck with like that.'

'That's how it starts.' I wink at her playfully to disguise my discomfort.

'Like I could never marry a girl.'

'*Righhhhht.*' I nod slowly, trying to tell if she's being serious.

'Are you upset about something?' I hope she doesn't think I've secretly been hoping we'll get married. I'm just shocked at the level of bullshit coming out of her mouth. We literally just fucked and now I'm sitting in her bed listening to what? Nonsense. And denial.

'Nah. It's just ... It is legal, you know. To fuck with girls. But there is also way more to life than babies and marriage. You're twenty-nine, not thirty-nine. And even if you were, there are other ways to have kids if that's something you really want to do.'

'You wouldn't understand . . .' She trails off and I can tell she's getting irritated.

'Why? Because I love pussy and I'm not afraid that people will find out?' I'm disappointed by how she's responded but simultaneously feel I have no right to be.

We drink our tea together in silence.

7

I sneak out of Bea's flat once she's fallen asleep and walk back to Juliet's. The temporary balm of Bea's body has completely worn off. The level of straight nonsense she was speaking was exhausting. And ironic, considering Bea's knowledge of vagina is instinctive.

It takes me an hour to make it back to Peckham, following a path of well-lit roads. I enjoy the tranquility that comes with walking undisturbed at this time. It's just the birds and me.

It's 6.45 a.m. when I get back and sunlight seeps through the barely there curtains that are draped scruffily across my bedroom window. Because of the size of the room I'm staying in, it has all become familiar quickly. I know which corners of the flat are doused in light throughout the day. There's a warmth about the space, though it's interrupted by the last cardboard boxes I refuse to unpack. Here, these boxes are a reminder that I'm on my way out, rather than settling in.

There's no point in sleeping now. And besides, I don't want to have another nightmare. They've been coming more frequently and start with a variation on the same theme. The most recent: me woken up in the middle of the night and led out of my old flat by two huge men with guns. Not very subtle.

Instead, I grab my laptop and get into bed, scrolling through the 'Arts & Heritage Jobs' section on the *Guardian* website. What I'm searching for is an advert that says: *Wanted: A live-in-poet. All you have to do is think and write and we'll pay you £1,000 a week.* Or: *Poet needed to write on Grammy-nominated artist's album.* I email Jamie explaining that I'm sick and won't be at work this evening. I know I shouldn't be missing shifts but I need to try and get my life back on track, find some reliable income. So, I plan to spend the evening applying for jobs and fantasising about my future as a best selling poet.

Juliet texts to say she's going out shopping with her mum on Columbia Road this morning. She's picked up on my anti-social mood this week and knows that when I'm feeling low, I'll eventually pull myself out of it. I just need a week or so to wallow and be left alone. I hear the front door slam as she leaves the flat.

Since visiting the housing association, I've been thinking about a lot of things, which has given me temporary paralysis. Two months ago, I had promised myself I'd do two things: make more friends in the spoken word community (not just acquaintances); and submit my work to at least three competitions before the end of the year. My current tally for both stands at zero, and it makes me feel unsure as to whether there will ever be an Elsie-sized space for me in the world. Everything is so uncertain. In my head, I create a map of all the outcomes. It's messy and evolves into a smudge of dizzying scribbles. I'm a couple of years off thirty. The beginning and end of my life, apparently.

None of the jobs listed are what I'm after, so I shut my laptop in frustration and pick up my journal instead. I stare at a blank page, completely unsure of what to write about. My routine for writing isn't particularly organised. I do some of my best writing with the TV on in the background. I'd watched an interview where Roxane Gay revealed she'd written some of her most poignant works with *CSI Miami* on, and I've taken this as justification for my approach. Today though I have a desire to shut out all external noise.

I drag my limbs out of bed, pop on the kettle and grab the herbs Juliet got for me to drink to enhance my creativity: a blend of lemon balm, green rooibos and something else I can't remember. She's really into loose leaf tea, which means I'm forever ending up with unidentifiable bits of bark in my teeth after I sip my drink.

I sit down at the table in the corner of the sitting room and press play on some Jill Scott, hoping the music will help my pen to move. There are clashing prints and ornaments dotted throughout. Juliet likes things to be loud. She says her space is a manifestation of the things she loves, but I think her presence is a lot more calming than the front room suggests. I position my chair so that my view is of the street. Watching people go by provides a solid foundation for stepping into the world of the people and places that pepper my prose. This way, I can analyse people's gestures and body language to gauge what might be going on for them, who they are. The blended family, with the girlfriend doing everything to win over her future step-daughter with little success, or the lovers disguised as friends who meet in the same spot every week in secret.

Jill Scott is serenading me through these passing thoughts. Her lyricism is my safe space and even though a lot of her poetry and songs are about men, the meanings behind her words transcend gender. In 'Love Rain', she makes delicious love, and I think of the first time I'd experienced those sensations, experienced another. Every line with her is intentional and it's impossible not to feel something when you listen to her music. She's a freak and I love that about her. I've never really been into poetry or music that focuses on romantic love, maybe because I don't think I've ever been in love myself. But Miss Scott makes everything she says taste sweet. She half-speaks half-sings, mimicking the staccato of her words.

Her dewy tones are interrupted when a call from my mum comes through. I busy the call immediately, not wanting to engage in stilted conversation to make her feel, for a moment, like a good mother reaching out. Or to take away from this rare moment of peace for me.

Juliet has cones of incense dotted in various corners of her house, and I light the one sitting on the table in front of me in the hope that the clouds of smoke and their woody notes will bring further clarity to my process. The only way to get over writer's block is to write. It doesn't matter if it is shit or won't form the basis for my next piece of work. I just have to write something. Anything.

But still nothing happens. So, I change my mind again and decide to tackle my mountain of emails instead. I go back into my room to grab my laptop and return to the sitting room table: 258 unread messages stare back at me. Up top is a series of job rejections. I have been trying to find a job that links back to my aspirations for writing in some tenuous way. I will do literally anything: work as a receptionist at a library, a writer's assistant, a copywriter, a book reviewer. But despite being completely capable of taking any of these roles, the recruitment teams at these companies favour applications based on education. I've considered lying on my applications, fabricating a degree from an obscure university to see if it will get me more interviews but the implausibly of me having studied abroad for three years and still not speaking a word of Spanish makes it entirely not worth the risk.

I apply for three more jobs: one as a waitress at a greasy-spoon café, one as a nanny (even though any mothers will be able to sniff out my disdain for children), and finally as a bookshop assistant.

Maybe it's completely mad that at twenty-eight, I still want to make a living as a poet. Juliet has tried to sit down with me at various points and give me the Helen treatment, interrogating whether I truly believe in my work and ability, or if I'm just self-sabotaging because of 'deep-seated childhood trauma'. I grit my teeth through those conversations.

Wading through the mountain of emails, there's one from Maggie titled: 'PRECIOUS BROWN'. I've become obsessed with hearing about the queer nights she used to go to, and she's been rooting through old event flyers from back in the day, scanning and sending them to me. This one is black and white, crumpled at the edges, and reads, 'Saturday 15th March 1997' in bold type. 'Precious Brown' is written in huge wavy lettering and the address for the now-extinct Candy Bar is at the bottom with lots of squiggly lines surrounding it. Underneath the main header, 'Black lesbian night' is repeatedly written in a soft type. And in the body of the email, Maggie writes, *This was one of the best*. I smirk at the thought of Maggie preening herself before a big night out. I take a mental note of the questions

I'll ask next time I see her, and after studying the poster for a final time, I continue sorting through my out-of-control inbox.

There are follow-up emails on a couple of overdue commissions I have, and then I see an email from the Poets of Colour Collective, and my heart jumps a little. The subject line reads: 'An Invitation to Perform at a Black-owned Café in Camberwell'. I immediately open it.

Hi Elsie,

We're huge fans of your work, especially your iconic poem 'Her Hands'. We would love to invite you to perform at an intimate gig we are hosting at 'Jennie' in Camberwell in two weeks' time. The event is called 'Verses' and we're asking each performer to share a verse or more from their most treasured poem, preferably your work but you can also share something that means a lot to you.

The Poets of Colour Collective is a totally self-funded group. We all have full-time jobs and do not currently receive funding from anyone (although we hope that this will soon change). At the moment, the most we can offer is to cover your travel to and from the café (so long as you don't live outside of London!).

The point of the space is to centre our voices. It's for us and by us. We hope that you'll consider our invitation.

We have confirmed Moira Harrow, Jal Dhar and Soraya Smith as performers so far.

Reply to this email or drop me a text on 07951343189 if it sounds like something you'd like to be a part of.

Love and solidarity,

Rina

I immediately google the other people performing. The first is a white-passing Black girl. I pull up Moira's Twitter and there's a TED Talk called 'The Oreo Complex'. I've seen the second guy before, and he's beautiful. Just as I'm stalking the final poet, the front door opens. It's Juliet in a long blue faux-fur coat clutching a spider plant and a huge bunch of yellow roses.

'Miss me?' she asks, grinning.

'I was just getting on with some life admin.'

'Oooh, exciting. Anything coming up?'

'Well . . . I've just been asked to do this show in Camberwell next week. But it's unpaid, and I can't tell if they're politically Black.'

'That would be very '80s of them,' Juliet says playfully. 'But you should definitely do it. You haven't performed in ages. This will be the thing to get you feeling like yourself again.' She lowers the last of what is bundled in her arms down onto the cluttered kitchen counter. She speaks to me through the rectangular '70s hatch in the wall between kitchen and sitting room.

'Smells nice back here,' Juliet continues. 'I see that you don't think the herbs are so bad after all.'

In spite of myself, I smile. 'Turns out they aren't.'

After a moment, she says, 'I don't hear you typing. Have you replied to their email yet?'

'Relax, mate.'

But before I can blink, Juliet is standing over me at the table, like she's made herself invisible and travelled through the wall. She grabs the laptop from me.

'Which one is it?' she asks, scrolling through my emails. 'Oh, this one, right . . . An invitation to perform at a Black-owned . . .'

'I'm not even sure I want to do it! It's just another unpaid gig. I doubt it will even lead to anything. And besides, I don't want to miss a shift at the club for something that won't pay.'

'Yes, but sometimes it is good to practise, put yourself out there. Hmm . . . how should we respond?'

'J!' I exclaim.

'I would absolutely love to accept your invitation,' she says in a mock posh accent, only slightly posher than her own. She's typing vigorously.

I let out a laugh. She doesn't stop.

'Okay. Okay. Okay. Let me write it. I'll do it, I promise! I don't want them to think I'm some sort of overenthusiastic weirdo.' I wrestle the laptop back from her grasp.

'They emailed you a week ago! They're hardly going to think that. You know, you have to grab every opportunity that comes your way. Don't be scared. Just go for it. Your talent speaks for itself.'

Juliet's right, so I reply telling Rina that I'd love to perform. It's not like I've shared my work in a long time, and this might even force me to write something new.

'Done.'

'Yeeeesssss,' says Juliet. She's cutting the leaves off the stems of her flowers and placing them into a variety of small glass jars and vases so that there will be bursts of sunshine throughout the flat. 'I'm so excited. I've missed watching you perform.'

'I only have a couple of days to refresh my memory! This performance might not be so cute.'

'You'll be fine, Els. It comes naturally to you.' She pauses. 'This is nice, isn't it?'

'What do you mean?'

'Us, back to being us.'

'Yeah, it's nice to hang out. But you know I won't be here for ever. I'm figuring things out.'

'Why don't you believe me when I say you can stay for as long as you need? And I don't mean purely for your benefit. It's nice having the company.'

'You're hardly short of the company! I didn't realise how much you went out and how many mates you have.'

'Nah, they're all recent. Met them over the past few months.' She pauses. 'I do want talk about it though, Els. You know, the fact that we haven't spoken for so long?' Ugh. I was wrong. She's been waiting to deliver this line.

'We don't need to talk about it, J.' I reply. 'I know you really want us to go there, but we're fine. It's fine. Don't make it weird.'

I flash her a pleading smile. I barely have enough energy to figure out what is going on with me right now, let alone anything else in the past. She looks defeated, but I change the conversation anyway and direct it away from me. I wonder how long it will be until she'll attempt to push a deep, meaningful conversation on me again.

'So, how's your week been?' I ask, hoping that she won't push the matter.

'It was okay. But there is this one teacher, a guy, Tom, and he thinks that because I teach the youngest kids in school, I lack all intelligence and therefore my opinions don't matter.' Her shoulders raise tensely. 'He thinks I'm just some sort of prop. I'm pretty sure he was hoping something might happen between us when I first joined the school, and it didn't, and now I think the way he is around me is his bruised ego coming to the surface.'

Juliet has always been good at her job. The kids love her and so do their parents. At the end of every term, she'll tell me about some cake, bottle of wine, or handmade piece of jewellery her children gave to her. I've never understood how she can develop such a deep bond with those kids. Children to me are the most annoying little things. I don't know how people manage to look after kids and themselves. As soon as I left home and was relieved of caring for the twins, I was adamant that I'd avoid any situation in which I'd have to look after small people again (except if I must and it's the only job that will accept me).

'It's nothing to do with you though. You know that, right? It's him projecting. Sounds like classic little-man syndrome to me.'

'I know, I know all of this,' she responds. 'But sometimes I just want to wring his neck.'

'Juliet turning to violence? Wouldn't that be a sight to behold?' I grin as I tap away on my laptop, checking to see if I've got any job interviews in the past twenty minutes. There is one reply from a dog walker I'd applied to. They want to meet, and I feel a burst of excitement, but when I look at Juliet she's still in her thoughts. It isn't worth mentioning to her right now.

'It's like he won't give me a break. Today he was trying to remind me of my place because I'd handled something with one of the boys in his class and hadn't told him about it. But there's a reason his parents came to me in the first place. God, I feel like I'm walking on eggshells sometimes.'

'I'm sorry, that sounds long and annoying and pointless.' I attempt to remedy the situation. 'Let's smoke?'

'Sure. I don't want to do anything else today.' She sighs despondently.

I wonder if I should delve deeper but I don't have the emotional energy to really get into it with her now. A spliff will provide a buffer and she'll lean in to her misery so that we can both sit in our feelings. I close my laptop for good and start to roll a joint. The intense fatigue I'm feeling forces me to give up on the thought of writing anything.

8

After completing one of two overdue commissions I sprint to the local corner shop, rummage through the shelves and line up a row of snacks at the till with precision. Fiery Nik Naks, Rubicon Mangoes, salt-and-sweet popcorn *and* a bag of Haribo Strawbs. My only plan this evening is to remain horizontal for as long as possible and watch *Set It Off* for the hundredth time. I need predictability.

As I walk through the door, Juliet is applying her signature blue flicks in the hallway mirror.

'Date night, is it? You look nice,' I say, slightly surprised, not because Juliet isn't attractive but because she's clearly made an extra effort tonight. More than is to be expected for a week-night. I wonder who she could be seeing. I was sort of hoping she'd stay in with me tonight.

'Hardly,' she responds, revelling in the compliment.

'In that case, I have a film lined up, and some of that gorilla weed you like if you want to join me.' I shake the blue plastic bag, which is overflowing with treats.

'Oh shit! Andrew, Sophie and Sarah are coming over soon. Sorry, I forgot to mention! Just for a couple of drinks, anyway ... Sophie is Andrew's new girlfriend. Did I tell you about her?' She looks at me in the mirror. I shake my head, the dread evident all over my face. 'She's cool, and I know they'd all love to get to know you. What do you think? Join us for one?' she asks, attempting to keep her hair out of her face as she applies her lip balm.

I haven't met the latest batch of Juliet's mates, but I can't say I like the ones I've encountered before. They don't feel like a good fit for her. Despite the fact that she finds them exciting and full of adventure, I think they are uninspiring and way out of touch. This evening is set to be a product of her loving the idea of all of her friends being friends. But saying no doesn't feel like an option. I am a guest.

'I'll have one drink. I've got that job interview tomorrow. Dog walkers, remember?'

'Babe, can you get the pot of vegan chilli from the fridge and put it on the stove for me,' Juliet says, going over her eyeliner for a second time. 'And you'll nail that interview.'

As instructed, I light the hob and place the pot of chilli on the stove, and after a couple of minutes the brown liquid is bubbling. It smells of cumin, paprika and fresh chillies, and my stomach gurgles. Then the doorbell rings.

'Can you grab the bottle of wine from the freezer?' Juliet shouts back to me as she goes to open the door.

Moments later, Andrew comes bounding into the sitting room. The two girls follow.

'Hey,' he says a little awkwardly as I enter the room, as though he's annoyed that I'm part of whatever four-way date night he'd imagined tonight would be. I manage a smile back.

Bottle of wine and glasses in hand, I make my way over to

the girls. I avoid any barely there hugs, but Sophie and Sarah seem friendly and smiley enough.

'Nice to meet you,' I nod, accommodatingly.

'We've met before!' Sarah exclaims and I pretend to remember.

I pour everyone a huge glass of wine.

'I've got some chilli on the go if you're all hungry?' Juliet ushers everyone over to the table. It's a tight squeeze. She puts out five bowls, some vegan sour cream, homemade guacamole, salsa and tortilla chips.

'This looks amazing, Juliet.' Andrew offers her a thirsty smile.

'Let me know if I can get anyone anything else. I have red wine in the rack and I think there's tequila hiding somewhere.'

'I actually have a margarita recipe down,' I say, looking for any excuse to leave the table.

'That would be lovely! I can help,' offers Sophie. She's plain with long mousy-brown hair and simple silver hoops in her ears. She's wearing dungarees covered in paint. Sophie must've come straight from her studio. 'I actually have something for you,' she says then, in Juliet's direction, and walks around the table to deliver her a gift bag.

'You didn't have to! How exciting. Don't tell me it's one of your beautiful creations ...' Juliet's beaming from ear to ear as she scrambles around in the tissue paper.

It's one of Sophie's pots, apparently. It's pretty cool – a pair of brown boobs with freckles on them. For a second, I wonder if they're supposed to be an imitation of Juliet's. 'Hope you like it.' Sophie's smile reveals silver train tracks on her bottom set of teeth, which instantly renders her cute.

'I love it. It's beautiful, isn't it, Els? We can put it right over here.' She places it on the hatch.

'It's really pretty, yeah. And who doesn't like boobs? They do sort of look like yours too, J,' I say.

I turn to Sophie and see her grinning, and then turn back to Juliet, whose cheeks are a little flushed.

'Can I take a closer look?' Andrew asks, and Juliet hands the sculpture over carefully. He pretends to consider it.

'The female form is just the most beautiful thing. It's to be celebrated. That's why I make the work that I do, you know. I'd never really felt comfortable in my body until I started making sculptures and pots.' Sophie pauses for a moment, as if remembering the exact moment this transformation took place. She retrieves the sculpture from Andrew's grip and places it back on the hatch.

'Best not to touch it while we're about to eat,' she says, annoyed that Andrew isn't taking enough care over her creation. Then she addresses me.

'You're also beautiful, Elsie. I'd love to make a sculpture of you some time. You've got the most perfectly shaped head.' Sophie grabs a tortilla chip and stabs it into the mound of guacamole. I suddenly feel a little self-conscious.

Seemingly devastated that he isn't the centre of attention for once, Andrew tucks his floppy mane behind his ear sulkily, revealing a silver hoop with a miniature guitar hanging from it. I smirk.

'Sophie, still want to give me a hand with those margaritas?'

We head into the kitchen. Juliet recently painted all of the cabinets lime green and replaced the old knobs with hand-crafted ones. After complimenting the gold signet ring my nan gave me, Sophie follows my instruction to squeeze all of the limes we have into a jug.

After straining, I add some sugar syrup, tequila and triple sec, which has been in the back of the cupboard so long that it resists my first attempt to open it. Finally, I salt the rim of some short green glasses and pour out five drinks.

We return to the sitting room, and when everyone has a drink in hand, we move away from the table. Juliet is sitting on the orange corduroy beanbag. Andrew is next to Sophie and Sarah on the colourful, mismatched sofa, and I perch on the arm of a chair, the only space left on this side of the room.

The conversation is largely dominated by Andrew, who can't wait to share the details of a project he's working on.

'So, my band, Saving Freddie, are supporting Black Magnolia in Japan. I can't wait. Juliet knows I've always wanted to go there.' He smiles softly in her direction as he speaks.

'That's . . . exciting,' says Sophie hesitantly, clearly surprised by the information.

'OMG!' Juliet opens her mouth wide, pretending to be offended. 'And you kept this a secret from me?' She leaps up from where she's sitting to give Andrew a congratulatory cuddle.

'We only just found out, I promise!'

'Andrew, that's amazing, I feel like I should put on that song you sent me, the new one'.

Juliet excitedly connects her phone to the speaker. A long drum intro radiates around the room. Juliet pours out a shot of tequila for each of us in celebration. 'To Andrew!' she says before backing hers.

'You should come with us, Juliet! You'd love it. I think a

bunch of us are going to go. I've heard such good things about the people there and the food . . . such a great culture. There's an amazing veggie place I've heard about and would love to take you to. Actually, yes, it would be incredible if you could come.' Andrew looks into Juliet's eyes as he speaks, as though he's forgotten he's in a room full of people. I size up Sophie to decipher if she's uncomfortable with his obvious display of affection. She's giving little away.

'Maybe, but I do have school to teach . . . Are you going too, Sophie?'

'Actually I can't because I have a commission that I'll be delivering around that time. But maybe we should all go another time. That could be fun.' She shrugs her shoulders with uncertainty and I roll my eyes into the back of my head because Andrew is obviously intending to use the trip as an opportunity to profess his undying love for Juliet.

'Just think about it,' he says, putting his arm around Juliet who is now perched next to him on the sofa. 'Sophie and I were watching the Vice *Gaycation* episode about Japan the other day and it was a really interesting insight into what it's like for queer people over there.'

'I'm pansexual,' Sophie adds with all the sincerity she can muster, 'and I can't imagine not being able to love who I choose openly and freely.'

'Must be so scary,' Sarah chimes in for the first time in a while. In fact, this might be the first time she's spoken all night.

'What's it been like for you?' Andrew asks, suddenly looking at me. 'Where is it that you're from again?'

'She's Guyanese,' Juliet says.

'Yeah, I'm Guyanese, via Bristol. I was born here in the UK

and I don't watch those documentaries because they're just made to provoke this exact sort of reaction.'

'What do you mean by that?' Andrew asks, sounding uninterested in his own question.

'I bet you the hosts got dressed up, didn't they? These programmes are just for people who aren't from a place to watch and comment on how savage the people are there over dinner.'

'This one wasn't so bad,' Sophie says defensively. 'Not like the Jamaican one.' I notice her cheeks are flushed and she slurs a little as she speaks.

'Oh yes, the Jamaican one was bad. It is pretty uncivilised though, isn't it? Treating friends and family or complete strangers in such a way that they have to live in the gutter?' Andrew joins the chorus.

'Andrew, your language choice is a bit off,' Juliet interjects, a little too graciously.

But rather than addressing me, he turns to her and says, 'Sorry, I'm a little tipsy. I just mean it's pretty sad that people aren't able to be who they are in the open, you know?'

I have to add: 'It's also pretty sad that white people colonised the Caribbean in the first place.'

Sensing a shift in mood, Juliet steers the conversation to smoother waters before Andrew has another chance to respond. Her eyes are flitting between the two of us, as though she's unsure of where to land.

'Does anyone want some more wine, or another drink? More tequila or we have rum, maybe?' She saunters around making a fuss and topping up drinks before disappearing into the kitchen and returning with a plastic bowl filled with ready-salted crisps.

'You're right though,' says Sophie once Juliet's returned.

'We, as white people, can be so unaware. I didn't mean to cause any offence.' I can tell she's decided I'm the authority on all things Black and gay and gay and Black.

'I'm going to go out for a smoke,' I announce.

'Do you mind if I come with you?' Sophie asks me.

I desperately want a moment of quiet but I can't be bothered with another argument, so all I say is, 'Sure'.

Sophie follows me onto the balcony, in a light orange puffer jacket.

'Do you think Andrew likes Juliet?' She gets straight to the point.

'Maybe, I don't know.' I'm cautious not to let my real thoughts spill out.

'I wouldn't mind if he did. But I'd rather he'd just be honest about it. I didn't even want to be in a closed relationship. It was him who was persistent. When we first started dating, he would always get really weird and possessive when I'd tell him about the girls I'd been seeing.'

'Is that you, yeah? One of us.' I take a swig of my margarita as she reveals herself to me.

Sophie's a lot more drunk than I am. Her pink lip gloss has ventured beyond the edges of her surprisingly rounded lips and she sways slightly.

'Can I have some of that?' She points to the roll-up I'm smoking.

'Sure.' She comes close and for a second, I feel like she's going to inhale directly from my mouth. I'm surprised to find that my heart races as I hand her the cigarette. I consider leaning in to kiss her, if only for the effect it would have on Andrew. The potential power. But she moves away again.

After taking a drag, she says, 'So, I hear you're a poet? What do you write about?'

I shrug.

'Anything and everything. Whatever I'm feeling, you know.'

'I bet you're super talented.' She smiles at me. It's bad, but I can tell it's definitely her attempt at flirtation.

'Just like you and those pots. Did you want to capture my face or do you—'

I'm interrupted by Sarah, who opens the door and joins us on the balcony.

'Sarah! Come join us angel. We haven't caught up all night. You must tell Elsie about your clothes. She's a dark horse this one!' Sophie whips out a packet of Marlboro Lights and hands Sarah one. 'She has her own fashion line. Can you believe that?'

I nod slowly as I exhale.

'It's a completely ethical and sustainable brand,' Sarah says proudly. 'Everything is made from recycled fabrics.'

'I think you'd love her stuff, Elsie. It's just amazing. Sarah was inspired after spending a year in Malaysia, weren't you honey?'

'Yeah, that's where our factories are actually. I get all the stuff made over there. By local women mainly.'

'She's modest but she's making an absolute killing.' Sophie leans in to tell me this, like she thinks I'll be impressed.

There are a million things I could say but I don't respond. There's no point. They wouldn't understand. I just close my eyes and take a long and slow inhale of my roll-up.

9

My alarm chimes loudly from under my pillow, despite Juliet
telling me time and time again that the radiation will give me
brain damage. My eyes open and even though I didn't have a
nightmare, I feel a distant, dreamy sense of unease. It's 10 a.m.
I pull on my tracksuit bottoms and an oversized black Levi's
T-shirt and plod into the kitchen, where I throw a generous
heap of Nescafé instant (an addition to the house that Juliet
is vehemently opposed to) into a handmade cup. The smell
of coffee starts to make me feel human again. Opening the
cluttered kitchen cupboards and surveying what's in stock, I
decide to make my signature fry-up as the wind whistles outside. The baby-blue cooker is on its way out, so I light the hob
with a match. I'm glad to be inside with the warmth from the
cooker. After chopping onions and adding them, along with
salt, pepper and chilli to some baked beans, I douse mush-
rooms and tomatoes in herbs and olive oil and then fry some
eggs. I know Juliet will be hanging after last night. Andrew
and Sophie didn't leave until 2 a.m. I make a little extra for her.

In Juliet's room, the curtains are still drawn, and a faint
smell of geranium radiates from the oil burner next to her bed.
I sit on the edge of it and hand her the plate.

'Mmm, this looks so yummy. Exactly what my hangover needs.' She sits up and looks at me with a contented smile on her face. 'I could get used to this. Thank you, Els.' I smile back at her.

We both polish off what's on our plates and I pile them up on Juliet's desk before squeezing into bed with her. She rests her head on my chest and I wrap my arms around her just how she likes it.

'Shall we put *Drag Race* on?' I offer.

'Yeah, but Els, I was thinking last night . . .' I hold my breath. 'About your poetry.' And exhale.

'About that old poem. You know the one you said isn't about me but is absolutely about me?' I think back to a couple of years ago when Juliet was at mine. I'd left one of my journals open – and after popping out to get some water, when I walked backed into my room, she was taking in the start of an unfinished poem, though she only caught a glimpse.

I'm glad that from where she's lying, she can't see my facial expression. Because it's frozen. I feel oddly nervous.

'Mmmmm. You mean, the one you *think* is about you?'

'The one I am ninety-nine-point-nine per cent sure is about me, yes.'

'What about it?'

'Well . . . I'd love to hear it again.'

'I don't remember it, J. I wrote it so long ago.'

'If it's about me, shouldn't I be allowed to request a performance?'

'Like I already said, it's not about you, J. And besides, I'm feeling a bit fragile right now. I can barely string a sentence together, let alone perform a poem.'

I can tell Juliet doesn't believe me, but she doesn't push it. And I'm thankful. I don't know why she needs to keep bringing up old stuff.

She manoeuvres herself so that she's facing me and smiles and whispers, 'Liar,' under her breath.

Juliet sets up the laptop so that it's balanced precariously on the corner of her desk. We've developed a little routine: every Saturday morning, we lie in Juliet's bed and watch the next episode of *Drag Race*. Even when one of us has had company the night before, we still tell them that we have something important to do that morning so we can remain on schedule. *And* prevent any awkward crossing of paths in the small hallway. This series, we are firmly in the Monét X Change camp, and if she doesn't win we'll be boycotting for sure this time.

Then, out of nowhere:

'Els, please read it to me.' I'm surprised that after endless glasses of margaritas and wine she even has the energy to keep asking.

'No, J.'

'Pretty please?' She flutters her eyelashes, knowing it's my weak spot.

'Don't do that thing with your eyes! Damn,' I respond playfully. 'It would be bad mind of me to deny you now, wouldn't it?'

'It would.' She wiggles around like a caterpillar in search of a comfortable spot.

'I'll read you a poem I wrote a month ago, how about that? You can be my guinea pig.' I'm hoping she'll say yes, so that we can avoid the conversation the other poem would bring up.

Juliet tries to disguise her disappointment and snuggles deeper in my arms. I keep talking.

'So, you know how wicked and bad my nan's pepperpot is? Before your vegan antics, you'd practically inhale that thick, sticky liquid. Anyway, I've been thinking about how our people make dishes out of nothing. The literal scraps, you know? Make them deep and rich and so that they feel like safety.' I retrieve my phone from the folds of the bed, go into my notes and start to recite the poem.

We have been handed scraps and asked to make a meal from the beginning of time. It's fine, because we do. We've been through things that have made us have to fend, can't pretend we ever thought we could rely on hands that weren't ours to know how to prepare a meal, a lineage, a history. They say it takes a village to raise a pickney. Takes a choir to raise a roof. But it takes one meal to know you are you:

PEPPERPOT RECIPE INC SPECIAL INGREDIENTS

3 pounds ah beef

(A grandma with gold teeth and a h that has been hung up to dry whilst three becomes tree and not the type up high, the type on your tongue, kinda sung)

1 teaspoon of salt

(Not the kinda sharpness that be bought just taught through stories of before and an uncle always afraid of a bang at the door)

1/2 teaspoon of black pepper

(In a hand that reminds us of tough but also tender and the sound of a fender that reaches us in a blues that restores us to our soil)

1 tablespoon of vegetable oil

(And an extra shot of intergenerational love)
1 large onion
(And the glimpse of seeing a Black man cry, if only standing
above the kitchen counter you might)
4 garlic cloves
(And no goodbyes, cos a house full of love is always full)
4 sprigs of thyme
(And a wish for extra time, here in the family. I mean this pot)
1/2 cup of cassareep
(And a whole long table and grandma at the top)
A stove lit of burning embers of what it is to be made of each
other, woven into wicker silhouettes of our past ancestors,
a protection from Georgetown to the Parish of Manchester.
Island to island. Over food we let bygones be bygones. 'Belief'
and 'belly full' are long-lost twins raised by the same mother,
I'm sure. One can make you trust in the other. I'm sure.

When I signal to Juliet that I've finished, she rolls over so we're facing each other. I can't read her expression.

'So, what did you think?'

'I love it, obviously.' She beams at me. 'It's beautiful. I'm sure Cherry will love it too.'

Juliet has always had a soft spot for my nan.

'I think she might, you know. Needs a bit more work but I'm feeling this one a lot.'

'You have such a good voice too. Soothing and slow and . . .' She pauses for thought.

'And . . . ?'

'You're loving this, aren't you?'

'Please don't let me interrupt you.'

'When you perform, it's like you're a different person.

You're not the bad gyal who doesn't take shit from anyone. Instead, you're . . .' Juliet gestures at the air, searching for the right word.

'I'm still a bad bitch. I'm just sexy and seductive with my lyricism.'

She laughs. 'Something like that, anyway.'

We stay in our position for another thirty minutes, not saying anything at all. It is only when the doorbell rings that our bodies are forced to part.

10

Bea, Jamie and Antonio are all at the bar when I arrive, as well as Katya and Ola, who both cover the occasional shift. Nobody berates me for being late, which seems off-key. It looks like an intervention is about to take place from the way they're all standing together, but I can't figure out for whom or what. I stand opposite Bea. She's annoyed that I left the other day without saying goodbye and every time our eyes meet, she deliberately looks away, demonstrating that she doesn't want to give me the time of day. I smile, which irritates her. Eventually, I divert my eyes so that I'm looking in the direction of the bar, which is when I notice that all the bottle spouts are still wrapped in cling film.

As we wait awkwardly for something to happen, I open my phone and scroll through my emails. There at the top of the inbox is a response from my most recent job interview.

Dear Elsie,

Whilst we loved meeting you and enjoyed hearing how much you loved your grandma's chihuahua, Chico (particularly the stories around how he was accustomed to the finer things in life!), the fact that you didn't have any experience of walking or owning dogs yourself has meant we've had to go in a different direction.

We wish you the best of luck in your continued search for employment!

Best wishes,

Kate at Walky Walkies

Even the fabrication of a family pet can't get me a fucking job.

'We've got some news,' Jamie says, gathering us all around. 'You know you're all family, right?'

Antonio squeezes his arm. It looks like they're going to announce they're getting married or having a baby. Both of their eyes are red, as if they've been crying. Jamie actually looks like he's holding back tears. After what feels like an eternity, Jamie opens his mouth again.

'We're closing the bar. We did everything we could to avoid this because we love this place, we love all of you, but the landlord has decided to put the rent up. You guys know that it's been incredibly slow for a long time, and we simply can't make the numbers work anymore.' Jamie can no longer conceal his anguish, and one by one tears fall down his face. He's full-on sobbing, acting like the widows who throw themselves on top of their husbands' graves after their death. He's devastated. Actually, so am I. I think back to my first day when Jamie told me all his grand plans for the place. How we never got to see them come true.

He continues. 'I wanted to create a space where members of our community would be able to hang out, and there was something particularly special about doing that in the area I grew up in. I thought we could convince people to stop going to central London for nights out and to invest in their local community but ... Well, I just can't believe this is happening to me ... to us,' he adds dramatically, remembering there are other people in the room who will be severely affected by this news.

Antonio tries to be positive, whispering in Jamie's ear. 'It will be okay, baby. We can even move to Italy like we've always talked about.'

'It's not okay though, is it? I've worked so hard to keep this place afloat. It's my life's work.' Jamie's tone grows increasingly shrill.

'What if we mix it up a little?' says Bea. 'You know there are all these collectives putting on incredible nights. We just need to revamp the place. Add some spice, maybe even change the décor? The night that collective threw was sick.'

'That's not a bad idea,' I say in agreement. 'With a bit of marketing to the right people, there is no saying that we can't completely turn this around.' This is probably the most interest Bea and I have ever taken in the business side of things, but the others are silent. I've always liked that the bar wasn't busy. So many empty tables and evenings when nobody but Maggie stopped by for drinks. It made me feel less short-changed by the pay.

'It's too late, guys.' Jamie hangs his head in shame, clearly turning over would-and-could-haves in his mind. He gazes up again. 'Look at how beautiful we made this place. And they're going to ruin it with their bland, boring interiors. I just know it,' he laments, covering his eyes with a flat palm.

I look up at the patch of damp, which, when I started, was barely noticeable. Now it consumes a solid area of the ceiling.

The paint on the walls is also peeling and the floor is in desperate need of replacement. Antonio and Jamie's decorations aren't flamboyant enough to disguise all the problems with the bar, but it was ours. And in our own way, we loved it.

'You never know,' says Ola, 'there could be hope for Boom yet. We could start a GoFundMe or something.'

'God forbid we beg for money – not on my watch. The rent hike is too much and they've already found someone to take the space over in a couple of months. They're turning it into a natural wine bar and pottery studio.' Jamie shudders and I catch his chill as he lets out a high-pitched, pained whimper.

There's nothing any of us can say to reassure him because the reality is that the system is broken. The people who should care don't actually give a shit about fixing things. Whatever end of the political system they claim to be from, they don't consider us, not really. We all know who is pulling the strings.

'We can only afford to keep Beatrice on until our lease ends, as she's worked here the longest,' Antonio says stoically. 'Jamie and I will pick up the rest of the shifts. I'm sorry that we're leaving the rest of you without a job. We hate this as much as you do, but there is nothing more we can do. This is the end of an era for Boom.' He kisses Jamie on the cheek reassuringly. The rest of us stand in silence, considering what our next moves should be.

Eventually we manage to leave the club, and on the way back to the station, all of us staff stop off at a pub for a drink. As I open my wallet to pay for a pint of cider, I find a crisp twenty-pound note resting between my bank and Nectar card. Juliet must have put it there. I've taken to hiding notes around the house, insisting she must have left them there and forgotten.

It's the only way to contribute towards anything other than the bills without her vehemently opposing. But these same notes seem to always find their way back to me. As if by magic I'm reminded that she's thinking of me.

On the ride home, I search online for old posters of nights at Boom. Just to reminisce. The image search mostly delivers pictures of the energy drink but sandwiched between them there's a picture of a younger, toned Jamie in a vest with a choker on. I click through to an old events board introducing the bar's opening night. It's from 2005. I pull out my phone and reply to Maggie's email from the other day. I have her number, but I don't want to come across as overfamiliar.

I type:

One for the archive: BOOM 2005–2018. RIP.

11

There are a couple of hours until the Poets of Colour Collective's Verses event starts, but whenever I try to read through my poems, I can't force the words out. I can't think of anything worse than standing up in a room full of people, wholly frozen because of all the conflicting feelings and anxiety swirling around inside of me. All I want to do is order a burger and sleep, but I can't justify the expense. And I don't have the time.

The blue walls and thick Artex ceiling of my room are enveloping me. I feel like I might drown or at least fuse into the mattress I'm lying on, never to return to the outside world again. To aid me in sinking deeper into my feelings, I play Joyce Wrice's *Stay Around* EP from beginning to end. I bury myself under the covers like a little girl hiding from the monster under her bed. To perform, to share, is to be vulnerable and that in itself fills me with dread. I don't know why I thought writing about belonging would be a good idea. Why I'd have any idea *where* I belong. The heaviness of the past few months weighs down on my eyelids and just like that I feel myself drifting off.

I drift in and out of consciousness so when I hear a familiar voice saying my name softly, over and over again, I think it must be part of my dream. But then the duvet is peeled back with care, my body is covered in cool air and Juliet's face comes into focus.

'Hey, sleepy.'

'Hey.' I rub my eyes and sit upright, leaning myself against the wooden frame of my single bed.

'Your event isn't too far off. Should you get up? I'll order a cab once you're ready.'

'I'm not going,' I say defiantly with all the strength I can induce. I'm holding in tears for fear that I'll lose control, completely overflow and drown in my melancholy.

'What do you mean?' Juliet probes with affection.

'I don't feel up to it. Think I've caught something.' I wonder if Juliet believes me.

She sits at the end of the bed looking at me, thinking about her next move.

'I know it's been a lot for you recently, but I think getting up and seeing the outside world might be good for you. Once you're outside, things might feel a little brighter.'

I know she's trying to guide me out of my indulgent self-pity, and I don't have the energy to put up a fight. I stay quiet.

'Why don't you get in the bath and soak for twenty minutes? I'll put some salts in it for you and then we can see how you feel?'

I nod only because I want to be left alone again. She goes to fill the tub, and the deep sadness is left lingering in the room with me.

Juliet helps me out of bed and guides me down the small hallway to the bathroom. The smell of grapefruit engulfs me, and slowly Juliet helps me take off my clothes. She avoids looking at my body, though she has seen it so many times before. Juliet starts by pulling the jumper over my head and then my T-shirt. Her gaze never leaves my eyes.

'Let me leave you to it,' she announces.

'No, stay.' Without her here I may submerge myself in the steaming tub and forget to come back up for air. She seems pleased.

I lean on her as I step out of the tracksuit bottoms I'm wearing and remove my underwear. Juliet averts her eyes and places her hand awkwardly on my back to steady me. Her hand feels cold against my skin. I pull her in closer for a cuddle but she feels stiff.

'Thank you for being here, J.' I say, letting go.

'In the bathroom?'

'No, you know, like . . . here. Here for me.' She squeezes my hand in response.

I get into the bath and am immediately overwhelmed by bubbles. The bubbles remind me of bath time at my nan's house and how much I loved how thoroughly she would massage my head with shampoo. I didn't have a bath in my old place, so this feels like a proper treat. My skin tingles with the heat, and I wriggle into a comfortable position. Juliet has attached a little waterproof pillow to the back of the bath, and even though I have to bend my knees slightly because the tub is small, I instantly feel relaxed. I notice that all the furniture in here is old. There are faded flowers on the toilet bowl sink and outside of the bath. The walls are bubblegum pink. Bubbles surround me, and for a moment, I bury myself underneath the foam.

Juliet perches on the floor, leaning against the edge of the bath so that we're facing each other.

'How are you feeling?' She asks as I resurface.

'Well, I think your plan might have backfired because this bath is really good. So good that I don't want to leave.'

Through a smile, she says, 'Let's go out, Els. Just long enough for you to recite a little bit of something you love. I promise you'll feel better for it. Plus, you know what you're like once you're out. I might never get you home.'

'I could be watching *Drag Race All Stars*, but fine. I'll do it for you.'

And we both know it's the truth.

We get a cab and my nan texts on the journey over, responding to my request for the recipe for her saltfish and bakes. She's written: 'How is it going at Juliet's? And I don't measure. You must come and I'll show you.' I smile. Nan's smart. This is her way of securing a visit.

We arrive at Jennie's, which isn't quite as I had envisioned it. I thought it was going to be a sexy, dimly lit poetic justice-type venue. But we are in a vegan juice bar filled with patterned scatter cushions and oddly shaped chairs. I'm wearing jeans, white trainers and a white jumper that an old friend embroidered for me. It features a hand with long nails except for one, the index finger.

A friendly man with dreads greets us at the door. He's proudly ushering guests in. 'Welcome, welcome, make yourself at home. And make sure to try one of our famous juices. They are all very, very fresh,' he says, making a point to speak to each person as they walk in. It's nice. The room is coated in nectar as the soothing tones of Raveena fill the space from a little pink speaker in the corner. The vibe is sweet and mellow as people greet each other, offering up gentle compliments.

A dark-skinned woman is sageing the space as she asks for blessings:

'Most honourable and loving ancestors, I ask that you help me to cleanse this space. Welcome a positive and supporting energy and rid it of all that does not serve us.'

The woman is wearing a bright green head wrap and is adorned with the most oversized rings I've ever seen – huge crystals in an array of colours that have been wrapped in bronze and copper bands. The combination of smoke and her green dress hypnotises me. Juliet asks which flavour juice I want, and I notice that several other people are staring at this woman as she weaves her way through the room smiling and nodding. The man from the door, who is now coughing amidst the haze, nervously asks her to stop what she's doing.

'It'll set the fire alarms off. So, if you don't mind . . .'

After a final orbit around the room, the woman obliges, putting out the sage stick into an empty scallop shell.

The venue is tiny and so the room feels full despite there being no more than thirty-five people here. I spot Malachai, a guy I know from back in the day when we performed at a lot of the same poetry showcases and open mic nights. He was a really good performer but I haven't seen him in a while.

'Elsie! My girl. Long time. You look good. Looking forward to seeing you do your thing later.' He hugs me.

'Yes, Malachai! Are you doing a little something too?'

'Nah, I gave in and got a regular job. Just been craving a

bit of old times. Makes me feel old being here but I've missed being in a room surrounded by wordsmiths.'

'Damn, no way. You and me both though. Looking kind of ancient right now.'

'Yeah, it just wasn't paying enough. Not all of us can be as big of a deal as you are.'

I look at the floor and nod uncomfortably. 'Needs to start paying real money though, you know?'

'Don't give up. It's rare for people to be able to do things with words like you can. We both know I was never as good as you.' I say nothing and after a pause, Malachai asks: 'Here, who's your friend?' He's gesturing towards Juliet, pulling a cheeky face.

'Oh, this is Juliet. Juliet, Malachai.' I point between them.

'Think I've heard a bit about you, nice to meet you. Right, I'm gonna go grab that bean bag in the corner before I end up having to stand at the back.'

'In a bit.'

Malachai runs off and Juliet and I survey the room. I recognise most of the faces here. There are a couple of poets I met at an evening of erotic readings put on by Prim Black. We all greet each other and make small talk about what we've been up to. I'm one of the oldest people in the room and this realisation fills my stomach with knots. Juliet hands me a ginger and carrot juice and we manage to find a couple of bean bags near the front. Eventually, an adorable human who I've not seen before stands up in front of everyone and introduces the evening.

'Hi everyone, my name's Leonie. My pronouns are she/they, and it's so beautiful to see everyone here in a room where we invite you to bring your authentic selves.' The amount that they are gesticulating tells me Leonie's nervous. Long red nails match their bright red lipstick but she's done the rest of her makeup to look like she has nothing on. I usually hate wigs but I don't mind theirs. She's wearing a perfectly installed lace front with two blonde streaks at the front, baby hairs and all. Their eyes are small and her cheekbones razor sharp. She looks good, maybe a little young for me, but good. Though the quality of the event she's pulled together makes me think they might be closer in age and experience than the dimple in the right cheek suggests.

'As a poet, I wanted to ensure that there were spaces where we could all come together and share our work in a non-judgemental environment. I think there are ways that we can all help shape each other's practice as creatives, share feedback, feelings and just be held.'

One of her friends whoops supportively.

'Tonight, we have invited some of our favourite poets of colour to share works with us on anything they like. We're in for a real treat. House rules are that we don't tolerate any ism – that's sexism, racism, ableism, classism . . . the list goes on. If you violate this, you will be removed immediately. Also, please do not assume anyone's pronouns. So, if everyone can introduce themselves before they start, that would be great.'

A round of applause from the crowd.

'Oh, and I'll give everyone a heads up when it's their turn. Thank you to Jimmy and Jennie for letting us use this space and to the rest of the Poets of Colour Collective for bringing this together. I love you all!'

With that, Leonie introduces the first poet. I haven't thought about boys since, well, ever, but even I find myself getting hot as he recites a poem purely about covering his skin in jojoba oil. Everyone's enamoured, and I hope that I'm not next.

'Next, we've got Radhika Khatri and then there will be a short break before Elsie Macintosh's performance. Please use the break as an opportunity to grab a juice and get to know each other better.'

Radhika's time on stage is short-lived. She skips the introductions and recites a singular haiku. The applause is stilted as the crowd cottons onto the fact that she's finished. Unless I totally fuck it, there's no way my delivery and response can be as bad as hers.

'How are you feeling?' Juliet turns to me. 'Have you still not decided what you're going to perform?'

'I don't know! I still don't know. I did write something new but I'm not sure about it.' She just squeezes my arm in support.

During the break, the café owner busies himself telling people about what can be found in each of his juices. A woman, who I assume must be Jennie, appears carrying a plate of small brown chocolates. She looks like the man at the door, just in female form. I decide they are siblings. She makes her way through the room, offering what's on her plate to everyone in her path. Eventually, she reaches us.

'Are these vegan?' asks Juliet.

'Yes, and I made them myself. All natural. Nothing synthetic about them.' Jennie smiles proudly at her creations.

We both take one, and as I bite into the little brown ball, a bitterness fills my mouth. I want to spit it out but instead wash down the flavour with the dregs of my juice.

One of the girls from the collective asks everyone to take

their seats again. Leonie gets up on stage, this time joined by someone else.

'So we have something very exciting to announce, and I'll let Nora explain more before we continue with the evening,' says Leonie, grinning from ear to ear and stepping aside.

'Thank you, Leonie.' Nora takes the stage. 'It's wonderful to be here this evening. I'm so impressed by the spirit of your generation, and I so wish that a space like this had existed when I was younger. As Leonie has said, my name is Nora, and my pronouns are they/them.' They look around the room as they speak and adjust their thick black frames.

'I'm from an organisation called The Diaspora Writes, and we have just launched a publishing prize called CRUSH with the support of the Arts Council. We'll be offering the winner of this prize a publishing deal. To enter, you need to submit a poem on the topic of intimacy – and this applies to all types of love and intimacy. We really encourage you to think outside of the box and celebrate the many different ways that we can crush on the people and things in our lives. There will also be two runner-up prizes of a thousand pounds each, and these include having your work published online. On 23 October there will be an event in which shortlisted poets will perform to a live audience, and these will be judged by a panel of industry and community leaders. A winner will be selected from these performances. Leonie will send an email around after the event with all the information about the prize, but you can also find it online at diasporawrites.org.uk. Thank you and enjoy the rest of the evening!' They take a seat.

'Thank you so much, Nora!' Leonie is back on stage. 'As they said, I'll be sure to share information on the prize after this evening. But up next, we have Elsie Macintosh.' She claps and the room joins in.

I stand up and find my way to the middle of the room. I'm now acutely aware of the person from The Diaspora Writes sitting to my right on a stool in the corner of the room. I take in a deep breath and make a sudden decision about what it is that I am going to share.

'Hey everyone, I'm Elsie. I've never been asked to introduce my pronouns before, but I've settled on she/her. I've spent a lot of time recently thinking about the significance of home and the weight that we place on its physicality. And between the shops selling orange wine and the fact that I can't even find a part-time job as a dog walker' – a few people laugh – 'I'm not sure London is the best place for me to be anymore. But then where else do I go? I don't know. It's hard. Perhaps some of you know what I mean.'

The Black and brown faces in the room amble between nodding and laughing softly. There's something comforting about this space. It's filled with kind eyes. It's sort of soothing and I notice that Nora is smiling too.

'Certain events have forced me to think about home in other ways. I'm still figuring it out. I haven't written anything in a really long time.' I pause. 'But this felt appropriate for tonight.'

I guess
You ask me where home is
And I say here . . .
Or here?
As if I don't know.
As if I ain't been shown a way home –
For a while.

Maybe it's wherever I can feel the bile in my stomach
*   settle. Or any room that's got a kettle*
And moment to pause.

Lost cause I know a little better
I guess home's wherever
I guess I find it wherever it is there to find.
Mine? No place fixed and every place I've missed.
Any girl I've kissed, at least twice.
Home? Sometimes wherever I have left a tear
Or the ear of any shoulder that bumps with mine
Whilst we are both trying to find the platform.
A platform?
A rave from back in the day?
The left side of a face?
Curved like a hammock in setting suns.
Setting suns.
Anywhere you can run to with your eyes
*   tightly closed.*
Home . . .
I actually don't know
To be honest,
If a tree falls in a forest
And nobody hears
Does it mean she's been kicked from home?
Or does it just mean you've outgrown the woods.
Home is where I don't have to keep my hood up.
Home is in whatever comes from the Dutch pot on
*   Nan's stove*
Home is on my own

But also has found a way to wickedly reside in a body.
If they are on me, or under
When outside there is thunder
But in interlocking arms there is slumber
And rest and neck kisses
And sex and anywhere that misses you more.
Homes they're the core
And life
Well that's like the apple
And sometimes
You gotta show some teet'
And bite all the way down.
And home is down
Any path
That feels like sunshine
And warm.
Home ain't cool.
Cos cool don't mean warm,
Home means far from the warning signs
And red flags
Home means I'm a slag so often some place I
    ain't know
Home's wherever the wind blows me
For that night
I guess?

I shrug all the way home

I realise I've made it to the end of the poem and come back
to my senses. I pause and realise nothing bad has happened.

In fact, the room fills with supportive cheers and claps and smiling faces, nodding, like I captured a little bit of what home means to them too. Juliet's whistling louder than everyone else in the room and even though this makes me self-conscious, I'm grateful for her support. I look over to the person from The Diaspora Writes and they are furiously making notes. The lady who was sageing earlier is standing up near the front of the room clicking, and the guy who read the poem about jojoba oil also looks impressed. I'm grinning now, and I wriggle my toes to remind myself that I'm in my body, alive.

I feel as though I could share more, ruminate in this moment for longer. But a little reluctantly, I rejoin Juliet on the bean bags to listen to the next poet, a Black woman with the most bewitching voice. It's properly baritone and commands everyone's attention. Throughout her performance, the room is clicking non-stop. 'Yes sis' and 'Mmms' fill the space. I enjoy the rest of the evening. Because of the size of the venue and where we are seated. It feels like people are performing directly to me, and I remember my love of poetry, glad Juliet dragged me out of my bed and bath. Everyone's styles are completely different and by the end, ideas are swimming through my head. A couple of times, I grab my phone to jot things down before they disappear.

At the end of the event, I see Leonie making their way over to us.

'Thank you so much for performing, Elsie. You were everything.' She brushes her hand across my arm as she speaks. 'Honestly, wow! We were all blown away. I think Nora wants to speak to you. They haven't stopped singing your praises.'

'Oh, thank you. That's so cool to hear.' I consciously try not to come across as desperate.

'Actually, one second.' Leonie gestures to Nora. Their short head of curls bounce a little as they walk in our direction.

They reach for my hand. 'That was fantastic. Your poem was great, and I'd highly recommend you apply for our prize if the rest of your work is just as strong.'

We chat for few more minutes and I write down my email in their phone, thanking them as they make a beeline for Jojoba Oil.

'See!' Juliet squeezes my hand.

Even though I know better than to get carried away about anything before it happens, I can't help but squeeze her hand back with excitement. Inside, it feels like a part of myself has come back to me. Like an old flame has been reignited. Leonie looks at Juliet, seemingly for the first time.

'And what's your name?' She asks, slightly suspicious. 'Are you a poet too?'

'No, not a poet. Elsie and I are best friends.'

Leonie nods intently.

'Well, Elsie, I'm supposed to wait to finish up here but I'm sure the others won't mind if I clock out a little early. Do you want to step out for some fresh air? I'd love to speak to you some more.'

Juliet raises her eyebrows and sticks out her tongue so that only I can see.

'We were gonna maybe grab a drink at the bar across the road if you fancy joining us?'

'No, you two go,' says Juliet, stepping back to give us some room. 'I've got some work I need to finish anyway. I can get a shift in before bed.'

'It's a bit late for a shift, isn't it?' Leonie asks curiously. 'What sort of work do you do?'

'I do a few things, but camming is one of them,' Juliet says playfully, swaying her body from side to side. 'So it's never too late for a shift. People are horny 24/7.'

I clock Leonie disguising their judgement with a smile. She isn't the first person to do this and I doubt she'll be the last. The way she's trying to seem cool is kind of amusing.

'I'll see you at home, Els,' Juliet says, eyebrows raised and with a downturned smile on her face. 'And thanks for a gorgeous evening, Leonie.'

Leonie nods at Juliet and then says to me, 'I'll be back in one sec.' She heads off to thank everyone for coming.

I turn to Juliet. 'Are you sure? You can come with?'

'As if I want to spend the rest of my night watching you seduce a woman with your same old routine. Are you going to also give this one your "favourite" book of poems and tell them that they're way too good for you? I've never understood how that makes them more, not less, persistent.'

I pull a pretend half-smile and pinch her arm playfully. 'I have game, you know I do.'

'Sureeee,' she responds, and then her second phone starts to ring. The one she keeps for her customers.

'Oh hello big boy, I was just thinking about you.' She employs a sultry accent and blows me a kiss, winking on her way out the door.

I gesture to Leonie that I'll meet her outside. She smiles, her red lipstick still perfectly intact as she follows me out.

'Ah, that was just so great, wasn't it? They're all happy to pack up so I'm good to go,' she says through a wide grin. It's evident she's gassed about how the night went.

'Shall we go to a bar a bit further down the road? There's a nice place I know around the corner,' I suggest.

We walk through the door of the dimly lit jazz-inspired bar. There are framed copies of sheet music on the wall, and Ella Fitzgerald's 'Over the Rainbow' is playing at a low enough level for us to still hear the buzz of laughing couples. It's a sexy venue. I've brought Leonie here because my friend, Tri, works on the bar, meaning that the wine is free. Tri has a fresh head of short baby locs, rings in each nostril and is wearing a crisp white T-shirt. As soon as she spots me, she stops polishing the glass she's been cradling.

'Elsie! What are you doing here?!'

'Yessss Tri. I was hoping I'd catch you.' We spud.

'I was at a gig at that vegan place. Leonie, wanna grab a table? I'll get us a bottle of wine.' I watch Tri assess the situation.

'She looks a bit young,' Tri whispers after Leonie wanders off.

'Do you think?'

Tri shakes her head. 'You're on that cougar shit. Love it.'

'Ha. It's just a drink. Look at her though, she knows she looks good.' I watch Leonie as she takes a seat in the corner.

'You know I only have eyes for one,' Tri replies.

'Yeah, you've been wifed so long, flirting is probably all a distant memory.'

'Yowwch.' She pretends to be offended. 'Anyway, what do you want to drink? I can comp you anything that is in this sort of price range.' She points to their extensive wine menu.

'Um, I wouldn't know where to start.'

'Okay, red or white?'

'White.'

'Sweet or dry?'

'Dry.'

'So we have this Lugana. It's light, crisp. Or we have a Pinot Blanc, which is my favourite, and a Côtes du Rhône Blanc, which people love. Vegan too.'

'I mean, whatever you recommend,' I say, but she looks a little disheartened that I'm not as enthused by the grapes as she is. So I add, 'The Pinot Blanc sounds great, Tri. Cheers.'

I return from the bar with two glasses, a bottle and a cooler. The table is so small that there is a custom-built bench attached to it. When I sit down, Leonie slides over so that she's practically sitting on my lap.

'So where did you go to uni?' she starts.

I let out a little sigh. 'I didn't.'

'Oh, is that because you took time out to travel? Or are you planning to go later on?' There's confusion on Leonie's face.

'Well . . .'

But before I can answer she dives in again. 'I took a year out to volunteer before I went to uni. I went to teach kids in Gambia. It was the most fulfilling thing I've ever done.' I momentarily wonder if the only thing we have in common is the colour of our skin.

'Those things are pretty sus, no? Very *West knows best*?'

'Not if you're Black,' they say with complete self-assuredness. I want to laugh or make a comment about their age, and how they might not know absolutely everything, but decide against it. They continue. 'So how come you didn't go to uni then?'

'It just wasn't really an option for me. There were other things that were more of a priority—'

'Fair enough!' She cuts me short again. 'How did you get into poetry?'

This is a question I'm happy to answer. 'I've always loved words. I wanted to be a musician at first.'

'Oh my God, no way! I bet whatever music you'd make would be amazing.'

'I'm not so sure about that . . . but yeah, poetry just fits. I've been writing for ever but properly since I was fourteen.'

'And how old are you now?'

'I'm twenty-eight. How old are you?'

'Twenty-three,' she says proudly. 'But I think I have an old soul so we're probably closer in age, you know, like spiritually speaking.' I want to laugh but I keep it in.

Ordinarily I'm not into younger girls, but despite the fact she's annoying me a little, she's also peng.

'How did you get into poetry then?' I ask, folding my arms on the table and leaning into them.

'Well, when I went to uni, I just had an awakening. I mean, my curriculum was *so* white.' Right. I'm curious to see what will happen when we reach the end of their ramble. She continues. 'I was studying English and I basically made my own reading list. You know, we can't wait for an institution to do it for us. It was definitely Audre Lorde who made me want to take poetry seriously.'

'Was it?' I lean back. 'Cool.'

'Where in London are you from anyway?' she asks. 'I'm a ride or die Southie.'

'I'm actually not from London. I was born in Bristol.'

'Oh my God, no way! Not from London! Why don't you have one of those West Country accents?' She's genuinely shocked.

'Well my parents came from Guyana, so they have hints of that in the way they speak. Though it's mostly faded now, and they were properly serious about me speaking the Queen's English. Basically, the blandest way of speaking possible. Also, I moved to London at sixteen.'

'Ahh. So your family moved to London at sixteen. Makes sense. You feel like one of us.' I nod, not wanting to get into the ins and outs of why, as a teen, I moved alone to this city.

We drink our wine and she talks at length about her ambitions for the collective and how happy she is with how their event went. I nod in all the right places but wonder when she's going to slow down.

Once we've made our way through the first bottle of wine, Leonie gets a glint in her eye and she starts to run one of her fingers up and down my arm. I like the change in vibe.

'Those are long.' I point to her nails and she continues down my body and onto my thigh. With my tongue, I wet my bottom lip.

'Want some more?' I hold up the empty bottle, keen for this evening to continue.

They nod and I head to the bar for another.

'Yo, Tri.'

'How's it going with red lips over there?'

'Ha, it's good. Can I get another bottle?'

'Yeah, but you'll have to pay for half of it this time. My manager is watching,' she whispers.

'No problem. We're probably gonna bounce after this.'

'How you been anyway, g?'

'All right. I had a gig at that little hippy café earlier. It was good. What's the latest with you?'

'You know, same old. Lisa and me are about to move into a new flat in Elephant. I think we might even get married soon.'

A moment later, she sinks her red claws into my thighs and our bodies convulse harmoniously. Our legs wrap around each other as a thin layer of sweat gathers between our torsos. We kiss, and Leonie's breathing grows more intense as I pull her onto my lap and tease my finger gently in circles around her clit. The sounds she's making and the moisture I can feel on my leg tell me what she wants. I keep my right hand where it is and with my left hand I brush my fingers against her stomach and then around her left breast. I lower them onto the bed before sliding one finger and then slowly a second inside. She guides in a third. Her moans are gentle and feeling her body react to my touch turns me on. I put in more work, but I don't mind. It's hot and sticky under the duvet and the bed is damp. We come up for air, and she kicks the duvet onto the floor and encourages me to take off what I'm wearing, which I do. She brushes her hand against the crevice of my thigh and I, in turn, position a pillow underneath her hips so that she's perfectly elevated. I lick her inner right thigh and pause for a moment.

'One second,' I whisper gently as I grab one of my straps from an unmarked box on the floor.

'What are you doing?' she asks.

'Getting this, if that's what you want?' I lift it up to show her.

She smiles knowingly and then nods in anticipation. I've finessed getting it on at a speed that doesn't interrupt the flow of things. Once everything is in place, I make my way back to Leonie and kiss her on the lips before brushing my hand over her in a slow and consistent rhythm. She closes her eyes and for a moment so do I, aware of the moisture gathering between my legs.

'Is this okay?' I ask before entering her slowly, gently, with the black silicone attachment.

'Mhmm.' She nods, pulling me close to her. She throws her head back and tightens her thighs around my own, increasing the speed of things. Our boobs stick together and with each motion, the top of the strap brushes against my clit at just the right angle.

'Wait!' Leonie suddenly jolts upright.

'Everything okay?' I ask, worried for a moment that my strap game is off.

'Yeah, no I'm fine. It's just . . . I need to use the loo.'

'Are you sure?' I say teasingly, leaning my head to one side.

'I was close but not *that* close. Definitely need a wee.'

'I mean, okay . . . If you've got to go!'

We separate ourselves slowly, careful not to cause any discomfort, and she jumps up off the bed.

Five minutes pass and I consider the possibility that maybe she's left the flat entirely. It's something I might do, but not something that's ever happened to me. But as I survey the room, all her clothes are still in here. I can't imagine her leaving the flat naked. I grab a pair of boxers and wander over to the bathroom. It's dark and she isn't in there. But I can hear noises coming from Juliet's room.

'I thought that your bedroom was the bathroom –'

'Well it isn't,' an angry Juliet responds. 'And you can't just walk into people's rooms unannounced!'

We are both still a bit drunk, but I do my best to appear attentive and sober.

'What's going on?' I ask, pushing Juliet's door further open. Leonie's wearing my shirt from earlier with nothing underneath, and Juliet is sitting on her bed in a full set of bright blue lingerie. Her laptop is closed but her ring light is on, which makes it look like there's a divine glow surrounding her.

'What's going on is that you need to stop bringing people back to the house who have no understanding of boundaries!' She looks really pissed off, which is a rarity. Her arms are flailing everywhere as she speaks, and she seems unfazed being honest in front of Leonie. Oh shit. She's pissed. I really didn't think about this. 'Apparently the door, which is labelled "bathroom", isn't as obvious as I had thought. I was in a private room with a client, who probably isn't even there anymore. It's just unprofessional to have someone walk in like this.' Juliet shakes her head.

I look over to Leonie for an explanation. Juliet catches my gaze.

'I'm not even irritated at them.' She signals at Leonie, standing awkwardly between us like she's caught in the middle of a long-standing family feud. 'I'm just irritated. I'm actually really fed up. I told you I had work tonight. Could you not have listened to me?'

'J, please relax. It's an honest mistake.' I'm not used to seeing her so angry, but I understand we have just fucked with her income.

'I'll pay you back whatever money you've lost out on. I'm sure Leonie's already apologised.'

'I have. I'm sorry. It was a mistake. I'm quite drunk,' she says, steadying herself against the wall to prove the inebriation.

Juliet looks at us sternly for a moment, then breaks the silence. 'It's not your fault, Leonie, don't worry about it. But I need to get back to my client now. Elsie, I'll see you tomorrow.'

Leonie and I make our way sheepishly back to my bedroom. I sit on the edge of the bed.

'What was that all about?' I frown at Leonie.

'Like I said, it was an accident,' she says coolly.

'Did you want to catch her in the act or something?' She was being weird with her at the event but the thought of her deliberately prying on her would be really fucking weird.

'It was a mistake. I didn't mean to go in there.'

I go to press the subject but then Leonie kisses me intensely and we're back on track. Their breathing is rapid and I can feel the rhythmic pumping of her heart racing as she presses up against me. She holds my face and kisses me, staring me dead in the eye for at least three seconds, which feels like an intimacy that should be reserved for encounters other than this. In response, I wriggle free and begin to kiss her neck. After a couple of minutes, I guide her legs open gently, using my left thigh to hold her in position. I lick my middle and index fingers and, using just my hands this time, they come quickly but loud enough for Juliet to hear.

I wait twenty minutes before saying, 'I have to be up really early for work tomorrow so it might be easiest for you to go now.' This may be a lie and look like a dickhead move but I don't know Leonie like Bea, or even Juliet – with whom I might be partial to a *little* squeeze. And besides, as much as the night was fun in an unexpected way, the thoughts of my ever-growing to-do list are creeping back in, ready to haunt my dreams.

'That's fine, I get up early anyway.' Leonie doesn't take the hint and instead curls into my arms, making the assumption that I want to be the big spoon.

12

I wake up early and pretend to get ready for the job I don't have. Leonie, who is still curled up in my bed, seems reluctant to move and I figure this is the only way to coax them out. She remains there, watching me as I pull clothes out of the green dresser in the corner of the room. I look in her direction to see if she's starting to show any signs of movement but she's just looking over at me in a dream-like state: half smiling, half snoozing. I pull on a pair of bright blue tracksuit bottoms and a matching jumper.

'I have to leave soon, Leonie. Otherwise, I'll be late.'

'Oh yeah, sorry. It's just that this bed is surprisingly comfy . . . I could always let myself out?'

Bit presumptuous of them.

'It isn't really my place, so I think it's best if you leave with me.'

'I was only joking,' she says then, a little defensively. She jumps up and retrieves her clothes from the floor. Her pink polka-dot pants first, jumpsuit second, and then she stuffs her bra into her pocket.

'Do you have a brush? I should've wrapped my hair last night.' She flattens out her wig, which is all over the place.

I point at my bald head and she laughs.

'Well, do you have a hat I could borrow then?' I scan the room for something I don't mind never seeing again. I hand her a plain black cap that was hanging on the back of the door. Once she's adjusted it and I've got my socks on, we make our way to the front door. I usher Leonie out quietly in the hope that her and Juliet's paths won't cross again. We successfully sneak out of the flat and make our way towards the Rye. I try and figure out what my next move is. It's that point in the year when the grass on the Rye is covered in a light mist. My head is feeling the cool air and I consider asking Leonie for my hat back.

'So, I'm actually going this way,' I say, pointing vaguely at the air, 'but it was nice hanging out.' Leonie surprisingly leans in for a kiss. I deliver a peck on their cheek and they look disappointed.

'Okay, well, I'll call you,' she says, and I smile and walk away before she can say anything else. I pause only to watch her enter the station, before doing a 180 and making my way back to the flat. Last night was fun, a distraction, but as ever, my thoughts are now creeping back in.

When I return, Juliet has surfaced from her room and I can feel the unresolved tension in the air. She bangs doors and moves around the kitchen heavy-footed. It's suddenly uncomfortable and I feel out of place in this flat that was almost starting to feel like a sort of home.

'Everything all right? Did you manage to sort things out with the client?' I ask her tentatively. 'I did try to get her to leave last night but I felt bad forcing her to go home on her own so late.' I'm trying to cover up my tracks.

'Mmm hmm, really sounded like it.'

'J, I'm sorry. If you don't want me to have people back here, I totally respect that. It's your place after all.'

'No, don't do that. You know that this is your place as much as it is mine, and I want you to feel completely at home here. I just want whoever you bring into this space to respect it too.'

'Noted.'

'I could literally hear her leaning against the door listening in before she *accidentally* found her way in.' Juliet makes air-quotes with her fingers. 'I think you need a better vetting process.'

That explains why Leonie was gone so long. It feels weird that she'd try and catch Juliet out like that.

'Since when do you care who I date anyway?'

'I don't.' Juliet has always been a terrible liar. The truth is that she doesn't *want* to care but I can tell a part of her does. I'm not sure why.

'Look, I know she was totally out of order and I spoke to her about it.'

Juliet glares at me. It's evident that this is going to take more than one apology. I wonder how long she'll be like this and after a long awkward silence I attempt to change tack.

'The good thing is that after last night, I'm feeling just a tiny bit more hopeful about my life. I scrolled through Instagram this morning and the amount of love that I'm getting is impressive, especially considering there were only a handful of people there. It looks like most of them shared my performance.'

Juliet softens. 'That's great, Els. You know I'm proud of you, always.' I can see her letting go of some of the anger as her shoulders release themselves from their upright position. 'And by the way, I've really been thinking about this Japan trip,' she continues. 'I think it might be good for me to get out of here, you know. Have a change of scenery. Also, the fact that it's happening during half-term makes it feel like I'm supposed to go. It's a universe move. You can obviously have the place to yourself while I'm gone. Just please don't burn the house down,' she quickly adds. And then she says more thoughtfully, 'I've always loved teaching, but I think I need a bit of time to figure out whether there is anything else I want to try out.'

'I'm sure Andrew will be delighted.' I mutter this under my breath but Juliet hears me.

'What does that mean?' She asks, having sniffed out the disapproval in my voice.

'Nothing, forget it.' After last night, it doesn't feel like the right time for me to judge her life choices.

'Are you sure?'

'Yes.' I side glance at her. 'So, when do you leave?'

'It would be in a couple of weeks' time.' She pauses. 'Are you sure that's okay?'

'Of course, why wouldn't it be? You deserve a holiday, J. I'm sure you'll have the best time. Plus, you've always wanted to go to Japan.'

My phone rings and in a bid to exit our conversation, I pick up straight away. Juliet shakes her head, the anger clearly seeping back in. She hates it when I leave conversations early.

'That's unlike you, to answer the phone as soon as I call,' Mum remarks before the word *Hello* has the opportunity to roll off my tongue. I should've checked the caller ID.

'We're coming to London next weekend, Elsie, and we want to see you.'

I sigh to myself. By 'see you' she means that they have plans to see their friends, and feel it's only right to make an obligatory stop off to see their only daughter. It happens once a year that my parents and I find ourselves in the same room. It's usually strained, and we never discuss anything real. But it's my token gift to them, a moment when they can perform parenthood and feel as though they're doing it – have always done it – right.

'Sure, Mum. I can book us a table somewhere.' I offer this up without much enthusiasm.

'We'd much rather come to yours, if that's all right?'

'Are you sure? I can pick somewhere that you'll like?'

They're both super fussy when it comes to food and anything I cook will inevitably fall short. I also don't really want them in mine and Juliet's space. A space that has come to feel safe.

'The least that you can do is host us in your home. We aren't strangers, Elsie.'

I see what she's doing. If they make a stop off at mine, they'll be able to pretend to their posse of church-going friends that everything is normal. I can already envision them spinning some lie about how I'm working as a teacher somewhere. Because that would be miles better than eating out in public and having to admit to themselves and the people around us that we are a) estranged and b) that I'm sofa-surfing at my best friend's house. The other reason they want to stop by is because Mum wants to see where I'm staying. This will be her only insight into my world.

'I'm with your father,' Mum says. There's a pause, and after a couple of seconds I hear him shout in the background.

'Hi baby. Looking forward to catching up,' he says with a faint, tender and awkward intonation.

'I'm actually living with Juliet at the moment. I'll need to ask her.' I gesture at Juliet but she can't hear what they're saying, and part of me is scared to put them on speakerphone in case they say something off.

'Okay, well I'm sure Juliet won't have a problem with your parents coming by.' Mum breathes heavily down the phone.

'Listen, I'll let you know if that works. What day are you here again?'

'Next Sunday would be good for lunch. We're going to a church service in the morning.'

'I'll get back to you. I have to go now, Mum.'

'Okay, Elsie. Bye, bye.'

I let out a sigh as she hangs up the phone. The thought of my parents visiting makes me feel wildly uncomfortable, especially when things are tense with Juliet.

'What do you need to ask me?' She looks up from the purple notebook she's been furiously scribbling in for the duration of my phone call. I hesitate and she looks suspicious.

'My mum and dad are coming to London. I mentioned that I'm staying with you and they said they want to pop by. Is that all right? If it's not, that's fine because I actually don't want them to come anyway.'

'Of course, that's fine. In fact, I'll invite Helen too to ease the tension.' It's actually always been weird to me that Juliet calls her mum by her first name. I imagine the piercing glare I'd get in my mind's eye if I ever tried to pull something similar.

'We can make it a reunion. I'll cook!' She jumps up like she's about to put together a plan. She's never been able to stay angry at me for too long. It was me who kept the silence for those three months after all, not her.

'What day are they coming?' Juliet's mind is clearly whirling.

'Next Sunday, for lunch.'

She takes out her phone.

'What are you doing?'

'Texting Mum.'

'Already? Wait, we don't have to . . .'

'Too late!'

My mum and Helen have never got on and I know for a fact that my parents won't like any of the vegan food that Juliet spends her life nibbling on. My parents need their food to contain a combination of meat and rice and if either of these component parts is missing, they'll spend the entire evening complaining. Once when they visited my old flat, I took them to a Trini place in Brixton and Dad moaned because there was no rice, just roti. They also didn't make their sorrel drink the way Mum liked it (she swore it was missing a special ingredient). I decide to tackle this problem first. I'll deal with Helen second.

'You know what, my parents love that Guyanese place in Herne Hill. There aren't any similar places near them. I'll do a big order,' I suggest, an attempt at a peace offering.

'Rude.' Juliet gives me her classic, exaggerated look with pursed lips and plenty of side-eye. 'But fine, your loss. You know I make a mean roasted cauli.'

The roast cauliflower she's referring to is a regular staple on her weekly menu. We've had it at least once a week since I've moved in. I don't enjoy anything about it: not the taste; not the texture. But when Juliet fixates on a new recipe, it becomes impossible to suggest that she cook anything else. When she isn't looking, I organise the food on my plate in the way a child does with their unwanted vegetables, pushed over to the side to give the illusion that they've eaten more than they actually have. The flaw in this plan is that Juliet thinks I love the dish and continues to cook it, and I continue to go to bed with a roaring stomach.

'This is a better idea because it means you won't spend the evening in the kitchen, J. *And* that will take some of the heat off me. You can absorb the stilted and painfully polite conversation . . . Mum will bond with you over teaching. You know that work is the only thing she's able to talk about. And that will free me up to prevent Helen from flirting with my dad.' Dad's always been amused by her stories. She's a rare bird seldom found in his neck of the woods. And because of this intrigue there has always been a feeling of unease between Helen and my mum. When they come for dinner, I'll make sure they are sitting as far away from each other as is possible in a small flat.

'Sounds like a plan,' Juliet laughs.

'How is Helen, by the way? You never talk about her.'

'She's, you know . . . She's Helen.' Juliet says this whilst letting out a sigh. I don't know why Juliet gets so exasperated by her mum. If I had a parent as uninterested in rules and tradition, I'd be lapping it up.

'And what does that mean exactly?'

'It means she's fine. She just continues to do what Helen does. You know she's a handful!' A fatigued look takes over Juliet's face. I move over to where she's standing in the kitchen and place my right hand on her sympathetically. For some reason I start to pat her on the shoulder in the way I imagine blokes do in the pub when they meet up to complain about their missus.

'What is that?' She turns to look at my hand, which remains, even though it's now still.

'I don't know. I just thought you looked stressed talking about her.' I remove my hand and quickly retreat to the other side of the kitchen, so that there's sufficient distance between us again.

'I can't believe you just patted me.' She laughs as she says this and I join in, swinging my awkward hand around in the air.

'But in all seriousness, the fact that you even had to mention her flirting with your dad is just . . .'

'I'm only joking, J . . .'

'I know you've always got along really well with her, but as a mum, she can be too involved.' Juliet goes into the sitting room.

'You do kind of act like best friends. I thought you liked it that way though? I used to be so jealous when we were kids.'

I notice that there is a stack of dirty dishes on the counter. I make my way over to the sink and we continue to speak through the hatch in the wall.

'Really? I think I might have preferred it if my parents were more like yours.'

'No. There's no way. Impossible.'

'I know they can't be compared or anything. I saw how difficult it was for you growing up. But sometimes I think just a little more parenting might have been good for me. My mum would love it if I invited her on a night out. She's suggested it more than once. Can you imagine? She's completely over the top about everything.'

'That is a little bit jokes, but I hear you.'

'Helen knows no boundaries.' She walks back into the kitchen then and pulls herself up so that she's sitting on the countertop next to me. 'And when I say no boundaries, I really do mean, none. She's the type of mum who couldn't wait to have the talk with me. Even made me watch a clip from my own birthing video. I'm still recovering from the trauma.'

'Naaaa, Helen! Mad. Thing is though, you wouldn't have been able to cope with the lack of freedom in my house. My parents were relentless.'

'Yeah, you were so exhausted by it. I wouldn't have been able to handle your never-ending list of responsibilities ... Gosh, parenting must be hard though, mustn't it?' She gestures at me to pass her the pink ceramic plate I've just finished washing up and starts drying it with a flamingo-patterned tea towel. 'It's why I'm not sure I ever want children.'

'Even despite the love you have for those little terrors you see every day?'

'Precisely because of that.' Juliet giggles. 'I see all of it. When you work as a teacher, you aren't just a teacher. You're also a therapist, and in my case a bridge between the school, the head-teacher and whatever is going on at home. I take so much of my work home with me. I know it looks adorable because they are small and cute *and* who else gets paid to make a papier-mâché turtle? But my goodness, at the end of the day, I can't imagine bringing one home with me. Besides, I've got too many places I want to travel to.' Juliet turns wistful.

'Well, you already know I'm not interested in the child thing. I'm scarred for life by the twins. And by my own mum. Honestly, some of us are meant to be mothers, and some of us are meant to be mothers of many things.'

'Oprah says it best.'

I flick a bit of water from the tap in her direction and she jumps down off the counter, whipping me on the bum with the tea towel as she descends. Any remaining tension in the air disappears.

13

As I step through the doors of the Jobcentre my feet crunch upon the autumnal leaves gathered at the entrance. I'm here to collect my weekly allowance of £74.34. The room is a stark white and there are small desks with flimsy blue Perspex partitions separating each unit. I note the amount of noise my DMs are making as I walk into the room. There is an underlying hum of tapping keyboards and mutterings and the smell of artificial apple fills the air. It's so cold in here that everyone – even the staff – is still wearing their jackets and coats.

I make my way over to a free station. The woman sitting there is the only affable-looking thing in here. She smiles and gestures at me to sit down.

'How can I help you?'

'I'm here to claim Jobseeker's for this week.'

'Okay, let me pull up your details. What's your name and date of birth?'

'Elsie Macintosh, and my date of birth is twenty-third of October 1990.'

'The computer is just taking a little while to load.' She's tapping away impatiently at the same button.

'No worries.'

'How's the job search going?'

'Not well, obviously.' Each word is doused in cynicism.

'Well, that's what I'm here for. There we go, looks like this thing is working now,' she says, slapping the cumbersome device on its side. 'I have a few jobs here that could work for you. From what I can see, your CV needs a refresh. You do know that for every job you're applying to, you should tailor your cover letter to that job, right? That's my number one tip.'

I grit my teeth into a smile, trying my best not to give her the satisfaction of my frustration.

'What sort of jobs are available?' I hope she doesn't make this process more painful than it already is.

'Why don't you tell me what you've been up to since we last saw you? That might be a useful place to start.'

It feels as though she's waiting for me to trip up.

'Well, I've applied to be a dog walker, a PA, waitress, bartender, librarian . . . oh, and kitchen porter.'

'Oh that is a lot, though we can always do more.' Her surprise doesn't last for long. 'And have you heard back from any of them?'

'Yep. I've been rejected by every single one. Either I'm told I have too much experience and would get bored, or I'm told I've not got enough experience. So, if you can magic something up for me that would be great.' I take in a couple of silent, deep breaths in an attempt to overcome how light-headed I'm suddenly feeling.

'Maybe we should work on some interview techniques.' The woman's brow almost joins in the middle of her forehead. 'And we should think about whether there are any jobs we can put you up for that feed into your overall career ambitions.' I place my hand on my chest in an attempt to self-soothe.

'My ambitions as a writer?' I say quietly.

'Oh, well . . .' She stutters as her eyes dart across the screen searching for a job I know doesn't exist.

'We don't seem to have anything like that here but what we do have are a couple of warehouse packing jobs. I'm going to forward them on to you now. I know it might feel disheartening to be rejected but you need to just keep applying. You'll get something eventually. This is Job*seeker*'s after all.' She emphasises her words to insinuate that I clearly haven't been searching hard enough.

'Do you have anything that needs strong customer service skills? I have loads of experience in those kind of positions.'

'Let's see ... No, not at the moment, sorry dear. In the meantime, take this,' she says, handing me a leaflet on the art of CV writing. 'And when you come back next week, I want to see that you've applied for at least three more jobs. Okay? And remember, when you have interviews, smile! Be friendly and personable. If they sense you really want it, you'll be in with a good chance.' I close my eyes as a wave of irritation overtakes my body. It's so powerful that I think it might drag me to the ground. I get up before the first frustrated tear has a chance to fall and I rush out of the building where I'm hit by fresh air as they come tumbling down.

'You all right?' A woman who is walking her dog on the path outside asks me.

I don't respond. I just nod at her Pomeranian, worried that I must look insane.

The walk home is blurry. There are figures everywhere

but none of them have clear features. I feel surrounded but I mustn't succumb to the miserable and rapid sensation of my chest tightening. I think I might faint but I don't stop, making it to the main road. I keep walking and wipe my tears as I go. They're blinding me but the more I scoop them away, the harder the next ones fall.

After weaving through the floating bodies, I'm finally outside Juliet's building. I decide to take a minute in the courtyard round the back where I let myself sob uncontrollably and lie on the cold, damp floor. When there is nothing left for me to let go of, I know it is safe to go inside. What the hell am I going to do?

Every time I think things are looking up, life decides to show me again that this isn't true, that I'm wasting my time. It's the way that fucking woman at the Jobcentre looked at me, the disappointment in my parents' voices when I never have a promotion to speak of and the fact that compliments about my poetry don't convert to cash or opportunities. I'm spiralling.

'Hi babe. How are you?' Juliet shouts from the sitting room before I've even pulled my key out of the door. She's wearing a pair of pyjamas covered in strawberries and flicking through a deck of daily inspiration cards. I hang my coat up in the hallway, not wanting to make eye contact with her.

'All right, just tired.'

She notices the wobble in my voice because she probes.

'Are you sure?'

She moves. I can hear her footsteps coming towards me but thankfully she just moves onto the sofa. I remain in the same position, facing the door, pretending to search for something in my jacket pocket.

'How are you feeling?' I ask her, hoping for a long-winded answer.

'I'm fine. I'm fine. Have you submitted your stuff for that poetry prize yet?'

'Oh, I haven't yet. I have a little bit of time left. I'll get it done.'

'The deadline is pretty soon, Els. It would be such a shame if you missed out on it.'

A new wave of anxiety comes over me, and I stand in the hallway another moment, closing my eyes and taking a deep breath. When I turn around, she is standing in front me. She looks concerned.

'Are you sure you're okay, Els? You know you can speak to me about anything, don't you?'

'I think . . . It's just . . . Maybe I need to pull my head out of the clouds with all this poetry stuff. The commissions I get at these indie publications are barely enough to get by. I'm only managing to hold everything together because I'm staying with you. There are no jobs anywhere. I've offered to clean, pack boxes, walk dogs, do anything! And there's nothing, J. It's hopeless. I'm hopeless. And I can't rely on you for ever.'

I walk past her into the sitting room and flop onto the sofa, totally defeated by this world. She sits beside me and guides my head so that it's in the middle of her lap. The sensation of her silk PJs against my scalp is luxurious and calming. I realise she must have pulled a sickie from work. I don't ask why. Juliet strokes me gently.

'It'll be okay, Els. I know it doesn't feel like it, but it's not been that long since everything happened with your flat. It's only been a couple of months and look! Having commissions is better than nothing. It's incredibly difficult to get your art commissioned for print, Els. And you're doing it! I know it's not paying a lot, but these are all good things and it's indicative of your talent. You just need to find a job to help fund your art until you get back on your feet and land a book deal. You'll get there, I promise. Don't give up.'

'I need something more reliable. I'm not eighteen anymore.'

'No, you're not. But you've worked ever since you were a kid. Ever since I can remember, Elsie. You're down on your luck right now but you'll find a job. You always do.' She pauses thoughtfully and bites her lip in that way she does when she's machinating some master plan. 'If you want a little bit of extra cash, what about camming?'

I tut at her impatiently.

'It's not as bad as you think it will be. It was a little awkward for me at first too, but then you sort of get used to it, and to be completely honest, it's up to you to determine what your boundaries are. You can always see if you like it and if you don't, then no worries.'

I sit up so we're at eye level.

'Look, you know it isn't that I have a problem with sex work, don't you? I just dunno if I can cope with seeing naked white willies flopping around everywhere. My straps are either multi-coloured or black. White just isn't my colour.' I let out a snigger.

'You can watch me with a client tonight if you like and then make a decision,' she says warmly. 'No pressure at all. Just watch. Why don't you pull a card and see what it says?' She guides me over to the table in the corner, covered with her daily inspiration cards.

'Pick a card, any card.'

I close my eyes and dramatically choose a card from the pile. The card I select reads, 'Be open to the possibility of the unknown'. It is written in a thick, pink, serif font, apparently for emphasis.

'Well, I suppose there's no harm in watching you if that is what the card wants me to do. But if it gets *really* weird, I'm outta there quick.'

'Since when were you such a prude? You've seen my boobs a million times.'

I think back to when we were at school. It was her who had backed me when the girls in the changing room started to make comments about not wanting to get changed in front of a lesbian. I wasn't as secure in my sexuality back then and even though I've always been attracted to women, I definitely identified as straight. I've come a long way since and Juliet is right. I have seen her naked before, just as much as you do your best friend when you stay the night or get ready to go out together. She has always been pretty free and open.

'All right, I'm gonna make myself a rum and ginger beer. You want one?' I say.

'Ooh yes, but make me a vodka tonic instead. I don't like clients thinking I'm drinking.'

I get up from the sofa and head into the kitchen, shaking my head at the mess. I love Juliet deeply but her idea of cleanliness is not up to my standards. I grew up in a home that was stiflingly ordered. But whenever I mention Juliet's organisational skills, she rolls her eyes and tells me to relax. She says that most people aren't as anal as me when it comes to cleaning and tidying and that I should really lighten up. Apparently a small amount of germs is good for the immune system. I'm still not so sure.

I pick up a couple of glasses and carefully inspect them to make sure they're clean. There's half a lime on the top shelf in the fridge. I think about all the tiny bits of bacteria that will have found their way onto its surface before banishing the thought and grabbing a couple of ice cubes from the freezer. I slice off the top layer of the germy lime and squeeze some of it into Juliet's glass, along with a generous glug of vodka and a splash of tonic.

'Are you ready?' I say, making my way over to her bedroom, 'Because your drink is. Should I enter?'

'Give me a minute ... okay ... hang on ... one sec. Three, two, one ... Okay, I'm ready for you,' she announces genially.

She opens her bedroom door. Her body looks tiny. She's wearing a red and white gingham underwear set with a pair of white thigh-high stockings. I was sort of expecting her to be wearing black lingerie with cut-outs in inconvenient places and to be holding a whip but instead, she's giving me full-on cutesy vibes. I really like it.

'You look cute,' I compliment her and she gives her outfit a twirl.

'Yeah? It's this brand, El Bras. She makes underwear out of scrap material and old T-shirts, that sort of thing.'

'Sounds sexy.' I hand her the vodka tonic, trying not to stare.

'Thanks. Okay, so if you sit there in the corner of the room,' she points, 'you can see what I'm doing. And you'll hear him without having to see the penis.'

'Cool.'

'Just don't say anything. Don't comment or laugh.' She stares me in the eyes to make sure I'm taking this seriously and then climbs on top of her bed, which is covered in a tropical orange and pink patterned duvet cover. There is a battered-looking teddy bear which she's had ever since I've known her.

'You probably wanna get rid of Bernie,' I say, nodding at her toy.

'Oww Bernie, you do not want to see what's about to happen here. That would scar you for quite some time.' She gently places him in an open box next to her bed.

'So, how do I look?' She asks as she poses on the bed. Her new bouncy, bleached pink curls rest on her collarbone. 'If I put red lipstick on, do you think that will be too much?'

'I think keep it simple, a bit of gloss or something.' I take her in one more time. 'You look good though.'

She grins at me and grabs a squeezy tube of gloss. 'Okay so today I have a regular client who requests a private session with me at the same time every week. He's actually not bad looking and he's also quite young. We usually speak for most of the time we have together and then he asks me to do some pretty standard playing with myself kind of stuff. Don't be weird or anything. It's just a body.'

'You know I love sex, J. I just haven't ever sat in a room watching you wank in front of a computer before.'

'Point taken.'

I take a big swig of my drink. I'd gone heavy on the rum – a habit I'd picked up on my one trip to Guyana in my late teens. If you go into a bar and order a spirit there, any sort of mixer is an optional extra.

'Okay, I'm going to sign in now. Don't wanna keep Jonathan waiting too long. He tips well. And I'm *so* close to having enough for my trip to South America next year.'

She winks playfully and gestures at me to *shhhh*, pushing her finger up against her lips. A couple of seconds later, she starts moving around, parting her lips and legs slightly. I assume that she's reading through comments in the chat and responding to their requests. She gently caresses her boobs and pushes her hair back slightly.

This is the first time I've seen her doing anything remotely sexual. We obviously speak about sex and I know she enjoys it just as much as I do, but I've never seen her perform or sell a fantasy. Turns out she's really good at it.

After a couple of minutes, Juliet stops moving and I hear the voice of a guy coming out of the computer.

'Jonathan, how are you?' she asks flirtatiously. 'I've missed you this week.'

'I've missed you too, Stephanie,' the guy responds excitedly, with what sounds like a New York accent.

I wonder why she's chosen Stephanie and try to suppress any laughs. I'd expect her to choose something more out there like Dandelion. After a few minutes of basic chat and generic touching, Jonathan says, 'You look so beautiful. Play with yourself for me. I want to see you take those off.'

'You mean these?' Juliet proceeds to rub the outside of her spotted knickers, making noises as she does.

'How wet are you? It sounds like you really like it.'

'I'm so wet right now,' Juliet says. 'So wet thinking about all the naughty things I would do to you if you were here.'

Jonathan is really enjoying it. That's clear from where I'm sitting. He's becoming increasingly out of breath as he speaks, a reminder that men have literally no idea if a girl is really into it or not. I don't feel weird about being in the room and watching Juliet, just a little turned on, but it doesn't feel wrong.

I know she's not looking at me but I do feel self-conscious, worried that if she does look in my direction, it will be written all over my face. She's doing a good job and the guy bashing himself off on the other end of the screen is here for it, which is the point, right?

After another few minutes, Juliet is completely stripped down and Jonathan has finished. They say their goodbyes.

'I'll see you next week, Steph. God, you are amazing. I wish more women could be like you.'

Juliet doesn't answer but does this little wave and then logs out of the call. An inexplicable tension is released from my body.

'I'm gonna stay on for a couple more hours, Els,' she says, starting to get dressed in the same outfit. 'We'll talk more about it later, but I told you, see? It isn't that big of a deal.'

'You were great,' I say, admiring her superpower ability to see men for the simpletons that they are and using that to her advantage.

'A lot of the guys are dickheads. Some try to demand things that I would never do, but it's mostly all right. And I'm glad you approve,' she says, tying up her hair. 'Did I make you horny baby?'

We both crack up. I'm laughing to hide the tingly feeling that emerged watching Juliet, though I'm sure that was due to the fact that it's been way too long since I last saw Bea. Or any girl, for that matter. Leonie was a whole week ago.

'I need another rum anyway. I'll leave you to it, J.'

I spend the rest of my evening in the next room. I'm thinking about Juliet and how much coin she'll make tonight – and who she'll perform for.

14

You still getting that food from Zionly?

Juliet texts me from her room. I'd promised I'd grab us lunch almost an hour ago.

'I'm going now! I swear!' I shout across the hallway as I reluctantly peel my limbs off the sofa. They've practically fused with the fabric because I haven't moved in hours.

I had another one of those dreams and this morning, the gunmen forced me outside onto my balcony, gag in my mouth. I was terrified and screaming through the fabric. They had balaclavas over their faces and I couldn't see their expressions. They pushed me over the balcony and I was about to plummet into the concrete when I woke up shaking. I spent the morning reading Juliet's dream dictionary but it was pretty useless. I found a couple of forums on PTSD and nightmares. They recommended therapy but I'm gonna have to search for a blend of tea or mindfulness app that can flush this shit out of me instead.

It's cool outside as I make my way down to Zionly Manna. I imagine the channa and delicious fried dumplings warming me from the inside out. Theirs is the only vegan food that I can say

I wholeheartedly enjoy. Everything they cook is packed with flavour and their sauces bang. I arrive before they've finished cooking today's menu, which is a common occurrence. I put in an order for two combination meals because everything sounds so good. There is a queue of similarly hungry and eager people forming behind me. While I wait for my food, I take a seat on one of the wooden benches at the restaurant's tiny front. I do my best to avoid drooling at the tantalising smells wafting from the kitchen.

My phone starts buzzing. It's Leonie.

> Hey all, just a reminder that you only have a couple more days to get your submissions in. Nora mentioned that they are yet to hear from a few of you (which I'd take as a good sign. It means they probably haven't found quite what they're looking for). This is your reminder that you're capable and powerful and that your words matter. Can't wait to see you at the showcase. In love and solidarity, Leonie xx

When I saw their name pop up, I was expecting it to be another one of her film recommendations. It's sweet that she thought to send a reminder. I get up and pace up and down the tiny space outside the food place to shake off my restlessness. I deliberate whether I can submit on time, whether there is anything in my head still to be teased out.

When our orders are ready, I grab the bags and speed down the high street back to the flat. I decide I can't waste any more time. Leonie's text is the kick up the arse I needed, telling me to get out of my feelings and write. I open the front door and hand Juliet her brown box, opening mine with haste.

'I have that deadline coming up. You were right. I've gotta do it. I'm locking myself away until I get it down.' I shovel a couple of spoons of food into my mouth while I speak.

'Calm down, your food isn't going anywhere!' Juliet replies. I march through the sitting room and into my bedroom.

I sit on the bed ready to write a poem about sex, the type of intimacy I'm most comfortable with. I know for a fact that it's possible to have mind-blowing sex without a deep spiritual connection. Sometimes there is pure fire, and it is what it is. I think about Audre Lorde's description of 'fingers whispering sound'. The image of warm breath dressing a body in desire. I stare down at my belly, so full that it's expanded, and think of the black vibrating wand in my bedside table. I need some inspiration. I slide under the covers in anticipation, hoping that the padding will mask the buzz.

I recently realised that masturbation has become a key part of my writing process, whether I'm writing about sex or not. Something is unleashed after you cum. As if the act of orgasming unlocks some secret crevice in your brain where all the creativity is stored. Not that I believe in magic, but I do feel my most powerful and assured after I've had sex, with myself or someone else. Sometimes I really take my time with it, and in those moments I usually just use my fingers, but today I want something more convenient.

Bea's body immediately comes to mind. We've been fucking for ages and so we each know what the other likes. We're never lazy with it either. I know that Bea loves it when I squeeze her nipples and she knows I love it when she parts her lips and legs in anticipation. We also know what the other person doesn't like. I can't stand being spanked because it reminds me of the sting and humiliation that came with getting beats as a child, and she doesn't like sex from behind. These things have changed and evolved over time, but we've remained pretty good at communicating things or clocking when we've picked up a new technique. Sex isn't seamless between us. We laugh a lot and things go wrong, but that comfort is what intimacy is about for me.

After gently placing the head of the wand on the hood of my clit, I turn it on at the lowest setting. The reverberations are immediately felt throughout my body and I tremble, turning so that I'm on all fours. I guide the vibrator in circular motions and my hips follow. My toes curl as the speed increases. I'm trying not to scream as I hold it in one spot, so that it is pressed against the right side of my clit, gently enough that it takes me more than just a few seconds to orgasm. I think of being in this position with Bea's thighs wrapped around my waist and the sound of silicone sliding gently in and out of her as we groan together, bodies hot and sweaty. I have one hand pushed against the wall now and the other remains in control of the vibrator, rubbing it backwards and forwards more intensely than before. I know it's about to happen because I can feel that my body is scared to succumb. It's overwhelming in a good way and the release is satisfying. I lie there breathlessly and wonder if Juliet has heard me, not that she'd mind. She always teases me about how long I spend in the bathroom and says the poor shower head is probably scarred from my antics.

I feel lighter now and once I've tucked the wand away, I take out my tattered brown notebook, bursting with Post-it Notes, additional sheets of paper and markers. My whole life, it seems, is in its pages. The poem practically writes itself.

there's curves on your body that create
      curves on mine
in time, your hips spread my cheeks
wide and grinning.
If sinning means laying here
then
I'm staying here
for as long as this air
smells like sweat
and all curves of mine are met by yours.
on all fours
you fall into a prayer
of some sorts. contort your spine
a level ground.
I've found my reflection in your wet back
at times.
You dive chest first into my mattress
Arch with attitude and ask me to show my gratitude
in a stroke or a soak.
I have been both the bender and the bent
spent nights swirling my duttiest desires against
      teeth and
back dimples and simple white sheets.
The kinda hot that starts at your feet
and somehow makes it to that sweet spot
      of your neck
where small pecks are welcome
and tongue trails are left.
I rest my best parts in you.
The parts I add on,

When I take a visit into the dark
You tag along.
We become a long outward sigh,
Your thighs frame my torso
I tiptoe my wishes southern on your stomach.
All vents blow a cold air but this room is a
        thick smog
When you rob me of my breath
in the power of getting undressed,
Head rolls into heaven
if ten is tops I'll give you eleven.
All sessions start with a smirk
all gardens require a thirst
And then hours
And hours
And Hours
Of endless
Continual
Hard flowing
        Rain.

I haven't felt this capable in a long time. Reading the lines over again, I make very few amends. As I prepare myself to submit, I read through the entry requirements for the competition and have this niggling feeling that I've gone down too obvious a route. Nora did keep banging on about a more unique approach to intimacy and where is resides. And the guidelines do say that you can submit up to three poems. I decide it might be good to show my perspective on intimacy outside of orgasms – as transformative as they are. I need to show that I have range if I want to win. I flick through my notebook in search of something else to include, and a quarter of the way through I find an untitled oldie. I decide that after holding it in the comfort of my heart for so long, it might be time to let it out. It's the right amount of honest and warm and unexpected. I'm not sure if it's impatience or excitement, but I type it up as it is before sending off my email.

15

I disinfect the entire flat. Mum and Dad are going to be round in a couple of hours.

Since I've left home, Dad keeps in touch by sending me a card at Christmas or on my birthday with a twenty pound note in it; fifty if he's feeling generous. This is his way of making himself feel like a good dad. Like that is all it takes. The only reason I started speaking to my parents again after I moved was because, after squeezing my phone number out of my nan, Mum had called me to say Dad was sick. In reality, all he had was high blood pressure.

'Everybody is always asking how is Elsie doing? And I don't know. My own daughter. You know, I've forgiven you for running off like that. You were a child but you're a grown woman now with more sense,' she had said, more concerned with how things looked than how they actually were. Our memories of how things transpired are very different. When I finally told her I was leaving Bristol, she'd practically said, 'go on then'. Maybe her invitation to leave was flippant for her, but it was literal for me. Later she told me that she'd never wanted to fight and she just wanted her daughter back. Once my anger subsided, I told her that we could try to maintain some sort of relationship but that there needed to be clearly defined boundaries. So here I am now, preparing for our annual charade.

'How are you feeling, Els? All right about lunch? It's going to be fine you know,' Juliet says, opening the windows to air out the scent of bleach and disinfectant. 'And by the way, I'd much rather you use the eco products I buy.'

I'm not convinced that they can do the job, but I nod back.

'What's on your mind, Els?'

'It's weird, actually. Do you remember the time Gemma saw me kissing Maya in the bathrooms at school?'

'Yeah, and she told the teachers and you got into loads of trouble?'

'Except I called the headteacher back pretending to be Mum.'

'Jokes. They believed it was her?'

'Yeah. They said I sounded young, but I pretended to take this as a compliment and they left it there.'

'Damn.'

'I know. All of the girls would kiss me in the toilets though. Remember Jodie? She's married with a million kids now. I follow her on Insta. She would literally drag me into the bathrooms whenever she could.'

'Jodie?! How did I never know this?! And to think your parents still have no idea about your way with girls.' Juliet closes the window now as it starts to rain.

'I was just thinking about the fact that they know *nothing* about me. They wouldn't know my favourite food. They wouldn't know what I like doing. My favourite colour. Plans for the future. Fucking nothing.'

'I'm sorry, Els.' Juliet looks sad as she moves her eyes down to where I'm scrubbing a small corner of the kitchen floor.

'It's fine. I was just transported back for a minute, you know. They are my parents but they're also strangers.'

'Look, today will be fine. You know I can speak as much or as little as needed.'

'You'll have to step in when they start asking me when I'm getting married.'

'I'm on it, babe.' She holds my hand and squeezes it in solidarity.

'Mum will definitely ask if I've found a nice Caribbean boy yet. My God. Just make sure Helen doesn't spill anything. You know how she gets after a couple of drinks.'

'Oi, she's not that bad, Els.'

I shrug and get back to my scrubbing. I need to wipe down every surface, door handle and light switch, but the bleach is starting to make me feel light-headed.

'Sit down!' Juliet eventually demands. 'I can practically see my reflection in the kitchen countertops. The one thing your parents won't have anything to talk about is how clean this flat is, but you should probably stop now or you might poison us all!'

I need to keep my hands busy to keep my anxiety at bay. I go to lay the dining table instead.

'No, you sit. I'll finish.' Juliet takes over, strategically placing chairs around the table and setting up a mismatch of plates, cutlery, and napkins.

'That looks nice,' I say, and I start to feel more relaxed once I've inspected the items she's laid out.

'Right, when you're done, can you quickly drive me down to Olive's kitchen to collect the food?'

*

We hop into Juliet's banger and drive over to the restaurant, which categorically serves the best roti in the whole of London. Guyanese, obviously. It has to be Guyanese for my parents. Food is how we've held onto our roots. My nan's cooking is how I've maintained my connection to Guyana. I've only been once. All of my family moved to Canada, the States or England once they left Guyana. I've never heard any of them speaking about returning there for retirement.

We can see through to the kitchen as we enter the shop.

'Maybe I'll make an exception today. The roti does look good.' Juliet licks her bottom lip.

'You sure? The ghee she uses isn't vegan.'

'That's why I said an exception, duh.'

The owner, Olive, slowly potters to the front of the shop. She's short and commands respect. 'Nice to see you, dears. Now remind me what you did order again?'

'Nice to see you too, Olive. I ordered a veggie curry for her,' pointing to Juliet beside me, 'two curry goats, two curry chicken, lots of rice and four roti. But we'd like five roti now, please.' The curry goat is for Mum and me, and the curry chicken is for Helen and Dad, who always asked why anyone would want to eat such old meat with brittle bone.

'You'll have to wait a little while for the extra roti. That okay?'

'Of course!' My food is never ready when I arrive at Olive's, not even when I call in advance. I know better than to ask how long it will take. It's just Olive who cooks everything herself. Occasionally her daughter helps out, but mostly she's on her own and she moves slowly. Nobody complains though. Her rich food and flaky roti is enough for anyone to wait patiently.

It's not uncommon for there to be a huge queue trailing out of the shop.

I look around and the interior of Olive's kitchen reminds me of my nan's house. Because I'm the first of all her grandchildren, she really did give me preferential treatment. She used to peel my grapes when I was a baby, and most importantly would let me sample the roti before everyone else. She'd wink and say, 'Go on, tell me what you think.' Nan cooks her perfect roti on a flat black pan that she always reminds me is older than me, older than my mother. She cooks all of her food on the hob that she would also use to hot comb my hair. Although I was never too fond of the smell or the hot metal and sound of my thoroughly greased scalp sizzling, it was a moment just for us, and at the time I wanted nothing more than to have a full head of straightened hair. And to be held in loving hands.

Just like Olive's, Nan's kitchen is all shades of brown: beige cupboards with dark brown handles; even the pots and pans and majority of utensils sit somewhere between those two shades. She keeps everything for ever and everything looks good as new.

'Almost ready, darling,' Olive says, popping out from the kitchen.

'Thank you, Miss Olive. It smells *so* good.'

'What are these?' asks Juliet, pointing to the fridge full of drinks.

'Everything is freshly made,' Olive shouts from the back room. 'I make all the juices myself.'

'Ooh, which would you recommend?'

'Well, the sorrel is good. The ginger is also a favourite.'

'Should we get some?' Juliet turns to me.

'Yes, we'll take a couple of the ginger and a couple of the sorrel too. Thanks Olive,' I reply.

Another fifteen minutes and our order is ready. I put the food on the back seat of the car because otherwise there will be no roti left when we get in.

By the time we return to the flat, Mum and Dad call to say they're close by and ask where the best place to park is. They bump into Helen at the front of the house. We hear them awkwardly saying their hellos before they knock on the door.

'J . . .' I take in a deep breath. 'This is going to be long. Very long. Pray for me.' I clasp my hands together and look up to the ceiling.

'It'll be fine,' she says, before opening the door to embrace our parents.

'Oh, it's so nice that you girls are living together, isn't it?' my mum says as she walks through the door.

'Yes, indeed,' says Helen, following behind and giving me a conscious smile. 'I knew that Juliet needed a bit of company. It was such a shame what happened with your flat, Elsie, but maybe it has worked out for the best. How are you, my darling?' She gives me a warm, earth-scented squeeze. She's a lighter-skinned version of her daughter and is wearing an arm full of bronze bangles, which clang together when she moves. Her similarly designed earrings are buried deep in a head of loose, dark curls. She always makes an effort, and today is no different. She looks like she belongs in a more tropical climate in her long, low-cut, silk emerald number. I return her hug, hoping she won't say anything more about my old flat to my parents.

I greet my mum first with a kiss on each cheek and then give my dad half a hug. He's a bit of an awkward guy. Even growing up, if I said 'I love you', he'd just tap the top of my head.

'You look different,' says Mum. She scans my body and then says, 'Eating more, maybe?'

I roll my eyes and move into the kitchen. My parents follow Juliet into the sitting room and I grab a bottle of six-pound prosecco from the fridge, pouring a glass for everyone but Dad. It's not vegan but Juliet makes an exception for booze. I pass a bottle of Guinness to Dad.

'Let's toast to new beginnings, eh? To our gorgeous girls being back together again,' says Helen.

'Cheers,' the rest of us say in unison. After I warm each of our meals in the microwave, we sit around the table, eating and making small talk. The smells of garlic, ginger and roasted meat waft through the room. I look over at Juliet, who is doing her best not to be repulsed by how Dad is attacking his chicken bone. I want to laugh as Mum picks up her knife and fork and attempts to tackle the crumbly pieces of goat meat on her plate. She wouldn't eat it like that at home. She's trying to be polite. Helen and Juliet take my lead and abandon their cutlery as I mop up the rice and glossy, rich liquid with my roti.

'You've always been able to put it away, haven't you, Elsie?' Dad says brightly as I wipe away the rice grains that cling on to the corner of my mouth. He's right. Curry goat is my happy place.

Juliet gets up and floats into the kitchen before returning with the drinks we bought earlier.

'Sorrel Bellini anyone?' Juliet offers but she's already adding a splash to everyone's glass.

Helen immediately takes a sip and, despite her face initially betraying her with a look of displeasure, she smiles at her daughter. My mum doesn't say anything about the Bellini or the roti, which means they probably don't meet her standards. Even though I agree that this isn't Olive's best, I avoid commenting and getting into a lecture on roti making.

At the end of the table, Mum leans into Juliet, who has sat back down. They're engrossed in a chat about her teaching work. The rest of us form our own club like a band of misfits who just happened to be at the same place at the same time.

Helen shifts the focus onto me. She doesn't realise I'm quite content with the spotlight being on someone else.

'And what about you, darling girl?' she says, out of nowhere. 'Such a talented orator. How is it all going?'

Mum stops speaking to Juliet to listen and Dad shifts uncomfortably in his seat, clearly feeling awkward that Helen has more of an insight into my life than them.

'I didn't know you were still writing that poetry stuff.' Mum side-eyes me. 'She would always be jotting down things as a child. I thought she'd grow out of it.' She laughs dismissively. No one joins in.

Helen squeezes my hand over the table. 'Her work is powerful. You should watch her perform some time. She had a gig the other day which I'm told went fabulously well.'

There's an awkward silence as I refuse to extend an invitation to my parents, who have never taken an interest in my creative output.

'You could even read one for us now?' Helen suggests. 'Oh gosh, it reminds me of my younger years when me and my friends would sit around listening to each other's work. Those nights would go on for hours.'

Juliet looks at Helen, willing her to stop. Helen just necks another glass of prosecco, without the sorrel this time. I'm surprised at the level of detail Juliet shares with Helen about my work, even if they do speak on the phone almost every day. Helen's monologue continues.

'Youth is such a fabulously free time, isn't it? It's wasted on the young. In my day we would have the wildest parties. Orgies. All sorts. We were so free. I worry about young people these days.' Helen's eyes close as she goes deep into her nostalgia, reminiscing on encounters with ex-lovers. Dad shifts again in his chair, and I catch Mum giving him a sharp look. He's careful as he moves, looking in my direction rather than at Helen, who is still in a world of her own.

'Anyway, what about you, Trevor? What's the latest with work?'

When we were younger, Helen and Dad always got along. As children, whenever it was Dad's turn to drop me at Helen's or Helen's turn to drop Juliet at mine, they would stand on the balcony, speaking until their spouses walked down the stairs. Mum would always be complaining that the cold air was making its way into the house. But after Juliet moved to London, our parents stopped speaking. They all haven't seen each other in a while.

Dad, being a man of few words, gives his usual response. 'Can't complain. Business is good.' There is more to say but he won't. Tonight, he opts for the tight-lipped Caribbean thing of not sharing too much of his business in case someone tries to use it against him. In this case, that someone is my mum.

'Is there any more rice?' asks Dad, who has the tiniest

spoonful of turmeric-stained curry chicken on his plate. In the role of dutiful host, Juliet goes to heat the last of the white rice in the microwave for him.

With Dad not giving much away, Helen abruptly changes topic.

'The girls are just so ... so ... how should I say? Entrepreneurial,' Helen says. I glance up from my roti, hoping Juliet hasn't told Helen that I'm thinking of trying out camming. Shit. Juliet seems to think the same thing.

'Mum!' Juliet says, practically running back in from the kitchen. 'Would you like some more prosecco? Anyone else want more prosecco?'

I attempt to gesture at her to stop filling up Helen's glass. The more she consumes, the more she is compelled to release. But Juliet's too preoccupied.

'I really think it's so empowering that as women they are able to use their bodies and it not be seen as a bad thing. In my day, there was so much animosity from my peers around sex work. It shouldn't have been as much a part of feminist discourse as it was. We should have been having a sexual revolution, not tearing down other women for their choices.'

I feel my face burning up and hope for an emergency phone call that can get me out of this situation, just like in those films where there's a timed call from a friend to tell them their made-up dog has died. Then the microwave beeps. The rice has been in there for far too long. Sheepishly, Juliet brings the steaming hot bowl wrapped in a tea towel from the kitchen and places it next to my dad, who is too stunned to acknowledge her. She busies herself serving him, avoiding my parents' eyes.

'Sorry but I don't understand?' Mum says, part-statement,

part-question. She has a look of utter disbelief across her face. She is a slender woman who has worn her hair slicked back in a relaxed bun ever since I was little. She smooths her hair down now, as though worried that her shock has dislodged her perfectly manicured hairstyle. Dad looks down at his plate.

'Nothing Mum. She's just had one too many,' I whisper so that Helen can't hear me.

'It's a completely radical act for women, especially in the age of fluidity, to be paid for work that women have been expected to do for free. We're all sexual beings, aren't we, Pauline?'

Fuck. Despite everyone's glasses remaining full, Juliet pops a cork and tops everyone up from the second bottle of prosecco. Besides the sound of Juliet pouring, the room is silent.

'Can you show me where the bathroom is?' Mum asks me directly.

I feel hot and sticky. Mum insists on me walking her to the bathroom door. Despite her being at least four inches shorter than me, she has a commanding presence. She turns to me, her eyes narrow and angry.

'I don't think you should be staying here, with these people. Helen is too wild. It's a shame that Juliet has such a bad influence, and I can see they are working on you too. This isn't a good place for my daughter,' she says in disapproval.

I scoff. 'I'm just fine here. And if it wasn't for these people, I would probably be out on the streets right now, not that you know anything about my life. And don't pretend that we're closer than we are, that you care about the people I'm with. When have you ever cared about "your daughter" before?' There is rage stewing in my core, and as much as I try to prevent it from surfacing, it can't be contained.

'And whose fault is that? You're so secretive. You tell me nothing!'

'Why would I?' I shout. 'All you do is judge and berate me!'

Not liking to cause a scene, Mum doesn't raise her voice or call me back as I storm down the hallway and sit down again at the table. When she returns, she whispers something to my dad who suddenly stands up and announces that they have to go. They find their coats and make their way to the door, both of them avoiding eye contact with me as they thank Juliet for having them.

Juliet, not managing to disguise her annoyance, whispers something to Helen as my parents head out the door. Helen, who is ordinarily full of life, shrinks as her daughter gives her a gentle talking to and orders her a taxi.

'Elsie, I'm so sorry darling if I said the wrong thing. Juliet's angry at me,' she slurs.

'It's fine, Helen. Don't worry about it, okay?'

Helen stumbles to give me a hug and Juliet escorts her outside. I peek through the window and see Juliet giving the driver strict instructions to look after her mum and make sure she makes it safely inside her house.

Before Juliet makes it back into the flat, I grab my things and dart out the door.

'I'm going out,' I shout as we pass each other.

'Els, I'm sorry! I shouldn't have mentioned anything to Mum. I should've known she wouldn't keep it together.'

But I don't stop because I don't want her to see how overwhelmed I am. She parts her lips, considering whether to stop me, but decides against it.

16

I've been wandering around aimlessly for a couple of hours and it's dark outside. There are no visible stars when I look up, just the dull glare of streetlights bringing the stillness of the night into focus. There is nothing on the road but the occasional motorbike or car passing by at dizzying speed. Peckham has a hazy glow that dances on the adjacent streets, providing a backdrop to the city's sirens. I decide to avoid the buzz of the high street and walk through the back roads in the direction of Peckham Rye. The last few autumn leaves are fluttering down from the trees that line my path. I want to sit somewhere I can be entirely still and undisturbed. The odd group of fifteen-year-olds drinking cans of K Cider and popping pills named after superheroes are the only people I see. My face is being sheltered in the hood of my jacket, the fur trim providing a comforting barrier between my scalp and the sharp night air.

In my haste to get out the door, I forgot to put on socks and my ankles are now painfully, fully exposed. I walk quickly. Halfway down the road, a voice from across the street calls out.

'Hey, wait!'

I can't see anyone else in front of me, but still I assume that their words are directed at someone outside of my eye-line.

'Elsie, wait! Is that you?' It definitely isn't Juliet's voice. I continue to walk, this time at a more urgent speed. A couple of days ago, I saw a video of a couple of girls being antagonised on the bus because they were gay. The thought crosses my mind that the person behind me is a homophobe who's found me online and is now coming to teach me a lesson. I can barely see anything in the darkness and immediately regret having avoided the high street. But if it is my time, it is my time. The only thing of value that I'd leave behind is my records. And maybe my journal. I hope Juliet will take them. My body is trembling a little, twitching as though I'm no longer in control of my muscles.

The voice, closer now, shouts my name again, and at that, I turn around to see who it is. My heart is pounding as I momentarily depart from the body that has carried me for twenty-eight years. At a distance, I see a Black person with broad shoulders and a short frame walking towards me. I breathe out a sigh of relief. Thank fuck. It's only Maggie.

'Maggie!?!! What the . . .' I refrain from swearing through my disjointed breaths. 'You properly scared me. I thought someone was coming to end me.'

'Who would possibly want to end you? It's just me, kid. No threat here. But what? Are you running from something?'

'I guess you could say that. I don't know.' I pause. 'What are you doing down here anyway? These aren't your usual ends.'

'My sister lives this way. Just there actually.' Maggie points to a grey four-storey-high block of flats across the road.

'I do leave Streatham sometimes, you know. That's just the only place you see me.' Maggie laughs, more lively than usual. I suspect she's a little tipsy. It is late.

'I'm surprised you recognised me from all the way over there.'

'It was those busy trainers that gave you away,' she says, looking down at my shoes.

Maggie is referring to the words written all over my black trainers. I'd customised them at an event a couple of years ago. I was sceptical of writing all over them. I thought they were better simple. People are forever trying to overcomplicate things, dress everything up, but there's power in simplicity. I know that's what I've been searching for, something beautiful and pure and easy, but life keeps getting in the way. But anyway, customising our shoes is what the brand had invited us to the event to do. So that's what I did.

Maggie keeps speaking.

'Do you want to talk about the reason you look as sad as you do? I was headed home but we can go to this pool club round the corner if you want to talk? They have a dartboard, and the beer's on me.'

I think about this offer for a moment, about Juliet alone at home, but decide that distraction would do me good.

'Sure, let's do it.'

Maggie's face lights up.

When we arrive, there are a couple of oldies playing pool, and they look like they've been coming here for years. After grabbing two bottles of Sol for us from the bar, Maggie finds what appears to be a familiar perch in the corner of the room. I can see that she's in her element.

'Have you ever played darts before?' I shake my head in response. 'You know they used to call me "bullseye" because of my streamlined approach and accuracy.' She smiles with pride at the memory.

'You have to show me what you've got then, Maggie,' I reply, playfully. Just being around her takes away some of the residual stress from this evening. She gives me a confident look, picks up a nearby dart and throws it into the middle of the board with casual precision. She takes a sip of her Sol and perches herself back next to me. I'm impressed.

'So, now that that's sorted, are you going to tell me what's up?'

'I don't even know where to begin.' I breathe in deeply and my belly rises.

'Just start at the beginning.'

'Well, my parents came to visit.'

'Where are you staying now? I was at the bar the other day and Bea mentioned that you lost your place. I'm sorry, Elsie.' She taps me on the shoulder, offering her sympathy.

'I'm staying with my best friend, my oldest friend. Which is a bit weird in itself because ... well ... we stopped speaking a few months ago. She told me she had feelings for me. I think maybe I had some feelings for her too, but I shut her down.' Now that I'm speaking, I can't stop. 'And then the day I got evicted was the first day in a while that I'd seen or spoken to her. And we've become so close again and ... and I don't know if something strange might be happening there ...'

Maggie nods at me to keep going.

'And then tonight, her mum got a little bit too drunk. She's a bit of a wild card. Usually, it's harmless but this time she mentioned that Juliet works as a cam girl and practically said I was too.'

'Oooof.' Maggie winces.

'I don't know why Juliet even told Helen that I was considering it. But, Maggie, you know what happened with the bar . . . I have to get creative about how I'm going to make money.' I look at her to see if her eyes hold judgement but the only thing I see is how intently she's listening, hanging on to my every word.

'My parents know nothing about my life or my poetry. They've never taken it seriously. So, when Helen mentioned sex work, Mum started acting like me staying with Juliet is bad for me. Like they're corrupting my innocence, which is ironic because it's her who stole my childhood from me. She doesn't have a fucking clue. And my Dad says nothing! Lets her treat me this way time and time again.'

'I see.'

'And I'm exhausted! I don't even know why I try to make it work with them. We are fundamentally strangers. If they hadn't given birth to me, there isn't even the slightest chance that we would choose to be in each other's lives, you know?'

There is so much I need to get off my chest. Maggie listens quietly.

'They don't have the right to judge who I am or my life choices, and they certainly don't have the right to judge the people who have supported me when they were absent. I was clearly never important to them outside of the services I could provide . . . I hate them, Maggie.' Tears stream down my face. I can hear myself and I sound like a teenager, but I can't help it. Maggie takes my hand.

'Oh, Elsie! You've had a heavy night. You know, our parents are just human. They are flawed, and even though it seems impossible now, at some point you'll make your peace with that.' Maggie pulls me to her and I rest my head on her shoulder.

'I thought I had but tonight brought up things I haven't dealt with properly, I guess.'

I sob and Maggie strokes the side of my face.

'Here, take this,' she says, passing me a dart and standing up. 'Focus your mind on this one thing for a second. Then let it go.'

I take in a deep breath and my dart lands just outside of the bullseye, in the green.

'Not bad. Now slow it down a bit.' Maggie guides my hand with her own. 'And remember, only you can decide what your limit with your family is. You've made the call before, and you might have to make it again.'

'I thought I'd found strategies to suppress that shit, to prevent it from bubbling over. Like breathing exercises and mindfulness. Precarious, but I thought I had a handle on letting it overtake me.'

'You young people think life is so straightforward. In reality, it's all a fucking mess.'

'I know it's a mess, Maggie. That much I get.'

'Then let it go.'

So I do. And this time the dart edges even closer to the middle of the board.

'Also, it might be good for you to tell people how you feel rather than keeping it in and assuming they should just know. Even if they don't respond how you want them to, at least you will have said it.'

'Maybe,' I say obstinately.

'Or if you don't want to talk about it, then put your skills to good use and write a letter. A poem, even! You'll feel better for it.'

I twist my lip in uncertainty.

'If, like me, you can't bring yourself to actually send the letter, just the act of writing will help. Trust me, I've been through it with my own.' I realise that Maggie has never shared this part of her life with me, despite the expansive stories she's told me.

'And it sounds as though Juliet and her mum, even with their messiness, do love you. You've gotta let them, Elsie. Let people love you.' Maggie wipes my tears and squeezes my shoulder as she says this. I feel helpless.

'I've been carrying around these feelings for so long, Maggie. It's weighing me down. The only family member I really care about is my nan, and I know I need to make more of an effort to see her. But going back to Bristol is so hard. There are too many memories there.' Maggie tries to interject but I'm not finished.

'And I *still* can't find a job. Nothing. Not even the most basic shit. I'm relying on my best friend, sleeping in her spare room, in a single bed, because I don't have four walls to call my own. It's fucked.'

'You have definitely had a rough time of it and it's not for me to tell you how to feel. This is tough stuff and it's happening all at once. But you've been holding on to so much and I can see it's all waiting to spill out of you. The one thing I will say, just on the family side of things, is that as hard as this might be to imagine, your mum has had things happen in her past that have shaped her into the person she is today.'

'Actually, the dynamic between her and my nan is quite weird . . .' I take a swig from my bottle as I think about this. 'I think there's a lot of resentment there. My nan brought my uncle with her when she moved to the UK but not Mum. Mum came over much later. And now they aren't close. They maintain a relationship out of obligation. A bit like me and her . . .'

'That's a tough pill to swallow. She probably feels just as abandoned by her mum as you do by her. She's had to learn what it means to love in her own way, and maybe that doesn't work for you, and maybe it looks different to Juliet and her mum. But she's probably trying. It's hard to put ourselves in other people's shoes.'

I'm suddenly irritated by Maggie's response. It feels like she's making excuses for my mum.

'It's not my responsibility to make amends though. She shouldn't have had a child if she couldn't see things through,' I say sulkily.

'Things aren't as straightforward as you might think, kid . . .'

My irritation flares but I'm saved by my phone buzzing in my pocket. 'One second, Maggie.' I pull my phone out and there's an unread message from Dad. He has never been able to stand up for me in person, so this is his signature weak move. Sending a text after the fact. And even though I know it's coming, it still stings. His daughter, the afterthought.

> I'm sorry we left things the way that we did. But please don't make any stupid decisions that will have a negative impact on your life moving forward. If you need money, all you have to do is ask. I can drop something in your account next week.

I pass the phone to Maggie to show her the text message.

She smiles and says, 'I didn't forgive my parents for their bullshit until I was much older. It wasn't until I reached my forties that I realised they were just as fucked up as the rest of us. Oh God, it reminds me of that Philip Larkin poem,' she says, offering a reassuring smile.

'You'll be all right, Elsie. You've made it this far.' I nod in acknowledgement. Unexpectedly, Maggie gives me a hug and I lean in to it. After a couple of seconds, we move around to an available pool table, and she orders a couple more Sols.

'I was sad to hear about what happened to the club,' Maggie continues. I'm glad for the change in conversation.

'So was I. Jamie could be a pain in the arse but that place sort of felt like home.'

'It's the same thing I saw happening in the '90s. Most of our events happened in other people's venues but there was this one bar in Euston station that we used to congregate at. It was a vibe. Didn't last a long time though.'

'Damn.'

'It was a different day but the same struggle.'

I take another swig from my bottle.

'You can mope for today, Elsie, but then I want you to go out there and hold your head up high. Don't think I haven't watched your performances online! You have a gift, and you do not want to wake up one day feeling as though you didn't use it. Trust me. At the peak of my darts career, I was in my forties, but if I'd known what my talent was, what would fill me up, I would've been reaching for it much earlier. The world is yours, especially when you're backed by love. Your friend, from the way that you've described her, loves you. And she's not going to leave. You have to learn to move through life without fear.'

Deep down, I know there's truth to what Maggie is saying. It's just easier said than done.

We spend the rest of the night playing pool and the conversation lightens. Under Maggie's watch, the tension I've been holding throughout my body softens, and for the next few hours, I don't think about Mum or Dad or Helen or what I'll say when I get back to the flat. Instead, I get Maggie speaking about the women in her life, past and present, and the events she's been sending me the posters of. She speaks and I laugh and soak it all in. Then, just as we are about to leave, I make my way to the toilet, and as I'm crouched over the toilet bowl, scrolling through my phone and a myriad of unread WhatsApps, I see another check in from Leonie.

> Elsie, check your emails!!! Nora said that they haven't heard back from you yet. You've got mail!! Let's meet up and celebrate sometime soon. Xx

For a second, my heart stops.

I check my inbox, but there's nothing there. Scrolling through my email folders, I click into spam and at the top sits an email from Nora with the subject, *CONGRATULATIONS*. It's from a week ago.

> Dear Elsie,
>
> Congratulations! We're writing to let you know that you have been shortlisted for CRUSH. We had an

overwhelming number of applications, and you are one of just five individuals who have made it through to the next stage of the process.

The poem we would like you to perform is your un-titled piece. It speaks to the brief perfectly.

In addition to the runner-up prizes, we will be offering mentorship opportunities for those who do not place on the evening.

A running order for the night will be shared with you next week, but the event will take place on 23 October at 6.30 p.m.

Winning would be a banging birthday present.

Please do not hesitate to get in touch if you have any questions.

Best wishes
Nora

I draft a quick reply.

Dear Nora,
This is such great news! Your message got caught in my spam folder, but I will definitely be there. Really look-ing forward to the event.

Thank you,
Elsie

I burst out of the toilet, barely able to contain my excitement. 'What are you smiling about?' asks Maggie.

'I've been shortlisted for a publishing prize, Maggie. This could be it!'

My phone rings and this time, it's Bea. She's drunk and wants me to come over. As ever, I welcome the distraction.

'You're popular tonight.' Maggie raises a suggestive eyebrow. 'Go and enjoy yourself. Celebrate your win. I'm too old to be nursing a hangover tomorrow.'

I'm out of the door before she even finishes speaking.

17

I wake up in Bea's bed for the third time that week, and she's in the kitchen making us tea. Karma is away and I don't ask where he's gone. Bea's empty flat has provided the perfect opportunity to keep out of Juliet's way. She has apologised about Helen every day (sometimes twice a day) since the lunch and even though I've told her over and over again that we're cool, I just need some time away. Time to figure out how I'm feeling.

'We really ought to stop meeting like this,' I say jokingly as Bea re-enters the room.

'Well you have to stop calling me in the middle of the night when you're drunk and want some of this.' She's wearing a baggy T-shirt and twirls as she walks so that what's underneath is just visible.

'You love it.'

'I do.' She hands me a cup of green tea and perches on the edge of the bed.

'Why are you smiling so much?'

'I just can't stop thinking about this publishing thing. The fact that I'm in with the chance of winning a book deal. The fact that in twenty-four hours, I'll be performing again. It's all mad. I think that maybe if I smile and think positively, I'll increase my chances of getting it.'

'Okay, weirdo. But that is amazing. And if you do get it, it will be because you're talented, not just because you're sitting up in bed manifesting with a lame grin plastered across your face.'

'I'm not beyond trying anything at this point.'

'Wait, is this what you're talking about? She points at an Instagram post advertising the CRUSH event. My name is right in the middle of the flyer in yellow writing. 'Why do you never invite me to your gigs?'

'If you absolutely insist, you can come.' I'm still unsure as to how much of my life I should let her into, and wonder what the shelf life is for our little arrangement, but I can't be bothered to argue with her now. 'In fact, you should come. You know I did write a poem inspired in part by your magnificent features.' I point to her bum.

'You did not!'

'I did.'

'It is poem worthy,' she says, looking smug.

'But don't worry, it isn't on the program for tomorrow.'

'So, what should I wear? All black and a beret? I've never been to a poetry night before.'

'Yeah, that's what everyone wears. Put on some black shades too. You should go all out.' I'm enjoying picturing her in this get up in the back of a low-key event.

'Sick. Okay.' She looks happy. 'We can go together, if you like?'

'Just as long as you keep me busy today,' I say.

I move to kiss Bea but a message pops up on my phone and

I pick it up. It's Juliet, sharing the Instagram flyer. I banish the uncertainty in my stomach. I've kind of been ignoring her.

J: AMAZING ELS. Can't believe you didn't tell me about this!!! And on your birthday!? Must be a sign.

E: I haven't even performed yet! But, yes, it feels good.

J: I feel like I haven't seen you properly in ages ... Can I come?

E: Yea, of course

J: I'll be with Andrew, if that's okay? We're headed for Japan in the early hours, so we won't be able to hang around for too long after. But I really want to be there.

I pause typing for a second and take a deep breath.

E: Sure. I'll see you tomorrow!

J: CONGRATS my superstar friend. Look at you go! Xoxoxox

E: Xxxxxx

I put my phone down and see that Bea is looking at me. 'Wanna jump in the shower with me?' she asks, and predicting my answer, she takes my hand and leads me out of the bedroom with authority.

The next day, it's the afternoon and we're finishing off the world's largest pizza on Bea's beige sofa. She's ordered a celebratory birthday feast. The flat is like one large nude lip palette. Variations on white and cream and brown are everywhere. Careful not to let any of the red sauce spill, I've spread a tea towel on my lap.

'We only have like two hours, right? I need to get ready.'

Bea heads to the bedroom and returns forty minutes later, making a dramatic entrance. She's got on high-waisted black jeans and a polo neck to match, a black beret and black lipstick. Her gold chains, usually swallowed by her cleavage, are nowhere to be seen.

'What do you think?' she asks, spinning around.

'Okay, Janet! You look hot.'

'You look fine, I guess.' She tilts her head to the side unconvincingly and laughs.

'I need to look more than fine. Have you got anything I can put on?'

'You can take literally take anything you want. I have some shirts and stuff in the back of my wardrobe. But you already know that,' Bea says, smiling.

On the other side of her bed is a shiny brown chest of drawers and I sort my way through her clothes. I find a fitted white vest and an expensive-looking oversized white shirt.

'Is this okay for me to wear? Looks fancy,' I say as I make my way back into the sitting room. She's holding a cupcake with a single candle in it. I blow it out and smile at her. No song, no fanfare. This is the sort of birthday I like. Twenty-nine. My smile disintegrates when I remember that I'm spending it in the flat Bea shares with someone else, and that it's the first birthday in a long time I've not celebrated with Juliet. But I try not to dwell for too long.

Bea takes her finger, dabs it in the icing and then places her finger in my mouth. 'Of course you can wear the shirt.

It's a big night for you. You couldn't show up in those rags
you had on.'

I kiss my teeth.

'Just try not to spill anything on it! You had to pick the
whitest thing in there, didn't you?'

'I won't, don't you worry. You got any white creps I can
wear with it?'

'Air Forces okay?'

'Yeah.'

'Okay, quick, hurry. You don't want to be late.'

I remove the T-shirt I'm wearing and pull the vest over my
head. The shirt follows. I ask Bea to do my eyeliner. She makes
perfect little black wings on each eye in record time and then
slips some lip gloss into the back of my trouser pocket and tells
me to apply it before I go on stage.

'Bus or train or cab?' Bea enquires.

'Let's get the train from Oval. We have time.'

As usual, the station's packed full of people, most of them
heading out for a big Thursday night. As we sit down on the
train, Bea pulls out two cans of a pre-mixed rum and Coke
cocktail from her black leather backpack. 'Thought you might
fancy a drink,' she says.

'Perfect.'

It's cute how excited she is for tonight.

As the train pulls into the next station, a guy sitting down
nearby gets up from his chair.

'You sit,' Bea says, before climbing on top of me. It's a corner
seat so I manage to avoid spreading out too much.

'You're getting heavy, Bea.'

'Oh, shut up,' she snaps back.

I can barely see what's happening around me, focused on Bea's body in my lap, but then I smell the familiar scent of fresh petals and a gentle voice says:

'Els, Happy birthday!' It's Juliet. She's wearing a long red coat and has lots of colourful clips in her hair which is pulled back into a loose, curly ponytail. She's got a healthy amount of blusher on her cheeks and bright red lipstick to match her outfit. She looks beautiful.

'You two look pretty cosy,' Andrew says snidely from beside her. I'm annoyed he's actually turned up. 'Happy birthday, Elsie.' I'm surprised as he hands me a card.

The other passengers on the train look irritated with the conversation we're having across the aisle of the tube. Andrew and Juliet have settled opposite us.

'Well, the lump sitting on my lap is Bea. Bea this is Andrew, Juliet's friend. And you know Juliet.'

'Hey.' Bea sends a disingenuous smile in Andrew's direction. She then offers Juliet a reserved smile, which is reciprocated.

'How's your day been?' Juliet tentatively asks me, searching for something to say.

'Yeah, fine. Nice actually. We had a chilled one.'

'What have you been up to lately?'

'Nothing much . . . you?'

'Yeah, same old.'

We're clunky after a week of not speaking in person. I don't want to say anything that will make things even worse. The main thing is that she's here, which is where I realise I want her to be.

'I'm looking forward to this evening,' she tries again.

'What can we expect?!' asks Andrew, filling the space.

'People will perform throughout the night, and at the end, they'll let us know who won, I guess.'

That's enough to satisfy him and then thankfully it's our stop.

'This is us,' I say, and we all disembark the tube. Bea and I hang back as Juliet and Andrew walk ahead.

'That's Juliet's man?' Bea was never very good at whispering, and she says this in a volume loud enough for the duo to hear.

'Not her man. Her friend,' I say, so quietly that I'm unsure if I'm really speaking, unsure if the words are true.

'Mmm,' Bea says, raising her brows in suspicion.

After a few minutes of walking, all of us step inside the large glass venue. I suddenly feel small because the ceilings are so high. Juliet turns around to check if we are still behind. I leave the three of them waiting in silence as I grab our comped tickets and Andrew offers to buy everyone a round of drinks. As he should, making himself useful. We find a table and sit as though we're on a double date. Andrew is living for it.

'So, how long have you two been dating?' he asks.

'We aren't dating,' I say and look at Juliet who is pretending that she isn't taking in Bea's outfit. I notice that whenever Bea looks in her direction, Juliet turns her head.

'Oh, you're not? You two would make a great couple. Don't you think, Juliet?'

'I guess,' she grumbles and pretends to fixate on a painting on the wall.

'We're just friends,' responds Bea, tracing my thigh with her finger and then squeezing it under the table. I move her hand away and she scrunches up her face dramatically.

'Oh, it's just that Juliet said you stayed at Bea's last night.'

'I didn't say that, Andrew.' Juliet's curt and avoids my eyes.

'Anyway, how are things with you and Sophie?' I shine the spotlight back on Andrew.

'We're fine. We're good. We're great, in fact.' Andrew is clearly flustered at the mention of her name. Just when he'd got Juliet all to himself.

'Great.' I raise my eyebrows.

'Soooo,' Bea says, trying to diffuse whatever is going on. 'What time are you performing?'

'I'm on second, I think.'

Andrew is about to speak again but he's interrupted by Juliet who, after downing her wine, slams her glass down with such force I think the table might crack.

'Um ... Everything all right?' Andrew asks her, a short, deep-set frown on his face.

'Yeah, I'm just really thirsty. Can I get everyone the same again? Birthday drinks!' She's being extra weird.

'That would be great. Thanks,' says Bea, and before I can put my order in, Juliet makes her way over to the bar.

'I was wondering, Elsie, what are you performing tonight?' Andrew asks.

'Oh, it's ... well, it's an old piece. It actually didn't have a name until recently, but I think I've finally found the right one now.' I gauge his reaction, and for once, Andrew appears to be genuinely interested in what it is that I'm saying.

I'm interrupted by Nora, who gets up on stage and starts to speak.

'Hello everyone! We are so incredibly excited to have you all here with us today for our CRUSH competition. By the end of the evening, you will have watched some breathtaking, funny and spectacularly thoughtful performances from five of the most exciting new poets in the UK, as well as a few musical interludes from some really exciting young jazz-talent from London. And someone is going to be leaving tonight's event with a book deal! It has truly been a pleasure to sift through the submissions and this lot certainly didn't make the task an easy one. Before we begin, can I ask all the poets to join us backstage? You can make your way through that door over there,' they say, gesturing at a blue door on the side of the stage.

I smile at Bea and get up from the table, making my way over. I recognise Jojoba Oil, who I'm surprised to see again. He follows and there are three faces behind who I don't recognise. A light-skinned girl with freckles and ginger hair. A short girl with her hair scraped up into two high buns, and someone else who is wearing the chicest outfit I've ever seen – a boxy pair of trousers, a jacket to match and a pair of lime green Sauconys. We sit together backstage in a room that's bare except for two squeaky leather sofas and the bottles of water laid out for us. After introducing ourselves, we retreat to various corners of the room and read through our poems. After a girl with a bluesy voice finishes performing with a saxophonist, the producer, dressed all in black, comes backstage and guides the person with the Sauconys to the stage.

'You're on next,' she says, pointing in my direction.

I wait in the wings silently, reciting the poem in my head one last time when I hear my name being called. I try to calm the nerves in my stomach.

'Thank you so much for that, Jodie,' Nora says, and the audience claps solidly.

'Up next, we have Elsie Macintosh.' They read off a list of accolades and published works that I don't recognise as my own. I force my legs to move.

Walking onto the stage, I notice how much the room has filled out since I left the table with Juliet and Andrew and Bea. They are sitting to the right of the stage. Bea and Juliet's faces light up as I go to the microphone.

'Hi everyone. My name is Elsie. It's great to be here and . . .'

I'm interrupted by a technical error that sees the light shining on me dim. Instead, a spotlight lands on an audience member, a man with thick black hair, probably in his mid-forties. He looks wildly uncomfortable, like the moment in a comedy show when someone decides to go to the loo, only to find themselves the butt of the next joke. Everyone is shuffling in their seats, trying to figure out whether this is a part of the show. I turn to the left of the stage, where I can see a tech team member trying to signal, in near darkness, to her colleague on the other side of the room. And then the spotlight suddenly lands on Juliet. I stare at her as she's blinded by the light, fiddling with her hair nervously. My heart flutters at the realisation that I'm about to read out a poem that no one's ever heard, that I haven't thought about for so long. I swallow, and just as I take a deep breath in, the lights come back on. I summon all my confidence.

'I thought I was going to have to perform in the dark for a moment. To be honest, that might have been the most appropriate given tonight's theme.' The audience offers me uncertain laughs. I continue.

'Thank you, Nora, for your generous introduction. I'm going to share some words tonight about a person who means a lot to me.' Bea shuffles excitedly in her chair, possibly forgetting that I won't be performing the poem about how juicy she is. I hope she isn't disappointed. I decide to focus my attention on the other half of the room.

'At first, when I was told the theme was "CRUSH", I wasn't really sure where to begin. But then I revisited something from the past – well the past and the present really – and it was obvious that ... Anyway, I'll let what I've written speak for itself. It didn't have a name until tonight. This is "Rosewater".'

She –
Who keeps the sweetest scent in her ever-
        changing curls
(sometimes we call them a rainbow).
She the girl –

I clear my throat and ground my feet.

Who smells like a rose and rose me from the ashes
        with boiling bubbling water.
She, the daughter of the scent too.
You, chant for me and I let you
I chant your name and you don't even know I do.
I chant for you and I'm not even sure I know how to.
She who placed petals in the parts of me
I thought were too barren to bloom.
Who pockets the sound of laughing lungs in her
        cheek dimples.

Soft faces smile back at me from the audience, and I hope they are thinking about the ones they have loved, love now.

Who in simple . . .
Is the reason thorns don't feel sharp
Even if they draw blood.
You my blood, or in my blood,
That I'm still trying to decipher.
She a cypher of Talking Heads and India Arie and
*   the Spice Girls and Angie Stone.*
What I mean is, you the epitome of soul
and how it fills a body like a smell fills a room.
Her room stores a camera and yet I have never
*   felt watched,*
Just felt like a necessity.
She's a necessity in an otherwise unnecessary world.
My world labelled messy and hectic and you taught
*   me the word eclectic*
And pointed to my heart and told me to protect it
At all costs
She scoffs whilst lighting a mawga roll-up.
She holds up when I fold up.
You told us that you stand for us both even when the
*   world don't toast to my label.*
You about as stable as the engine of that car
But far means nothing with four wheels, nostalgia
*   and a word stupid and big like destiny.*
She selected me,
(4L)
She who holds all her best ideas in that blue flick,
*   that sits just above her upper lashes*
She
Magic

You magic
You who create havoc in traffic in that car
But that car reminds me of Tracy Chapman and
     getting a ticket to anywhere.
She that ticket.
Which means you that ticket.
Without you it's wicked, this world, home, here.
If you are not here, I got your spirit.
Don't worry,
When I can't see you.
I inhale
And I won't worry.
You.
You.
You.
The rose to my water.
The water to my rose.

I stop speaking and bring my eyes up to the crowd, swivelling my body so that I'm facing the direction of our table. Juliet is staring intensely at me. I think her eyes are wet though it's hard to tell through the lights on stage. I can't tell whether they are good or bad tears. I want her to smile or blink or give some indication that we are okay. That she understands.

The audience erupts into rapturous applause. Juliet isn't whooping as she usually does. Instead, she's sitting there, with her hand over her mouth. Andrew, confused, looks from Juliet to me and back to her again. He pulls in closer to where she is sitting. For a moment, I'm paralysed, trying to read her expression, completely unaware of the rest of the room.

'Thank you, Elsie!' says Nora, gently guiding me off the stage and bringing me back to reality. 'Next we have Suyin Tai.'

Walking off stage my mind is being pulled in a thousand different directions – uncertainty, pride and hopefulness swells. The remaining performances go by in a blur. I sit backstage, numb, nervous, brilliantly alive.

The judges adjourn for thirty minutes, which seems like such a short amount of time to determine my fate. The producer delivers a carafe of wine backstage and all of us furiously chuck back a glass as we compliment each other on our performances. Time moves slowly.

'Your poem was really moving,' Suyin says to me. 'It was exactly how love feels. Beautiful.'

'Ah, thank you. Yours was really great too. I feel like all our styles are so different.'

'Yeah, the interpretation of art is so subjective. What moves us might not move the judges, you know?' says Jojoba Oil.

'For real,' I respond.

'And whatever happens, I'm glad I've met you all. I'll be following you from now on.' Suyin takes out her phone and gestures for each of us, starting with Jojoba Oil, to bring up our Instagram accounts. I think she's using this as an excuse to get to know him.

We all shrink into ourselves then for a moment of quiet. I imagine that everyone is doing the same as me, trying to think about what I might say if I win. What I'll say to Juliet once I'm off stage. I'm trying to practise that visualisation stuff she told me about, but the only thing I can picture is her weepy, beautiful face.

I'm lost in my thoughts and so the minutes pass quickly. The producer comes back into the room to ask us all to follow them and we do. We line up like schoolchildren in assembly. Nora joins us on stage.

'What an incredible night it has been. It was such a tough decision, but we've settled on our winner and runners-up. And I also want to say a massive congratulations to everyone who entered the competition, to everyone who performed this evening and to yourselves for being the most supportive and attentive audience!'

We're waiting anxiously to see whose name they will call first. I try to pretend that the audience isn't there even though the heat from the bright lights is causing me to sweat. As much as being a runner-up is better than nothing, I need a proper win. For once.

'Our runners-up are Jal Dhar and Barbara Nash. They will each receive a thousand pounds and have the works you heard here tonight published online.' Both poets step forward to receive a triangular-shaped glass award and envelope. Jal is grinning, while Barbara wears a disappointed half-smile across their face.

'Remember that for those of you who don't receive an award tonight, we have organised a year of mentorship by two well-established poets,' Nora announces, knowing full well that it's not mentorship any of us are after.

The anticipation is killing me. But finally, she gets to the reason we are all here, cramped on stage, melting under the lights.

'The winner is someone whose work spoke perfectly to the brief. It was honest and moving and whoever "Rosewater" is dedicated to is clearly very loved.' My heart stops beating. 'Our winner is Elsie Macintosh!'

It takes me a moment to register that my name has been called. When I don't move, the producer ushers me over in Nora's direction and I feel full of unadulterated joy. I've done it. Oh my God, I've actually done it.

'Thank you so much! Oh my God, oh my God.' I'm gushing as they hand me the award and envelope. I can hear Bea cheering loudly above the rest of the room.

I want to run over to the others, but Nora asks us all to wait to pose for some photos. We take it in turns to smile alongside them. I have the biggest grin on my face. It's so big that my cheeks are starting to ache. I want to run out of here and scream that I've fucking done it. I want to present my win to every person who didn't hire me, every person who laughed when I told them I was a poet, to my parents! But mostly I want to share the news with my nan. And with Juliet. I've been so scared for so long that my moment would never come and now it is here. I'm overflowing with ecstasy.

As soon as we're done with the photos, I walk through the crowd, searching for my friends, and as I do, I'm greeted by friendly face after friendly face, congratulating me on my achievement. Some clap me on the back and others offer smiles. I feel like a celeb. I reach our table and no one is there. Someone squeezes my shoulders and I turn around to see Bea.

'Babe,' she says, grabbing me by both arms. 'You did it!!' She's smiling widely and it's infectious. Then she lowers her voice. 'By the way, when did you realise you were madly in love with Juliet?'

I'm stunned, but before I can say anything, Bea continues.

'I can't lie, I'm a little offended that the winning poem wasn't about me. But it's cool.' She tilts her head to one side and smiles at me. 'Don't worry. You don't have to say anything'.

I scan the room in the hope that Juliet might be lingering somewhere, also hoping that she didn't hear Bea. I'm expecting to see her come from around the corner and give me the biggest embrace. I want to hear her tell me she's proud, that she knew I'd win all along, that she loved it.

Bea catches me looking.

'They had to go and catch their flight,' she says, wrapping her arms around me, squeezing out the disappointment she can tell is there. Just as she lets me go, she says, 'Listen, I have to go sort out the flat for when Karma gets back. Hope that's okay.'

I manage to spit out a few words. 'Oh, of course. Cool, yeah. I'll see you soon. Thanks for coming.' Bea congratulates me again and makes her way through the crowd following a clear, decisive path.

And even though I'm in a room full of people, I feel completely alone.

18

'Eh, eh. I'm surprised you remember me,' my nan proclaims as soon as I answer the phone. I've missed the gentle authority with which she speaks and the way she seamlessly weaves Guyanese and English vernacular together. Both belong to her.

'Nan, I'm so so so so sorry. I've been meaning to call. Things have just been really busy.'

'No point in being so so so so sorry.'

'I know.'

'And when was the last you speak to you mudda? She seems in more of a bad mood than normal. Those boys must be driving her mad.'

I sigh. 'I don't want to talk about her. How are *you*?' I say, shepherding the conversation away from Mum.

'I'm all right. Just aches and pains. Inside I'm as young as you, but when I look in the mirror, I don't recognise the old fool looking back at me.'

'Anything serious?' I feel panic rise in my chest at the smallest bit of new information.

'No, no. It's just what happens.'

'Okay, well, I'm glad it's nothing out of the ordinary.'

'You remember where I live? You never know how long I have left.'

'Nan!' She does this whenever she feels neglected by me.

'It's true.'

'Don't say that! I know I've been rubbish, but I'll come and see you soon, okay?' As usual, I resist committing to a specific time or place. I hate disappointing her so only agree on a date if I am absolutely sure I'll make it.

'Don't say it if you don't mean it! I'll just be waiting for you to remember that I exist.' She huffs down the line.

'Nan, how could I ever forget you exist? That's impossible. Look, I'm sorry. Don't make me feel bad. I'll make it up to you.'

'You have to live your life but I'm not joking about you coming to see me. Mi nuh see you for tree months. Nuh mek me wait so long next time.' Her tone softens and I feel a twinge of guilt. I know I should feel bad but I smile at the Guyanese that comes through in her voice when she's mad.

'I know, I know.'

'Perline has some rum, seasoning and Julie mangoes for me. Can you pick them up and bring them before they spoil?' Her sister, Perline, still regularly visits the Caribbean and, upon Nan's request, is required to bring back underripe Julie mangoes and escovitch for her.

She's good at this.

'Anything for you,' I say, not wanting to disappoint her any more than my absence already has.

'How's Juliet?'

'She's good, Nan.'

'How you two get on?'

'Not bad at all. She's in Japan at the moment.' A little sadness creeps unexpectedly into my voice.

'Bring her when you come next time'

'Sure.'

'You better. Ah lovely girl that Juliet be. Mi know her since she little you know. Bring her and lemme see what she looks like these days. Will be wonderful to see you both.'

'I won't forget. But Nan, guess what?'

'What?'

'I got a book deal!' I beam down the phone, still not quite believing it. I haven't said it out loud to anyone yet.

'Ah, you mek mi head feel so big. Mi proud of you. First published author in the family.'

She pauses, soaking in the significance of this.

'I'm so happy, Nan.' Tears gather in the corners of my eyes.

'How come you wait till you're nearly done before you tell me the good news? Let mi sit down and make sure I take it in. Tell me again. Lord me have to brag to all mi friends.'

'It's good news, isn't it? Finally, some good news.'

'I can rest now knowing that you've made it.'

'Well, there's still a way to go yet . . .'

'I always knew you had it in you, child. From since you little. You must go out and celebrate!' I'm still beaming. She's my father, mother and grandfather rolled into one. All the family I've ever needed.

'I love you! Let me know if there's anything else you need me to bring from London.'

'Love you too. But Elsie, before you go, let me tell you something . . .'

'Nan, what is it? I thought you said everything was fine?' Panic rushes through me again.

'Don't worry. Everyting fine.' Nan says slowly, enunciating each word clearly and deliberately. 'Mi go move out you know.

This house is too big. Everybody gon, they grow up so it's time for me to cut down. Less gas, less everything, something I can manage.'

I wonder if she's chosen to have this conversation over the phone so that she doesn't have to witness my dramatic response. I collapse onto the sofa. The thought of no longer being able to visit her house is crushing. Nan's is the first place I ever felt safe in.

'But Nan . . . I love your house.' My voice is quiet, my earlier joy suddenly gone.

'I know you do, Elsie, but this house is too big for me alone. So when you come, you gotta help me pack up all this stuff.'

'Where will you even go?' I ask quietly, with faint desperation.

She kisses her teeth gently. 'The council go find somewhere for me. Something more suitable where I don't have to go up and down the stairs all the time. They already looking for me.' The way she elongates her words lets me know that the decision is final. I only hope the council is better at helping her than they are at helping me.

'Why don't you come to London to be close to me?'

'London? No suh. I have my doctor here, the bus route. You're the young one, you come and run back and forth. I will come and visit but I will never live in London. I've got good neighbours, friend, the little market, everything.'

Even though I know she's right, it still stings. I say nothing.

'Elsie, enjoy your win. I'm so proud of you. I can die happy now, knowing you're gonna be just fine.'

'Thanks, Nan. And I promise I'll see you soon.'

I hang up the phone and sit in my feelings for a few

minutes. Then, unsure of who to tell my news to next, I pick up the phone and call backup (Leonie) to see if she's down for a couple of drinks. We arrange to meet at Pelican Bar in Queens Road.

The inside of the bar is a light, soft grey and filled with high seating in a similar tone. There is no art on the walls, just a list of ten cocktails printed out on massive sheets of paper and stuck to the sides of the bar. The only available seats are in the window. I order a champagne colada for twelve pounds and take a seat in full view of the rest of the street and wait for Leonie and my drink to arrive. The distraction from my feelings is, as ever, welcome.

After five minutes, one of the servers brings over my cocktail in a short tumbler. My immediate thought is whether it's truly possible to fit twelve pounds' worth of alcohol into a glass so small. I take a sip and as much as I want to be annoyed by the pretentiousness of it all, it is delicious. Leonie appears in front of me and smiles through the window before walking inside and giving me an enormous embrace. She smells like bubblegum and is wearing a fitted black skirt with a cropped black cardigan to match. The first couple of buttons are undone, and this time their hair is in a short black bob. She has a simple manicure of short black nails to match.

'I can't believe I wasn't there to witness what I heard was the most breathtaking performance ever,' she says. I smile.

'Thank you. It's all very mad. You have to let me get you a drink.'

'I'll have whatever you're having.' They point to my glass, now half-empty, and I walk over to the bar and order another two. The bartender says that someone will bring them over.

'How does it feel?' Leonie asks as I return to where we're seated.

'It feels fucking good. Like really fucking good.' I'm beaming again. 'How have you been though? How come you weren't able to make it?' I'd assumed, given her involvement with the prize, that she'd have been at the event.

'Life has been a lot. My aunty hasn't been very well, so I've been visiting her mostly. But other than that, I guess things are good.' She quickly brushes over what she's just said and when the cocktails are delivered to our table, she takes a swig and shifts the conversation in a direction she is more comfortable with.

'We've got some events coming up with the collective that I'm excited about. But actually, enough of that. Tonight is all about celebrating *you*.' They raise their glass and we cheers.

'Hey, make sure you look me in the eye.' She offers up a cheeky and inviting smile which I return.

The conversation flows easily, and I'm glad I called her. She seems more relaxed than last time we hung out. An hour into the evening, someone comes up to us. I don't recognise them. They say hello and expectantly turn towards me. I do a quick mental search in an attempt to place this person's face. Their eyes are large and intense. I think I would've remembered them. They're not picking up on the fact that I seem confused, but then they say,

'I just had to tell you how incredible you were the other night. Like wow. Your poem was beautiful.' Then they turn to Leonie. 'Was it you that poem was about?'

I mean, that's a bit presumptive.

'It would make perfect sense,' the person continues. 'You're stunning.'

Leonie is more than enjoying the compliment. I don't want to embarrass them, or be rude to this stranger, so I just nod and smile and thank them for saying such lovely things about my work. I think about Juliet, what she's up to in Japan and whether she's thinking about me as much as I'm thinking about her. She hasn't messaged me with travel updates like she ordinarily does. Like she promised to do. I haven't reached out either, unsure of what to say.

I take a couple more sips of my drink and while Leonie continues to entertain this person, I turn my mind to my publishing deal. I daydream momentarily about my as-of-yet unwritten poetry book, and how it will feel to hold in my hands. I return to reality and it's just me and Leonie again. We are on our third cocktail now, and Leonie has a tipsy glaze in her eyes.

'I think I might head,' I say, surprising myself with my lack of desire for any after-dinner activities. My mind is elsewhere.

'Yeah, let's go back to yours?'

'I'm actually not feeling too well.' I lie because I'm acutely aware that the person I want to be celebrating with isn't here, and that as much as me and Leonie could go back to the flat and have fun, all I'd do is think about Juliet.

So, we say our goodbyes. Leonie pulls on her black puffer jacket and kisses me on the cheek before we make our way out of the bar.

When I arrive back at the flat, it's freezing and I can't get the heating to switch on. I use this as an opportunity. I call her on WhatsApp and when she doesn't answer, I send her a message instead.

Hope you're having the best time, J! The boiler is playing
up again and I can't remember how to reset it. It's probably
really early where you are but text me when you can. Xxx

Searching for a reminder of her, I open the card Andrew had given me. It says 'BITCH YOU'RE OLD' with an illustration of RuPaul underneath. I chuckle. At least I know who picked the card. There isn't a long message inside. Just a note that reads: *Happy birthday love, Andrew and Juliet x*

I fall asleep on the sofa wrapped in Juliet's jumper.

19

Sorry Els, it's been non-stop here. Andrew and I
are having the best time. Boiler manual is in the top
drawer in the kitchen. And congrats, by the way, on the
book deal.

So, she did watch me win. I've been wondering if she left
immediately after I performed 'Rosewater' or if she hid in the
corner while I was on stage accepting the accolade. It's been
eight days since Juliet left and she's only just responding to my
message – and congratulating me. She must really resent me
because she didn't even send a kiss or love heart or sunshine
emoji, which is out of character for her. She just ended her message with a full-stop, and without giving any real instructions.
Yes, I did manage to google the boiler reset days ago, but she
doesn't know that. For all, she knows, I could be sitting here
with frozen toes. AND a frozen heart. If this is what it is to
really care about a person, I'm not sure I want it.

I know I'm being dramatic but I can't make it stop. Over the
past few days, I've been checking my phone obsessively. I've
become someone I don't recognise. Moist. Full of feelings. I

knew that something was wrong when even a session with Bea
and a string of dating app hook-ups weren't enough to take my
mind off things. This is a hundred per cent pathetic – being in
Juliet's flat moping around like a love-sick puppy. It's not like I
didn't just get a book deal and don't have a million other things
to channel my energy into. It's just that none of those things
are her and it's weird that if she did feel uncomfortable by my
performance, she hasn't said anything. Also, who says 'congrats' these days? Strangers say congrats, not best friends who
should be genuinely happy for you. It's so formal. And . . . Oh
my God. What if one day soon, I'm the one saying 'congrats'
to her on her engagement to Andrew? What if he's proposing
to her right now?

I crash into the sofa and pull out my phone to reread the text
message she sent. Of course, she's been busy. She's probably
busy hanging out with Andrew's pretentious friends, busy
eating the best vegan sushi at the best vegan restaurant in the
world that he's taken her to, or, I don't want to think it but I
can't help myself. She could be busy in bed with him. Because,
well, I can't compete with that, with Japan. I consider replying
immediately but decide against it. I don't want to look like I'm
thinking about her as much as I am. And if I respond straight
away, that might freak her out even more. I think about what
Bea said, about how obvious my feelings for Juliet have been,
and I'm totally fucking embarrassed. The more I think about
that night, the more a feeling of dread overcomes me. I jump
off the sofa. It feels as though there is a little person doing
somersaults inside my stomach.

I summarise the situation in my head. I end up winning a
book deal off the back of a poem I wrote about my best friend,

who I'm realizing I'm a little bit in love with, and if that love isn't reciprocated, I'm still going to have to work on a book exploring the topic because without it I'll be stuck here, in her flat, in love. I imagine this to be one of those things where people say, 'you'll laugh about this one day,' and I can't wait for said day to come because right now I'm struggling to find the humour in it. If there wasn't rain driving against the window, I'd go for a walk to clear my head. Instead, I decide to put on an exercise video. Apparently it helps with anxiety.

I dart across the hallway and into my room. I don't have proper gym gear, but a pair of boxers and a sports bra will suffice. I open my laptop and rest it on the wooden table opposite my bed, and unroll one of Juliet's yoga mats that is stashed tightly behind the wardrobe. I lie here for several minutes and then, in my continued state of agitation, carry my laptop back into the sitting room. Opening up YouTube, I opt for an intense fifteen-minute work-out, but after the fourth set of crunches, I am sprawled out on the floor, defeated, my arm throbbing. Netflix suggests I watch the next episode of *Drag Race All Stars* instead, and just like that, I'm spiralling again. All roads lead to Juliet.

My phone rings and it's Maggie.

'Hey kid. How are you doing?'

'Hi Maggie. I'm fine.' My voice sounds pathetically distant.

'Oh? Guessing the prize didn't go so well then? There is always next time,' she says reassuringly.

'Oh. No. Actually, I won, I got the book deal.'

'What? That's wicked!'

'Yeah.'

'So then, what's up? You sound small.'

'I'm fine.' I hesitate. 'I think.'

'I won't force you to speak if you don't want to but sometimes it helps. Remember last time?'

'Well.' I gulp. An invitation is all I need. 'The poem I won the competition with was a poem I wrote about Juliet. I thought it would be harmless . . . you know what, maybe the issue was that I didn't really think at all. Now everything's mad.'

'Mad?'

'Like . . . maybe . . . I am a bit in love with her. That is, if love makes you feel like you want to throw up. Never in my life has a girl made me feel this unhinged.'

'Those will be the nerves. Have you spoken to her?'

'She's on holiday with this guy and his friends, and she also ran off after the performance without saying a word. I think she's freaked.'

'Or maybe she just needs a little time to process?'

'Yeah, I guess.'

'Maybe when she comes back, you should be honest with her about where you're at?' A voice inside of me screams that's a terrible idea. The worst. Because if she felt the same she would speak up. She has done it before. But if I speak up and it doesn't land there is a lot to lose. What if she recoils at the thought and we don't speak for another three months and I end up more homeless than I am now?

'Maybe,' I murmur reluctantly.

'You can't hold onto this for ever and to be honest, Elsie, it sounds like the cat's out of the bag.' Maggie laughs gently, and despite myself, I join her. 'I think you'll be surprised at how understanding she will be. Just go gentle.'

As much as I don't want her to be, I know she's right. She's always right. We say our goodbyes.

I find myself walking towards Juliet's bedroom and getting undressed, dousing myself in her rosewater perfume and lying in the middle of her bed. Her laptop is on the bottom of it and for some reason my mind is transported to watching her on webcam. Without thinking, I lick my fingers and take my time, thinking of the freckles on Juliet's face and body and her big hair. I imagine she's here with me, eyes closed. I imagine her kisses all over me and me asking her what feels right. I'm really in it, the fictional moment in which all that matters is us attentively unearthing what makes the other feel good. The more aroused I am, the clearer she becomes. And when I cum, I don't move, just stay in the middle of her bed, using the pillow as a stand-in for Juliet.

20

The warm, woody smell of nag champa is competing with the harsh scent of my cleaning products. I've been on a scrubbing spree. The bathroom has been freshly bleached, the sitting room hoovered, and I've now moved on to the kitchen. I start with the cupboards, unloading all the shelves and wiping each bottle individually before placing them back in their rightful position.

Juliet will be home soon.

I take out a pair of yellow washing-up gloves from under the sink and clean a few cups and plates, and once I've finished, I spray and wipe down the rest of the kitchen surfaces and cupboard handles. Once I've completed the kitchen, I light an additional stick of nag champa and position it so that it's wedged between the window's opening. I've made sure that the cupboards are filled with oat milk, dried lentils and whole-wheat pasta. Her favourites. I've got rid of the evidence of all the meat I've consumed in her absence.

After circling back around into the sitting room, I position myself on the sofa. My eyes dart around the room, searching for anything that might be out of place. But unable to sit still, I get up and fiddle with the curtains, and arrange the art that lines the walls so that the frames are all perfectly straight. The flat is very ready for Juliet's arrival. I'm not.

The sound of a key turning in the lock startles me and is followed by Juliet practically skipping inside. Despite a twenty-four-hour-long journey back from Japan, she looks happy. I tentatively move towards her.

'Hi! It's so nice to see you!' She gives me the type of squeeze that is usually reserved for a long-lost relative. It's a hug that says: *I've missed you, it's good to be home.* I'm surprised. And relieved. Although she's a little frantic, practically flying through the house, and I'm not sure if this deliberate, so she can avoid making eye contact for now.

'Oh wow,' she says, looking over my shoulder. 'You've really cleaned. Even more than usual. It's immaculate in here.'

I take Juliet in. Breathe in her scent. It steadies me. The fact that she's been on the world's longest flight hasn't stopped her from dressing as flamboyantly as she usually does. She's wearing a green coat with fluffy rims and a giant fluffy collar, and an orange chunky-knitted scarf.

'So ... How was it?' I help her bring her heavy suitcase into the flat.

'Oh, it was amazing. It was magical. I love it there so much. The food was amazing. I actually strayed from my diet on more than one occasion!' She looks sheepish. 'Don't judge me but the sushi, the sashimi? Oh my God, it was all too tempting. You would have loved it.' She's rotating around the room, recounting her trip, and slowly shedding her bag and coat before finding her way to the floral armchair nestled between the bookshelf and the table. She's still not looking at me.

'I knew that eventually you'd come to your senses. What did you do while you were over there?'

'So much. I went to most of the shows that the band played, and Andrew and I went out to eat a bunch of times. The rest of the guys in the band, as lovely as they were, were a lot. But really, spending time with Andy was glorious.' She smiles into a memory of him, and I wince at the affection that comes when she abbreviates his name.

'But well done you!' She's being overly blasé, trying to continue on as normal. 'I'm sorry I had to rush off after your big event. I'd left my passport at the flat and you know how painfully early the flight was. I had to head back and get it before we went to Andy's.'

'It's cool, J.'

'I got this for you though!' She jumps up and flips her suitcase down on the ground, hastily unzipping it and pulling out a medium-sized object wrapped in brown paper. She hands it to me.

As I carefully unwrap the package, a blue embroidered journal with gold detailing appears. She's had my initials embossed on the front. It's beautiful.

'And I also have one of these for you.' She hands me a little bottle of saké.

I smile and place the bottle on the side table. It's the book I'm most interested in. I trace my fingers against its intricate design and flick through the blank pages. She's left a note on the first page: *For all the universes you are yet to imagine. All my love, Juliet x*

I close the book again and clutch it close to my chest.

'Thank you,' I whisper. 'This is perfect.'

We stare at each other for several seconds, the first time Juliet has looked me in the eye since she came in, but as my attention shifts to her lips, Juliet breaks focus.

'So, what did you get up to while I was away, Els?'

'Umm, I spent a lot of time thinking and writing. It was good. I had a chance to sit and reflect on a lot of things. And there is something I feel as though maybe, well, we should talk about ...'

'Reflection, really?' Juliette sounds uninterested, picking up the brown wrapping paper and walking over to the bin. Just as she opens the lid, much to my horror, she pulls out a lacy pink bra. It belongs to Bea, and I thought I'd buried it deep enough to prevent this moment. I knew I should have made the journey to the refuse chute outside.

'What is this?' She twists the bra in her fingers as she speaks.

'Um, that must be mine. Awkward.'

'You and I both know that bras do not feature in Elsie's wardrobe unless they were left by one of Elsie's conquests.'

I ignore the comment and try to steer the conversation.

'No but honestly, about what I was saying before, I have had a lot of time to think about life and what I want out of it. And the thing is—'

'Me first!' she interrupts, either overly eager to share her own news or trying to avoid what I was about to say. 'There's something I need to tell you.'

'Okay ...'

'While we were in Japan, Andy and I spent a lot of time speaking, more than usual. He's actually a great guy. You know I'm open to trying new things and I wasn't sure when he said it at first, and maybe it was something to do with being in a completely new and beautiful and different place, but anyway, we got really close.' She speaks without pausing to breathe.

'What do you mean, close?' I ask defensively. 'What about Sophie?'

'Yes, well, things had started to cool off between them before we flew out there. He said he's always wanted for us to give things a go. I mean, I had no idea! Did you? I couldn't believe it.'

'Yes, I could have told you that. The way that he practically salivates when you walk into the room kind of gives it away.' I snap back.

I hate the idea of them together. Literally can't stand the thought of it. He's obnoxious and narrow-minded and she's a free spirit. I picture mini-Andrews walking around. If they got pregnant or married or any of the things that straight people do, I'll be forced to endure him until he keels over. The thought is horrifying.

'Els, I know you don't like Andrew, but I thought you would at least be happy for me. Maybe that was too much to hope for.' She turns cold. 'I've found someone who wants to give it a go. That's what I want too. I need you to support me.'

'Of course I do, I want you to be happy,' I say, summoning all my strength. 'And besides, they say friendships make the best foundations for romantic relationships, don't they?' I have to stop myself rolling my eyes at the irony.

'Exactly. And it's not as though ...' Juliet pauses mid-sentence.

'It's not as though what?' I press her.

'Nothing. Never mind.' I see her take a deep breath. She

turns upbeat again. 'I'm so proud of you for winning the competition. You're going to be a published author, Elsie! Can you believe it? Your own name, printed on a big ol' book. I am proud of you. I really am.'

I only smile. I can't quite find the words for everything I'm feeling right now.

'I was going to ask if you fancied dinner from that vegan burger place you like tonight, J? My treat. But I suppose maybe now, you might fancy something fishier?'

She laughs. 'No, that sounds great.'

'Oh and J. My nan wanted to see if you would come up to hers next week with me. You don't have to, obviously. She just won't let it go if I don't ask.'

For the first time since she came in, she looks at me warmly.

'Why would I not want to come? I love Cherry. I can't wait to see her.' This is her way of proving that everything is fine. 'Unless . . . you'd rather I wasn't there? It's up to you.'

'No, that sounds great, J.' I wonder how long this charade will last for.

21

A week later, we board the train at Paddington station and because I've purchased the cheapest tickets I could find, we don't have assigned seats. Juliet goes to scour the carriages for two seats together. I wait awkwardly at the entrance, keeping watch over our luggage as people squeeze past me in annoyance. After a couple of minutes, Juliet comes to get me.

'I've put my coat down on a couple of seats, but they are quite far up.' She grabs her luggage and I follow her down the aisle of the moving train, trying to avoid tripping on small pooches and the legs of men encroaching in what is already a narrow space. After hoisting our luggage onto one of the racks, Juliet tucks herself in the window seat and immediately plugs her headphones in. We've barely talked all week. I was hoping that by her choosing to come on this trip, this train journey would provide neutral ground on which we could reconnect properly. But instead, she offers me only a weak smile when I sit down next to her. She's buried herself in an explainer podcast called 'Rooted', which looks at the origins of spiritual practices before they became twenty-first-century fads popularised by white influencers.

Ten minutes into the journey, Andrew calls.

'Hi babe,' she says, perking up.

A pause.

'Yes, yes, we're good. Just on our way to Elsie's nan's.'

A longer pause.

'Well, I already told you, I've known her for ever.' She says this defensively.

'No, it's not like that. What is wrong with you? Why are you being so strange?'

I risk a glance over at her.

'Look, you've called at a bad time. I'll talk to you when you've calmed down.' She hangs up the phone and shakes her head, and before I can say anything she loses herself in the podcast again.

Fifteen minutes later, her love of sharing facts drives her to unplug and acknowledge I'm actually here with her.

'Okay, so did you know that . . .'

I put down my copy of *Here Comes the Sun*, taking the rare opportunity to speak.

'J, listen, I'm feeling really stressed that this might be the last time I see my nan's house. It's like I'm losing a piece of my safety net and I'm scared. And I don't even know if you actually want to be here with me because you've been plugged into that thing for the past thirty minutes. I need you today. Why did you say you'd come if you won't be there for me?'

After failing to conceal her disappointment at being interrupted, Juliet puts her phone away and twists her body so that she's looking directly at me – for the first time in days. She takes a deep breath.

'I understand how you must be feeling. It has been a lot of change for you.' Juliet squeezes my hand and I nearly jump.

'But remember that Cherry makes the house, not the other way around. And to your other point . . .' She lets go of my hand and starts playing with the '70s-style rings on her fingers, her gaze focused on the patterns housed within them. 'I don't know exactly why I'm here, to be honest. At first, I was trying to prove something. You know . . . that everything is A-okay.' I freeze but she doesn't notice and continues speaking. 'Which goes completely against the principles I try to live by . . .'

She looks at me and I notice that her shoulders have dropped. She's more relaxed and the air between us has softened. No resolutions are being found, but we're both being honest with each other for the first time in ages.

'But . . . I don't know, Els . . . I can't imagine doing this life thing without you in whatever capacity. So, I'm here.'

All I can say in response is, 'Same'. What she's said sounds like an invitation for us remain as we always have: best friends.

'So, let's make the most of the next couple of days. Let's enjoy being at your nan's for the last time.' This lifts my mood a little.

'Fucking life. Never stops, does it?'

'It doesn't, and Elsie? You know how moody you can get. Don't take your upset out on your nan. She won't have made the decision about the house lightly. Try and see it from her perspective.'

I flinch. Juliet means well but her comments are cutting. I resume reading and she plugs herself back in, instead opting to share what she's learnt with one of her many friends over text.

Arriving at Bristol Temple Meads feels like stepping back in time. Although the houses surrounding the station look different, it still feels weirdly familiar. This is the station I spent so much time hanging around as a teenager, meeting up with girls from MSN at the age of fourteen. It is also the station where I'd departed to London for good to start a new life. It's a lot to take in.

My arms ache with the pressure of my bags. These mangoes and all the other bits of shopping Nan asked me to pick up are weighing me down. There's no way of saying no to her though; it isn't a word that exists in the dictionary of grandmother and granddaughter.

As we emerge from the station, I'm reminded that people outside London actually smile at each other on the street and that this doesn't necessarily mean that they are plotting to chop you up into tiny little pieces. I withdraw cash from the ATM for our bus fares, and when the bus arrives, a stranger helps lug my bag inside.

'Oooof, what you got in here?' he asks.

'Mangoes.'

Unsure of how to respond, he just gives me a curious smile.

Juliet and I ride on the bus in silence.

Nan lives in St Pauls. She's one of the originals in the area. I still have a key to her house and I am half-expecting it not to fit. But after some manoeuvring, Juliet and I are in and I'm immediately hit by the smell of saltfish and bakes as the front door swings open.

'Elsie, is that you?' Nan calls out from the kitchen, her rich Guyanese accent sunny and familiar.

'It's us! I'm coming.' I drop the bags hastily in the hall and make my way down to the kitchen, the corridor still carpeted with the same floral pattern that she's had since the '70s. She's standing in the middle of the kitchen with her arms wide open and I dive straight into them. She squeezes me deep. She feels smaller than before, more fragile. I used to be convinced that my superhero nan would never age but I can see that time is enveloping her. She lets go, holding me at arm's length as she takes in my face, and I take in hers. She has some new lines and wrinkles, and I feel bad that I've been so consumed by my own shit that I've missed the moments when these had formed.

'Don't fret,' she says, reading my mind. 'You here now.'

I smile at her, and all the tension in my body is replaced with warmth and comfort.

'Ah cooking your favourite today.'

I grin.

Nan nods her head. 'Where you friend?' she says loud enough for Juliet to hear, making it clear that she's welcome inside.

'I'm here!' Juliet announces and Nan gives her a similarly warm embrace. I see Juliet fold into her arms. When she lets Juliet go, we just stand awkwardly side by side.

Nan turns her attention to frying the last of the bakes in a black cast-iron pan, and she then spreads them on a paper towel. I immediately reach for one; even though it's piping hot, I can't stop myself. Her kitchen table is covered in the same plastic cover she's always had. While still munching on the bake, I offer to help her prepare the last bit of the food but she swats me away like a fly.

'I may be old but I'm not dead,' she says. 'You two just sit down. I'm gon do the cooking because I know where everything is.'

I'm already guzzling down my second bake when I realise that Juliet hasn't eaten any of hers.

'Oh, damn. J is vegan. I forgot to mention that.'

Juliet smiles awkwardly, clearly not wanting to in-convenience Nan.

'Let me fry up some pepper and onions for you to have with the bake. You're looking mawga, unlike my granddaughter over there. She can eat and eat and eat. If you done look sharp, she can eat you and all. You must leave here with your belly full.'

Nan is already halfway out of her chair. 'You girls will have to go out and get me some more vegetable though. I'd planned to cook curry goat, pig tail and rice and all them tings there. Your favourites,' she says, smiling in my direction.

'No, honestly it's fine, Cherry, I'm not hungry,' says Juliet, but Nan doesn't listen.

Once she has finished frying up the veg, we all sit together at the table again, eating and talking, sharing the various updates in our lives. I take the opportunity to tell them both that I have a job interview when we get back to London, this time for a role I might actually get.

'Lord, have mercy. That is good news.' Nan nods her head and Juliet turns to look at me. She looks disappointed that I haven't shared this information with her.

'What is it?' Juliet asks, wanting to be let in.

'A café job. Waitressing.'

'That's great, Els.' Unsure of how to congratulate me, she touches me on the shoulder as though this is neutral territory. I place my hand on the spot she just touched, wishing she would rest her hand on my skin for a little longer.

'First the book, now a job. You really make me proud, likkle one. Keep it up.'

Nan's called me 'likkle one' ever since I was actually little and hasn't stopped even though I now tower over her. I love it.

'Yeah, it's a good thing. It is a good thing,' Juliet chimes in, and I look up to see her fiddling with her hair. In record time, Nan has finished frying up a heap of spring onion, tomato and sweet peppers for Juliet and places it in a bowl on the table next to where she's sitting.

In the corner of the room, I spot an old picture of Nan, my brothers, Dad, Mum and me. It looks like one of those staged photographs taken in a studio. There are also images of my nan on her various travels, and these have been there so long that they've practically become part of the walls. I still can't believe that she's moving.

'You look like you've seen jumbie,' Nan says as I zone back into the conversation. She catches my eye. 'The memories in this house won't fade, you know. They live in here.' Nan turns to me and gently presses her finger against my temple and then holds my cheeks in her two, small hands. 'And wherever I am, you'll always have a place to come back to.' Tears prickle at the corner of my eyes. 'Now, finish your food.'

I obey.

'When was the last time you talk to your mother?' Nan asks as she squeezes my leg, changing tack.

'I haven't seen her since she came over to J's for lunch.'

'It didn't go well,' Juliet joins in.

'So I haven't heard from her since then. But it's not like we speak every day anyway.'

'I don't know why your mother is so uptight,' Nan says, shaking her head in anguish. 'And your dad ... that man has never had much to say.'

Nan has never been my dad's biggest fan. She doesn't trust people who are quiet and always agreeable. She says that she can't be sure of anything that comes out of their mouths and that it's always the quiet ones who snap one day or shoot up the place, nobody seeing it coming.

'I raised my children to be freer than we were taught back home. But you mother? I was hoping she'd be more relaxed and independent and go for her own dreams and never mind what people say, especially in the church. That's how I lived my life. I dunno where she got her attitude from. I suppose it's my fault for leaving her out deh for so long.' She kisses her teeth lightly with regret.

I have nothing to add so say instead, 'You know your saltfish is unrivalled, Nan.' I mop up the final bake and remnants of fish and she revels in the praise.

'It's a shame you and your mother can't cook and I know you like my kind of food. My road is running out of bricks.'

This is Nan beckoning me to take note of her recipes and spend more time with her. My guilt hits again.

'You know nothing will ever be as good as your cooking, Nan. But I agree. I'm gonna start writing stuff down.'

Her raised eyebrows are sceptical. I probably said something similar the last time I visited.

'What did you think of the food?' she asks Juliet, searching for more praise.

'Delicious as usual. Reminds me of Sundays at yours when we were young. I used to really look forward to it. My mum had me on such a strict healthy diet back then.'

'Good. I'm glad. Now that you've been fed and watered, I have a few little jobs for you. My shoulder's killing me. I've been moving as many boxes around as I can but there are a couple in the attic that I need you to bring down for me. There should be some travel bags up there too that I'll need to use to pack things into.' She's never shy of putting me to work.

'Of course. Shall we drop our things and then head up to the attic?' asks Juliet.

'Yes dear, and Elsie? You bring the mango?'

After unloading a mountain of mangoes and assorted seasonings from my bag, which I am sure can be purchased in multiple places in the UK, Juliet and I head up into the attic, which is a museum of everything my nan has ever owned. I recognise a red kite, a game of backgammon, and there's even a box containing her wedding dress. There are also lots of things I don't recognise amidst the piles and beams. There isn't a working light up here, so we've wedged a torch upright in an old shoe. It casts a glow across the bottom half of Juliet's face. We're sitting close together, our legs hanging through the hatch. Neither of us speaks. We just look around the room until our eyes meet again. I want to pull her in close, to kiss her even, but she starts to cough.

'Think it's my dust allergies playing up.' Juliet physically leans away from me. I try to offer a solution.

'Why don't you wait at the bottom of the ladder, and I'll pass things down to you?' She nods her head and quickly gets up, making her way out of the loft.

I stand up, making sure not to bang my head as I manoeuvre my way through the small space. It's a little creepy up here and I wonder if there are lost souls lingering under these beams – the house's previous owners, trapped memories, and the likes.

In the middle of the loft, there is a series of empty brown travel bags and cases. One by one I pass these down to Juliet, who is shielding her eyes from the incoming dust.

As I grab the final bag, I knock the torch over and the light shines onto an unlabelled black box. Curious and not wanting to miss anything before Nan moves, I open it and find a stack of photographs and some old letters inside. I notice that several of the photographs are of my nan and Alison on holiday together. I remember how they used to do everything together. Alison was always at family birthday parties and spent Christmas with us most years. In the photos, she looks the same as she did when I bumped into her a few weeks ago. She's barely aged. The only difference in this particular image is that her hair is styled in two perfectly parted braids. She looks glamorous standing next to my nan. I turn the photograph over and written on the back is '1999, Turkey', which explains why they're both wearing blacked-out '90s sunglasses. Nan is in denim shorts and a T-shirt, and Alison is in a flowing yellow summer dress. There's another photo of them together in Berlin at Christmas. This one is labelled 2003. They're both smiling underneath a Christmas tree, clutching pitchers of beer. They look happy.

I keep going through the photos and there are several more taken in similar backdrops. I even find one where Alison, Nan and Dad stand around me as I blow out candles on Alison's infamous fruitcake.

Then there's . . .

'Everything all right?' Juliet calls out, and it takes me a minute to respond. These images, tens of them, have my brain spinning. I'm not sure if I'm really seeing what I think I am. Can't be.

'Yeah, give me a second. Just trying to organise a bit before I bring stuff down.' I buy myself a little more time.

Searching for an explanation, I move the photos aside and turn my attention to the letters. I love the thought of people sending notes to each other by hand. It's part of the reason why I enjoy writing my poems down in my journal first. There's something thoughtful and intimate about putting pen to paper. And the things I'm trying to make sense of feel stronger when I write them down.

There are letters from and to my nan's eight brothers and sisters, sharing information about their new lives in different parts of England, Canada and the US in the early days after leaving Guyana. They speak about who is courting who, cold weather, and how despite some of them having had decent jobs in Guyana, it was proving difficult to find 'respectable' work.

After wading through the top few letters, I spot a note in different handwriting. It's harder to read, but I make out that it's a letter from Alison. A gasp leaves my mouth once I open it. I'm not sure why I didn't connect the dots years ago. It suddenly makes so much sense.

It's a love letter.

Nan didn't date anyone after Grandad left her for another woman. It wasn't something we spoke about, ever. Whenever I'd ask about him, she'd quickly shut it down. I don't even think they officially got divorced, but Alison was always there. Nan had a spare bedroom once my mum and uncle had moved out. I'd always presumed that this was where Alison slept on the nights I'd stay over, as most of the time she'd still be there in the morning when I woke up. Now the realisations come flooding in.

'Juliet, grab this,' I say in a half-whisper, suddenly apprehensive of what my nan will say when she realises I've been looking through her stuff. I pass the first box down.

'Be careful with this one too.' I hand down the smaller box of letters.

'Why are you whispering?' she asks, holding her ear in a bid to hear me better. I bring my fingers to my lips, telling her to ssh, and we move quietly downstairs into the front room.

This is the only room in the house where there is noticeably new furniture. There is a purple sofa and a new television, which wasn't there the last time I'd visited. Nan is sitting down watching her favourite show, *Judge Judy*. I can hear her saying, 'Save the drama for your Mama', in her uncompromising tone. We used to watch the show back-to-back. She would laugh at Judge Judy's fervour and ability to call total bullshit on the people who thought that she wouldn't be able to read them for filth.

As soon as Nan clocks the boxes Juliet and I have brought in, her facial expression changes and she turns down the television. She pauses for a moment. Juliet looks at me and I stare at the nan whose life I thought I had all figured out.

'Where you get those?' Nan asks suspiciously. I'm still unable to predict how she'll respond to the questions dancing on the tip of my tongue.

'The attic, Nan. I thought these were the boxes you asked me to bring down.'

I can tell from her expression that she already knows I've looked inside.

'Mmmhmm,' she says, in possible disapproval.

My poker face dissipates, and she once again has direct insight into my thought processes.

'What did you find then?' Her brown eyes spark with new energy.

Juliet doesn't say anything, totally confused. She perches herself on the brown leather sofa opposite my nan, as if subconsciously trying to give us space for whatever is about to unfold.

'Nan, you and Alison?'

'What you want to know?' She's really going to make me say it. For a moment, nothing comes out.

'Elsie, you know I don't like it when you don't speak up. I raised you to use your voice, not swallow it.'

I walk towards her.

'Nan, were you and Alison ... You know ... ?' I don't look her in the eye. I'm confused and comforted all at once.

'Eh, are you going to spit it out? But yes, me and Alison. Just like you and Juliet.'

'Do you mean you were good friends who hung out together a lot, a bit like sisters? Or were, you know, the kind of mates who *really* liked each other?'

Juliet fidgets on the sofa.

'We were in love.' Nan says this so casually that I involuntarily let out a giggle.

'Oh my God, Nan. This is huge!'

'What? I had a life. I know you assume that I was only ever just your nan, here on this earth to look after you, but I loved people too you know. You aren't the first.'

I can barely cope with this new information and can see that Juliet is in shock too, even though she's trying her best to play it cool. How could I never have seen that she and Alison were together?

'Me and Juliet aren't like you and Alison. Just by the way,' I say then, to set the record straight.

Juliet looks taken aback by how bluntly I clear this up. Nan catches her look.

'Oh, well you two have always been very close. I thought it was bound to happen some day.'

I say nothing, not sure where to take the conversation from here, and Juliet fiddles nervously with her hair. Even though we are forever finding ourselves mistaken for a couple, this time feels thornier because we now exist on shakier ground.

'I'm going to pop to the shops,' Juliet suddenly asserts. 'Is there anything I can get you, Cherry?'

Nan gestures towards the door with her long, bony, brown fingers. 'There's a list hanging up just over there, if you don't mind. Do you remember where the shop is from here, Juliet?'

'Yeah, I'll find it. Don't worry,' she says, already halfway out the door.

Once she's gone, my nan gives me that familiar stern expression.

'Tell me bout you and Juliet. What's happening there?' She gestures to me to come and sit down next to her.

'Nan!'

'Come on, you know you can tell me anything.'

I perch on the edge of the sofa.

'I don't know . . . It's all got so complicated.'

'Why's everything got to be so complicated with your generation, eh? Either you like someone or you nuh like them. You tell them or you keep it in. Come now, which is it my girl?'

'I think about her a lot . . .' I find myself replaying our cuddles in bed and watching her on webcam. I forget where I am for a moment and Nan clears her throat with authority, as though warning me not to get into any intimate details. I run my hand over my head and look down at my feet.

'No. It's too late anyway. She has a boyfriend and he's the worst,' I murmur.

'It's never too late.' Nan turns up her bottom lip to suggest that I should think again. 'Why do you mention the boy with such discontent?'

'He's just not a very nice person. He's not right for her. He's arrogant.'

'The fact that you have quite so much to say about what is right for her suggests that you feel like you are what is right for her. I'll let you work it out.'

I turn the conversation back to her.

'Nan, how on earth did you tell Mum about you and Alison? She doesn't even know about me.'

'Your mother ... well, she's a different kettle of fish. Alison and I, we never let anybody know our business. You know how it goes. Mattie tell Mattie and Tara tell Tara. Not worth the stress. And it was a different time then. Only my brother Godfrey knows about me. He's the only one who could take it. The rest of them got their own ideas. To be honest, I was scared at first when I developed feelings for Alison. I was never taught that it was okay. But after a while both of us surrendered to it. We didn't want to make any of our families feel uncomfortable, so we kept it to ourselves. What we do behind closed doors is nobody's business. Unless they're bedroom inspectors.'

She would never admit it, but I'm wondering if Nan sending me up to the attic might have been deliberate. Maybe she wanted to show her true self to me, her dyke granddaughter.

'Elsie, you look like I've just told you I'm dying. Be sure to change your face quick, before the wind blows and meks it stay that way for ever. Pick up your jaw.'

'Sorry, Nan, I just wasn't expecting any of this, you know. I spent so long growing up wanting to share parts of myself with you all but I didn't know how. It's not that I thought it was wrong or that I was wrong, but you know what Mum's like. She's proper strict and it was hardly like the Sundays we spent together at church were the perfect opportunity to say, *Hey, by the way, I'm gay.* I always used to feel like I was gonna catch fire when I sat in those pews. And now, you too?'

We both belly laugh, giggling so hard that our eyes water. My nan, big dyke, and me, baby dyke, laughing in all our gay.

'I always had an inkling about you child, but it wasn't for me to ask you how you felt and I didn't want to come between you and your mother. She always seemed to have an issue with how close we were. Jealousy,' my nan says, with a strong sense of fatigue.

'But Nan, what happened with you and Alison?'

'Oh, only what happens sometimes in love. You fall out of it.'

22

'It's odd how so many people, your nan included, seem to think there's something else going on between us.'

Juliet hangs her head off the top bunk in the spare room. Little blue bows line the wallpaper. Her voice is cautious.

'I guess it's what happens when two girls are as close as we are. Especially when one is gay with a capital G,' I say, trying to lighten the mood.

'You know what I think? I think you're secretly in love with Bea.'

I can't tell what game Juliet is playing.

'She's practically married,' I respond. 'Plus, it's not like that with me and Bea. You and I are different.'

'Mmm . . .'

I change the subject.

'It's been really nice having you here, you know, before this place is gone. I didn't think I'd being doing this again so soon, packing up. Even though I know it's not the same and I know both you and Nan have reminded me that this house isn't her or me or all of us, it kind of is, you know. That's how I see it anyway. It's like this house contains spirits within it but it also is a spirit in its own right. Feels like it chose us.'

Silence hangs in the air.

'Can I jump in?' she asks suddenly. I assume she's yearning for the same closeness I am.

'Of course.'

She clambers down from the top bunk and into my bed. It's a tight squeeze as she nuzzles her head directly into my chest. In this moment we are back to being us.

'Comfortable?'

'Always.'

'Els, how weird is it being back at your nan's? I feel like we're in school again. I still dream about her homemade fudge and pineapple slices.'

'Me too. I can't believe this whole house is no longer going to be hers.'

'So many memories.'

'But it might mean that *finally* she'll let me have some of her records.' I giggle softly before being brought back to the reality of what is happening. 'She finds it hard to let go of things and apparently I do too.'

'I'm sure she'll let you have whatever you want. She adores you and everything you do,' Juliet says fondly. 'Goodbyes are hard but honestly, Elsie, just enjoy every little moment with your nan while she's here. I'm not saying she'll be going any-where any time soon. But I miss mine, so badly and that's the thing I wish I'd done differently. Spent more time.' Juliet saw her grandma way more than I see mine so this is a welcome yet sad reminder of how impermanent everything is.

'Remember how you told me your grandma, Caroline, told you that she'd continue to find you in all the lifetimes she was yet to live. I think that's true, J. She's with you. But I'm sorry if a day like today makes it even more real that she isn't here anymore.' I feel her body exhale.

'I think it's true too,' she says gently, with a crack in her voice.

We're so close that it feels like our bodies will only be separated if someone unstitches us.

'J, your breath . . .' I say pulling in my chin and holding my nose emphatically, trying to lighten the mood.

'Rude. Yours is awful too.'

'Move then.'

'I want to stay for a little longer. It feels good here.' She nuzzles deeper into my chest.

There's a comfortable silence for a moment. I'm loving having her beside me but I also can't tell why Juliet changed her mood so quickly.

'Els, did you never suspect your nan and Alison?'

'Never. Not even once. I was hardly thinking about my nan's dating history as a kid. She was just my nan. I didn't think about her having a whole life outside of that.'

'It's weird, isn't it? We don't really see our parents as having lives as messy as ours.'

'I wonder what happened between them. But now that I think about it, when I saw Alison the other week, I thought she was acting so strange about my nan.'

'Maybe Cherry is as much of a womaniser as you are. Or . . . maybe it's a cautionary tale about what happens when you fall in love with your best friend.'

I have no idea how to respond properly. The words leave my mouth too quickly.

'It's probably a good thing I never got in your knickers

then, isn't it? I'd probably have broken your heart.' My words tumble out without grace and Juliet's forehead crinkles, the mood shifting.

'No, my heart broke when you stopped speaking to me.'

'Oh Juliet, you know I love you, don't you? I'll always love you. It's just . . .'

'You don't need you to say anything, not now. Let's just be still.'

23

Lining the walls of a gallery in east London is a series of self-portraits by visual activist Zanele Muholi. The exhibition is called 'Somnyama Ngonyama, Hail the Dark Lioness'. The images are both regal and striking. Muholi is the subject and the one archiving a queer, Black history that is both theirs and ours to share. We're walking through the space side by side, stopping to take in each image. I'm grateful to Maggie for the invitation.

'How do they manage to create something that feels so otherworldly and yet still rooted in something so real?' I'm staring at an image of Muholi with blown-up latex gloves attached to their head and body.

As with the other objects and accessories in the other photographs in the series, the gloves match their skin. They are all Black.

'Some people have just got that thing.' Maggie nods as she inspects every corner of this particular picture.

'A thing that can't be described, only felt,' she continues.

'That's true, though I'm frustrated that I can't find words that adequately capture it.'

'Of course you would be.' Maggie chuckles. 'But this is one

of those shows that you need to ruminate on for a little while. It's the sort of exhibition that encourages you to hold a mirror up to yourself. To question things.'

'It's that ting.' I'm making light but I get what she's saying.

We continue walking through the space, mostly in silence, taking it all in and feeling things. When we're finished, Maggie insists on taking me for a lunch. After queuing outside for twenty minutes, we are now sitting side by side in the middle of a tiny trendy restaurant, waiting for two spicy pepperoni pizzas to arrive.

'Maggie?'

'Yes?' She takes off her cap and places it delicately on the side of her chair.

'You know the flyer you sent me the other day? Are you telling me that there was a Black queer centre that existed on Bellenden Road? Like that was really a thing?'

'Yep.' Maggie had scanned in and sent me a newsletter from May 1995. In Times New Roman font, in the middle of the page, *Save the centre ... by any means necessary* was written, and at the top of the page, *Black Lesbian & Gay Centre* was written next to two stick figures with round faces and oval features.

'It didn't last long though,' Maggie goes on. 'One day there was enough funding for all, but things quickly changed. No financial support. Politics.' She shrugs emphatically.

'Mad. I still can't get my head around the fact that there was an actual, physical safe space for us ... and in Peckham.'

'You're really interested in this stuff, aren't you? I thought you'd get bored eventually but you've always got something to ask me.'

'Bored? More people should know about this! This is literally our history, and you know me! I love to get lost in a good story.'

Maggie looks a little sad.

'I do wonder when these things will completely fade from memory. So many people thinking they were the first, but if you just look a little bit further back, there's a lot that existed. We only ever build on each other's achievements.'

'I feel that. Like when you talk about how people dressed or what you were listening to, I just think about how that evolves over time. It's like we're all shapeshifting. Trying to figure out what our thing is. We're all connected. You. Me. The artist. Even my nan . . .' My brain is moving at a thousand miles an hour, creating a timeline of events.

'Your nan?'

'Found out this weekend that Nan's oldest pal wasn't just a friend.' Maggie is unfazed by my revelation. She just says, 'I see.'

The waiter brings over our pizzas and after covering them in garlic oil and black pepper, we get stuck in.

'I'm gonna write about you one day, Maggie. That is, if you'll let me.' She smiles as I speak, and that's all the permission I need. Being around Maggie is reliably restorative, in the way I imagine people feel revitalised after a weekend of being pampered at their mum's place. She gives that comfort to me.

When I arrive back at the flat, I have a phone interview for a role at some bougie new store opening in Peckham. It's a wine shop slash bar slash 'doesn't quite know what it is'. It hasn't opened yet but they also want to programme events, which sounds cool. *And* it's a job. The interview goes well, I think, better than the interview for that café. The woman seemed to like me and the fact that I write poetry got her particularly interested. Since I didn't get the waitressing job, I'm hoping this one comes through. When I'm finished I sit out on the balcony and make a roll-up – a habit I've picked up since living at Juliet's. It's early evening and chilly, so I wrap myself in a blanket. November is my favourite time of year. There's a tranquility about the city ahead of the buzz of Christmas festivities. I've made it to the end of the year; things are happening for me and my nightmares are finally becoming less distressing.

I light the cig and the first drag makes me feel light-headed. I check my emails. I've been going back and forth with the publisher on payment schedules, though the conclusion is that under no circumstances should I give up the day job I'm still yet to find. I've been thinking about moving out and how good it would be for both me and Juliet. It would enable us to process, move past our feelings and find our friendship again, like we did at my nan's, but this will never happen if I can't even get a fucking job. And anyway, a large chunk of my publishing advance will be used to pay off the debt I've been trying to forget about.

From the balcony, I spot Juliet walking up the road, alone and lugging several bags of shopping. I go and meet her halfway up the stairwell and take the bags from her. She's tired but seems happy to see me. She's in purple high-waisted jeans and a bright jumper in multiple shades of pink.

'Long day, J?'

'I'll tell you about it when we get inside. I only meant to pick up a few bits but ended up with the whole shop.'

'Every time!' I smile back at her.

We haven't had a *Drag Race* Saturday in ages, and I've been missing the tenderness and warmth in the moments of it being just us. I can't believe that just as I was starting to come to terms with the fact that our relationship could be more than a friendship, she got a boyfriend. Classic Elsie luck.

I have to say that this week, J and Andrew have been mindful of keeping space between us. I'm sure that it's Juliet's doing. Even though I know she doesn't love his flatmates, she's been making a conscious effort to spend as much time as possible at his. Occasionally, if they've been out for the night in Peckham, they've come back to the flat. The other night, I could tell they were drunk and I heard them fucking. It filled my stomach with an overpowering nausea. I wanted so badly to walk into her bedroom and untangle their bodies and find the place where Juliet and I fit. He was all groans and huffing and puffing; she was surprisingly quiet. He made a weird comment the other day about her giving up camming, which I didn't like. Something about him having enough money that she doesn't need to do it, because she couldn't really like it. I heard the tail end of what he was saying as I walked into the kitchen. Just as, 'What are you talking about?' left my mouth and I was ready to get into it, Juliet shut the conversation down, clearly not wanting us to go head-to-head. Juliet is the sunniest person I know, and I don't want this insecure bandy making her shine any less brightly.

I decide that today I'll ask her about camming in the hope that we will be able to have a moment of even performed closeness. She seems pretty comfortable doing it around me and also at this stage, I need work that pays real money. So I might as well give it a go. I want to have enough cash in my pocket to know that I can sustain rent for the year ahead – but I am worried that something will leak and end up being shown to my mum or dad. Or my nan, though I don't think she spends much of her time on X-rated websites. She can only just wrap her head around how to use her burner.

'So, tell me about your day then,' I say as I walk into the flat and begin unpacking the quinoa, chickpeas and green juice from the shopping bags. Juliet peels off her layers.

'Gah, so long actually. There was this kid who took a shit in the middle of the classroom. An actual turd. I didn't know children could produce such adult-sized poo. And then, if that wasn't bad enough, I had to cover breakfast club today because as usual Rachel was late for work.' She exhales as she speaks, and I can see her unravelling as she lets it all out.

'Ah, man. That is nasty. Can I get you a cup of tea or something?'

'That would be lovely . . .' She pauses and looks at me suspiciously. 'You're being extra nice today. What do you want?' She flashes a smile my way.

'Why must you assume that I want something because I'm being nice?' I purse my lips.

Juliet shrugs, bowing her head and using her teeth to pull off a fingerless glove. She continues taking off her layers of knitted things and I realise I'm just standing, staring at her. I quickly look for something else to do and pop on the kettle, reaching to the top cupboard for her favourite blend.

'So, J . . . I was thinking about what you said, about me trying out camming. I'm not saying I'm a hundred per cent down but I kind of want to try it once. Just to see if it could be a nice little earner for me. The publishing prize sorts me as far as a deposit is concerned, but I'll never be able to keep up rent with the amount I'm making at the moment.'

She comes into the kitchen looking genuinely surprised.

'Wow. Okay. I didn't think you would ever come around.' Juliet is tired but perks up with this conversation. 'I mean, if you want to try it, we'll need to go out and buy you some undies. Those old boxers you love so much won't be a vibe.' She giggles.

'Are you calling my boxers dusty?'

'Yes. I absolutely am.' She enjoys delivering this line.

'Rude.'

Then, tentatively, she says, 'We can do it together, if you like? I'm supposed to have a session with one of my regulars tonight and he's asked me before if I have a friend. German guy. Business type. Wants the convenience of intimacy with a woman without having any sort of commitment. A bit like you, actually.'

The last bit takes me by surprise, but just as I'm about to say something, Juliet keeps talking.

'Once I've had a cuppa, we can head down to the high street and grab you something to wear.'

'One of your regulars so soon? Are you sure I'm ready?'

'You saw what I did last time. And anyway, we'll just be enacting a standard fantasy. Nothing too difficult. I thought you had all the moves,' she teases, winking at me.

'Obviously I do.' I twist my body inwards and then realise my pathetic (and involuntary) attempt to flirt with her.

She doesn't seem to notice, just looks down at her phone and says, 'Actually, we only have an hour till the shop closes. We'd better go. Come on.'

She finishes her tea in record time, and we leave the house and roll down to the shop just before closing. This is a time for just us. After whizzing down the high street, we find ourselves in a shop that is lined with rows of lacy bras and crotchless underwear. There's nothing sexy about how everything is laid out, and there are buckets of discounted thongs dotted throughout the shop and adorning every surface. It's cluttered and I don't know where to begin.

'Goddayum,' I say with an Americanised twang. 'I like seeing this stuff on other people but I'm not sure how it'll look on me. You know me, I'm a simple gal.'

There's a sales assistant ready to pack up. She seems put out that we've walked in just before closing. I remember that feeling from the club.

'Just grab a couple of bits that you like the look of,' Juliet orders. 'I always feel so guilty for coming here. I can only imagine the conditions under which everything is made.' She looks around the shop sadly.

'J, we don't have time for your commitment to save the world right now! I've gotta get paid.'

'Okay, you're right. Let's make it quick. I think the changing rooms are closed so try to choose something you know will fit.'

We stand at opposite sides of a black wire underwear rack. There are the world's smallest thongs, red laced underwear sets and love-heart-shaped nipple covers, none of which are things I can wear. I opt for a simple black two-piece because it comes with the only unpadded bra I can find in the shop. I feel uncomfortable and want this part to be over as quickly as possible. Juliet has picked out a couple of options on the other side.

'Um, what do you think of this?' I show her what I've picked up.

'No, no, no,' she laughs. 'It's not that you wouldn't look, you know, good in it, it's just that I think we can do better.'

'You're enjoying this too much, J.' I frown, feeling a little silly, self-conscious and out of my depth.

'Who, me? Teaching you, Elsie Macintosh, self-professed sex god, how to choose something sexy to wear? Yes, yes I am.' Her smile is far reaching.

Juliet holds up a black lace body suit with roses on the tits. 'What about this?'

'Really?' I look at her, unconvinced.

'It's black like your other set and simple, but not too simple. The roses add something. I think you'll look great in it.' She gives me a look I haven't seen before, and I suddenly feel a little nervous.

She continues. 'Let's pick out another option, just in case this one doesn't fit. Something red, maybe?'

'Now you're pushing it.'

'Okay, what about this one then?' She holds up another black lacy two-piece. It looks virtually the same as all the others.

'I'm trusting you here, J.'

My eyes catch on a green corset and matching thong set.

'I'd like to see you in this.' I point to it, unsure of how she'll respond. I want her to smile at me.

Her cheeks gain colour and she looks away, though she does pick up the suggested outfit and place it onto the counter.

Everything adds up to £35, which means that it probably won't survive more than two washes. The sales assistant happily sees us out of the shop and locks the doors behind us.

'I can't believe you've convinced me to wear a piece of candy floss,' I say as we wander back down the high street. She raises her eyebrows as though she's not buying my nervousness.

'I feel surprisingly shook, all things considered.'

'It'll be fine, and like I said, if you feel uncomfortable we'll just shut it down. But I believe in you. You'll be great.' She brushes her arm against my shoulder and even though I try not to react, my hairs stand on end.

When we get back to the flat, I jump straight into the bath so that I can shave my legs, edges of my fanny and armpits, which have been left to grow wild. I have a feeling that most of the men who pay to watch women fuck each other online probably subscribe to a hairless vision of womanhood. Today isn't the day to try to convince them otherwise.

'You better wash too, J,' I say jokily after getting out of the shower.

She offers me a dirty look in response. But wrapped in a tiny towel, she shoves me out of her way as she enters the steam-filled bathroom.

I paint my toenails black, just in case this guy is into feet. After we've both changed, preened and moisturised, I make my way into Juliet's bedroom where she's busy positioning the camera. I take her and her green corset in. For a moment, I don't know what to say.

'Wow, Els. You look good. Like really good,' Juliet says slowly, looking me up and down. My heart speeds up a little.

'Do you think? I think I look like an alien.'

'Nope ... I don't think so ...' She is still looking directly at me, holding my gaze. I break the moment.

'I can't believe we're doing this. *I'm* doing this. Have I lost the plot?'

'It'll be fine. I'm kind of looking forward to it,' she says as she plumps up the pillows on her bed and gets rid of Bernie.

'Okay, so, what do I need to know? I'm actually kinda terrified. What if I laugh or move or say the wrong thing and break character?'

'You don't need to overly perform. Try to make it feel as natural as possible, like it's just me and you. But, at the same time, do remember that there's a camera and try to stay in frame.' She tilts her laptop screen. 'If I set it up like this, then we should be able to get a good amount of us in.'

'Will Andrew be funny about this?'

She sighs. 'It's my job. If he isn't able to accept it, he'll have to find someone else.' This is the first time I've heard Juliet say anything that isn't entirely complimentary about Andrew. 'We don't have to do this unless you feel comfortable and want to, Els. If anything gets too much, or too awkward at any point, you have to let me know. Let's set up a safe word. You choose one.'

'Cauliflower.' There is no indecision as I say this, knowing that if cauliflower is mentioned, it will be an instant mood kill on my part. I go on. 'Okay well, let's get to werkkk. I'm ready. Also, you don't look so bad yourself. You make that corset look like it could be from Agent Provocateur.' I say this in a mock French accent and Juliet smiles, enjoying the praise. She does look beautiful. My frantic pulse agrees.

'Come here then.' She turns the camera on and enters us into the chatroom. She then turns to me and smiles reassuringly. Slowly, she touches my face and traces her hands down my

core before leaning in and kissing me. My body is on fire and
without hesitation, I kiss her back. Her mouth is warm and
our kiss is deeper than I expected it to be. She pulls away and
we stare at each other. She smiles, and with my fingers, I trace
the spot where her lips landed.

'Was that okay?' she asks.

'Fucking hell . . .'

'What?'

'Yeah, it was more than okay.' I'm gawking at her.

'That was just the warm-up,' says Juliet, and I wonder if
she's deliberately teasing me, making my mind and body beg
for whatever could come next.

It's weird. We're both sitting on her bed, in our underwear,
in this chatroom, waiting to receive our instructions from a
client. We sit still, not quite knowing if – where – to touch
each other. I want to laugh, my feelings all over the place, and
I think she does too, but we manage to keep it together while
we wait for her client to request a private session. I feel goofy,
stiffer than usual, and like I've forgotten what the rules are.
I'm aware that the camera is on, but Juliet is doing her best to
guide the situation gently. I wonder if she can tell how much I
want her and how much I'm savouring each time our skin or
fingers meet. I feel a little pathetic, sitting here, imagining that
this moment of packaged fantasy is in fact real. I've tried to
push my feelings away but they're only getting louder. For the
general camroom, she kisses my stomach tenderly and, afraid
to make eye contact with her, I face the camera directly instead.
I'm not sure what this must look like for the people watching.

The request comes in and Juliet whispers gently in my ear,
'Just follow my lead.'

I nod back. I'm not used to someone else being in control yet I'm enjoying how comfortable Juliet is. Her warmth is putting me at ease. She does most of the talking to her client, who is very excited to see us. The worst part of the whole thing is having to smile and pretend that he is the one I want to impress.

'Just focus on me,' Juliet says quietly, sensing my discomfort.

'Imagine it is just us, or that I'm one of your many wives.' She's speaking quietly enough that only I can hear what she's saying.

I want to tell her that in this moment I'm not thinking about anyone else but instead, I decide to show her. We spend a brief moment just kissing and as we part, Juliet checks to see if I'm okay through her eyes alone. I'm glad that I can't see the guy on the other side of the camera; he asks for remarkably little, but still I'm acutely aware that it isn't just us.

Juliet removes the straps on the bra I'm wearing and slowly and gently engulfs my nipples in her mouth. I'm taken aback by this but then I remember the guy on the other side of the camera isn't just paying to watch us kiss.

'J,' I say, gently through stilted breaths.

'Are you okay?' She says quietly as she moves her way back up and kisses my collar bone. 'I'm fine, Els. Are you fine?'

Suddenly I think I might burst into tears. I close the laptop and get up.

'Elsie!'

I pace up and down the room for a moment and then I can't stop the words from tumbling out.

'I really want to kiss you and I really don't want to do it with other people watching. I mean it, J. All I want is to be with you. I've been trying to firm it, you know, convince myself that

I'll be happy just being your friend for ever. Especially after my performance because I felt like that was what you wanted. But it's like I'm obsessed with you or something. I want to be around you all the time. Breathe you in. And I know I ran away for those three months and I'm sorry it's taken me so long to realise but I'm back now and literally all I want is to be with you.' I speak so fast, eventually running out of breath.

She looks at me for a second, saying nothing, and I can't read her expression. Then finally:

'I want to kiss you too. I want to do more than kiss you.' She says this with urgency and I'm filled with relief as she speaks.

Juliet grabs me and pulls me into her. She doesn't have to do a lot to turn me on. The anticipation is enough. It feels strange to be close like this – not because it's wrong but because it's new. And this time, we're actually alone.

We take it slow and kiss like teenagers discovering each other in a completely new way. Juliet pulls me onto the bed. Our bodies are interlinked as we roll around, giggling through our shared giddiness. Our kisses are full and warm and messy and long. We part lips just long enough for us to take in a breath, and our eyes open and meet, the creases in the corner of hers telling me she's as happy as I am. It's intense but then she kisses the tip of my nose and I think I might melt. Taking it in turns, I kiss her cheek and she kisses my chin. I kiss her ear lobe and then her neck. She has little dark brown beauty spots that I've never seen before – on her face and neck and next to her belly button, which sticks out only slightly. She giggles when I kiss her here and this makes me smile. After a second, she taps me and I worry that I've done something to disrupt the serenity of this moment, but her eyes are wet when I look up.

'I've wanted this for so long,' she whispers.

'Me too.'

'I thought it might be weird if it ever happened, but it feels exactly how it's supposed to feel.' She pulls me close again and bites her lip as she guides my hand to the small of her back and then lower. I can't stop watching her as her eyes close and lips part.

It's hot underneath the covers and my palms are sticky. Juliet kicks part of the duvet off us, and with her index finger, traces the top of my scalp down to my bum.

'I want to taste you,' I say, pointing between her legs.

Juliet's eyes grant me permission. 'So do I.'

She gently licks my neck and nipples and then my inner thigh. She starts by kissing me gently. Her lips are soft. My eyes close and my whole body convulses and rolls back. I allow myself to let go completely as she takes her time to kiss and lick and suck in response to my body's needs. Wants. She's in total rhythm with me and at first I try to muffle the sounds my body is making, but then I scream uncontrollably because it has never felt this good and the sounds she's making are inviting me to join in. I don't think she's done this before, but it's euphoric. For all the sex I've had, never have I felt this much like I'm able to let go and focus on my pleasure as much as the other person's. In this moment I'm not in control, we're paying equal attention to each other's desires.

Our bodies continue to dance, seamlessly moving from one position to another. Both of us tasting each other at the same time, wriggling with pleasure. Her sitting on my face, directing me to where it feels best. Me on all fours as she fingers me from behind and kisses the arch of my back. Her legs enmeshed with mine. Us, just kissing, holding, squeezing each other tight, telling each other over and over again how happy we are to be here.

We don't give in to sleep until 3 a.m., by which time we are blissfully drifting in and out of consciousness, both of us occasionally saying the other's name to remind ourselves that we are really here, that this is really happening. I'm usually the big spoon but tonight she holds me tight.

24

I wake up in Juliet's bed and she's still holding me. Her legs are intertwined with mine and her face is pressed up against my back. Our bodies have kept the bed warm. Even though I need to pee, I don't want to leave. I turn around so that I'm facing her, and I feel the softness of her breath on my face. She wriggles slightly but doesn't open her eyes.

Usually, we're together passed out after a night out, but there is nothing messy about this moment. I want us to talk and laugh and continue to explore skin, picking up where we left off last night. I'm ready for her to wake up, open her eyes and see her smirk in a way that will reassure me she has no regrets. As I'm fantasising, she wakes up and my anxiety rises with the fact that I can't read the expression on her face. I try desperately to hold her gaze through a soft smile.

'Hi,' she says sheepishly, pushing a couple of strands of hair out of her face.

'Hi,' I say back, and I feel giddy, like it's the first time meeting my biggest crush.

'I wasn't expecting that to happen last night,' she says nervously, maybe even coldly. I'm not sure which. I'm taken aback by how the energy in the room has shifted.

'Neither was I.' I run my fingers through her hair, trying to commit this moment to memory.

'Els, I . . . I feel great but . . . I also feel terrible, you know . . . because of Andrew . . . We crossed a line from working to *not* working last night – and really quickly.'

'J, why are you bringing Andrew up?' I move my hand away from her, shuffling so that there is some space between us.

'Because he's my boyfriend, Els.' She sounds defensive, and grabs the duvet to cover her top half.

I'm suddenly confused. 'I thought you wanted last night to happen?'

'I thought I did too, but Elsie, now I don't know . . .' I close my eyes, willing her to go no further. To take back what she's just said. But she keeps speaking.

'I don't want to lie to him . . . and I don't like playing games.' Her voice is quiet.

'What are you talking about? What games? You're moving mad right now.' I fail to conceal the anger that has suddenly risen in my chest.

'We both know you don't really want me.'

I'm visibly shocked. 'What was last night then?'

'You just wanting to fuck. I bet I was a back-up to Bea or whoever else you usually hook up with. And I was next best thing. Also you probably wanted to take the opportunity to piss off Andrew.'

'This is insane.' I can feel myself deflating; surely she knows that none of what she's saying is true.

'No, you're insane. You used me last night to get back at my boyfriend. I can't stand how you two incessantly bitch about each other.' She shifts, sitting upright.

'What does he say about me?'

'See?' Juliet rolls her eyes dramatically. 'That's such a classic Elsie response. Everything always about you. Why do you even care?'

'You brought it up and now I want to know.'

Juliet moves so that our bodies are as far away from each other as they can be in her double bed. I know I'm pushing it but at this point I'm so mad I can't help it. After everything, I can't believe she's doubting me like this.

'He's threatened by you, which is ridiculous because like I said, there's nothing actually going on.'

'Last night was hardly nothing, was it?' My posture changes. I fold my arms and crumple my face. The conversation we're having now is worlds apart from the one we had last night, the one that didn't require words.

She mirrors me in protest and looks out of the window to where the sun is streaming in through the curtains. Even though I'm angry, she looks beautiful in this light.

'I don't understand how you can sit there and listen to him talk shit about me anyway.'

'We don't sit around speaking about you, Elsie. You're not the centre of the universe, contrary to popular belief. In fact, I actively avoid the subject. Sometimes these things just come up. And also let's not forget the things you say about him that you force me to listen to.'

'Stop beating around the bush, J.' My breathing becomes heavier as I speak. 'What has he actually said about me?'

Juliet throws her hands up in the air. She's furious. So am I. 'Fine! He thinks that you can be abrasive, dismissive and that you project your misery onto everyone around you. Mainly me ... and to be honest, that's exactly what you're doing right now.'

'Jesus, you even sound like him. I don't know who you are right now.' My mind is whirling, trying to make sense of all my conflicting emotions: sadness, anger, disappointment. 'I'm tired. I'm going back to my room. Sorry – *your* room.' I get up and storm in the direction of the door, completely naked.

I'm panicked. I must be really fucking naive because I wasn't expecting to wake up to this. I thought last night was the thing that was going to finally take us to the next level. I don't know what to do other than leave the room. I struggle to catch my breath as I feel her slipping away.

As I close the door, Juliet says quietly behind me, 'You know how I used to feel about you.'

I stop. She goes on.

'But you've always done nothing but throw it back in my face. You cut me off for months. You hook up with other girls in front of me all the time. You perform a poem about me to a room full of people without so much as mentioning how you feel to me first. Who does that? And then last night? What was that? You fuck me because you feel alone and take advantage of my feelings again?'

'Why are you doing this?!' I turn around and shout this back at her.

'Because, Els, I've been completely fucking in love with you, but now I love Andrew. You can't be mad at me because, after waiting for you for so long, I've finally moved on and found someone who actually wants to be with me. I confused things last night; I let you kiss me, and for that I'm sorry. But this isn't fair. It shouldn't be me apologising. It's you who uses me for attention and comfort and support whenever you choose, no matter how I'm feeling or what I'm going through, and so it should be you saying sorry!' Her voice is shrill.

Juliet sits up in bed, looking at me intently and waiting for me to say something, but my whole body has frozen into submission. I feel myself shutting down, the words I've practised saying to her in my head for weeks evaporating. I feel completely caught off guard, like there is nothing I can say to remedy the situation.

Juliet shakes her head in disappointment. 'You can't decide that you don't want me and also not want anyone else to have me.'

Each word that she says merges messily into the next. As my heartbeat grows louder, her voice becomes quieter. I know that what she's saying is important, but I am less and less able to take it in.

'Me and Andrew, it's for the best. And I still need you. I really, absolutely need you to be there for me. I need you to support me in this relationship in the same ways that I always support you. I can't take any more of this pushing me away and only pulling me back in when it's convenient for *you*. I don't want to be blindsided by things you never tell me. That's not how relationships work, Elsie!' She grabs a pink T-shirt from the floor on her side of the bed and pulls it over her head and then scans the room for her pants. She puts them on under the duvet, hiding herself from me, then makes her way out of the bed and puts on a long-sleeved purple dress.

I desperately try and grasp at the words that are splayed messily on the floor of my mind. I feel self-conscious now that

I'm the only one not wearing any clothes. I pull the door so that it's covering me, clutching at what's left of my dignity.

'Why didn't you tell me this is how you felt?' I ask her then, all coy.

'I did, Elsie! Are you kidding me? I did then and I have again now! It took a lot for me to be honest with you about how I feel all those months ago, and it wasn't that you even had to say you felt the same. I just wanted you to acknowledge my feelings, you know? And to show me some respect. But you ran away, Els. Like you always do. You literally shut me out of your life.'

Before I can say anything, Juliet is up and out of bed.

'The truth is what happened last night can't happen again,' she says. Everything has found its way to the surface and is now spilling out of her. Tears stream down her face.

I feel a wave of sickness as I swallow the saliva gathering in my throat. None of this makes sense and I'm not sure how to respond. I'm still clinging onto the handle, as if her bed-room door is the only thing holding me up. My knees feel as though they're about to give in. Anything that comes out of my mouth will miss the mark. Maybe she's right. I've been selfish. I squeeze the handle tighter with my fist. Eventually, all I'm able to say is:

'I'm sorry. I'm so sorry. I want you to know that I do love you though. I really do.'

'That's it?' She looks at me with a deadpan expression.

There's a pained look in her eyes and I know I'm doing this all wrong. 'What else do you want me to say, J?'

'Maybe more than just a "sorry"?!'

I know what I want to say is that my love for her consumes at least ninety per cent of my waking day. That I think about her all the time, and I can't imagine a world that she's not in. I want to say that I wish she'd end things with Andrew so that we could have space to figure us out. That she'd give us the chance to do last night again, so I could really prove myself to her.

But none of these things come out. I bite my bottom lip.

'Do you really not have anything else to say?'

The silence is deafening. My palms are sweaty.

'J, I'm—' but just as I start speaking, her phone rings. Talking Heads' 'Once in a Lifetime' has been her ringtone for the past three years. Juliet looks at me for a moment, disappointment all over her face, and then she answers.

'I'm sorry I didn't answer babe ... I was sleeping. Yes, everything is fine ... No, I didn't mean to worry you ... I understand ... I can meet you there in fifteen? Sorry, okay ... Love you too.' She holds the phone against her shoulder and wipes away the tears stuck to her lashes with her hands. She doesn't make eye contact with me. She grabs her jacket and without saying anything else, breezes past me and slams the front door on her way out.

My legs give way from under me, and I'm left sitting on her bedroom floor shaking, alone again.

25

A bell rings, notifying us that a red-headed man and woman have walked into the café. They are both soaking wet and I imagine them shaking off like dogs fresh out of the sea as they peel off their coats and wring out their hair. A couple of seconds pass and the waitress greets them, guiding them to a part of the café that isn't visible from where Bea and I are sitting. It's packed in here so we've been forced to share a table with two other people. Bea and I are sitting opposite each other, as are the others. We're all doing our best to pretend as though this arrangement isn't as awkward as it is. I would much rather be at Bea's right now, doing my usual routine of taking my mind off my very real and very current dilemmas by focusing on her body – but her boyfriend is at home. The waitress resurfaces from the back of the café and she's flustered. It's clear they're understaffed.

'Hi, so sorry about the wait. What can I get you?' She smiles sweetly as she pulls out a pen and notepad.

'I would like scrambled eggs and smoked salmon with toast,' says Bea.

'And I'll have an English breakfast with orange juice.'

'Would you like anything to drink?' she says to Bea as she

finishes jotting down our order. Her eyes momentarily dart across the room as she checks to see where her next stop should be.

'Tea. Green. Thank you.'

The waitress recites our order before greeting the next set of guests.

Bea has her hair tied up in a bun that sits in the middle of her head. She has on a glossy lip and individually applied lashes. Unusually, she's wearing an oversized blue jumper that envelops her body.

'How you doing?' Bea asks.

'Fine, I guess.' I sigh.

'How's Juliet?'

'Do you really want to know? Is it not awkward that we keep doing what we're doing in secret, and now we're sitting down ready to have a chinwag like a couple of aunties? I know I personally don't want to hear about you and Karma.'

'Well, that's on you. People have casual sex all the time, Elsie, and besides, you know there's nothing here for us in the long run. I thought you were the queen of no-strings? And until we have to stop, why would we?' She reaches out and strokes my arm. We're both clinging on to the comfort of this messy familiarity.

'Right, right.' I twizzle a sachet of sugar between my forefinger and thumb.

'So ... ?'

'So, what?' I'm deliberately obstinate.

'You're going to have to speak like a normal person, Elsie. What's going on with Juliet?'

I say nothing and she pulls the sugar packet out of my hand and puts it back in the pot in the middle of the table.

'You can't just shut down because things get real. You're in love with Juliet and she's clearly in love with you too. L-o-v-e is beautiful. Do you know that, Elsie? It doesn't always have to hurt. There's nothing like what me and Karma have. You deserve that too.'

I scoff involuntarily at the comparison. 'Things aren't as simple with me and J.'

'Well, isn't that your favourite line! Things are as simple, or in your case, as complicated as you make them. You think you know everything, but you don't.'

'What would you do in my situation? It's all a mess. I don't even know how J feels anymore.'

'I would use this and this and this' – in an almost rehearsed combination, she points to her head and then to her heart and then presses her finger on her lips – 'And I would speak. I would be honest with myself and also with her. You're con-fused because I bet you said things to protect yourself, and she said some things to protect herself, and probably none of them were true. Now, I would open my heart and tell her how I feel, and invite her to be honest in return.'

Trying to avoid Bea's advice, I look around the room. Everything in the café is deliberately mismatched – all of the chairs and cups and tables – and although everything is slightly different, the space still feels happy and harmonious. I look around at the tables of couples flirting over baked beans, and happy families eating off colourful plates. There are children in high chairs with scrambled egg in their fingers and the distant sound of a cook shouting 'service' from the kitchen.

'We're not in a good place right now, Bea. And besides, she has a boyfriend. Not that that stopped you.' I grumble the last part in near silence. Bea looks unconvinced so I quickly add: 'And besides, we're best friends. She doesn't want that to change.'

'Your complete inability to say how you feel has left you stuck and moping, and that boyfriend, not to gas you up unnecessarily, but he is punchinggg. He's just a guy, and she's not even really that into him. You have to know she's gonna decide to dead it off at some point. She's just convincing herself otherwise so she doesn't have to keep guessing at your feelings.'

I slump onto the table and rest my head in my hands. Bea rubs my hand gently and by the time I lift my chin and open my eyes, our food has arrived.

Bea licks her lips in anticipation, looks at me and then takes a large mouthful of her eggs.

Tentatively, she says, 'I think, maybe, that you've already crossed the best friend line and there's no going back now, regardless of whether you both try to make it work.'

I sigh loudly, pushing my food around my plate.

'I could be wrong', she says, throwing her palms up, her tone informing me and the people sitting next to us that she does not think for a second that she's wrong.

'Every time we speak about things it goes so badly. Every time, I freeze. And maybe she's right. I don't wanna lose her for good, and getting into "something" could break us once and for all. Like if it didn't work or if I let her down.'

'God, Elsie, not everything has to be so bleak, you know. Not everything ends badly. I'm friends with loads of my exes. I'm even sitting here coaching you.' She's well pleased with herself and I consider the fact that if Juliet and I were to happen, Bea and me would also cease to exist.

'You don't know what's going to happen. Stop being such a pussy,' she says, shovelling the salmon and toast into her mouth.

The woman next to us looks at her as she speaks, and I glug back my orange juice.

'I wish this was something stronger,' I say, looking into my glass. Bea extends her arm and strokes my hand with her fingers. I go on. 'I think you might be right. I am being a fucking pussy. There is a lot I would have done differently, but I can't turn back the clock.'

'No, but you can decide how to handle things moving forward. Listen, I have to get back soon,' she says, looking at my half-full plate. 'Are you gonna eat that?' Before I say no, she takes a sausage and bites into it, staring me dead in the face.

'Nah,' I joke, 'I'm not hungry.'

Bea stands up and throws her jacket over her jumper, looking around for the waitress as she munches through the last bit of sausage.

'I'll get this,' I say. 'I'm an almost-published author, didn't you know?'

'That is true. Now, remember what I said: don't be a pussy.' She blows me a kiss before walking back out onto the street.

The waitress eventually makes her way around to me and I settle the bill.

When I step out of the café, the sky is completely grey and it's started to rain. Groups of people are sheltering under bus stops and shop fronts, waiting for the shower to pass. I put up my hood, and without thinking, pull my phone out of my back pocket. I call my mum for the first time in years. Even with all the 'I don't care either way' energy I put out towards my mum, a part of me wonders if here, at this moment, she might be happy for me and whether it might make her genuinely happy to hear good news about her daughter – now the 'soon-to-be-published author' instead of 'the poet who hasn't got her shit figured out'.

'Elsie?' She sounds shocked. 'Is everything okay?'

'Hi Mum. Um, yes. Yeah, everything's fine. How are you?'

'I'm all right, it's so good to hear your voice.' She pauses for a moment. 'What are you doing? Are you sure everything is okay?' Her surprise morphs into concern.

'No, I'm fine. Really. I just thought you might want to know some good news. I got a book deal.'

'A book deal? Oh wow, Elsie that is very good news indeed. Well done! You'll have to tell your father. Let me go get him.'

Even though she doesn't say a lot, I hear her voice for the first time full of pride.

26

The next two weeks at Juliet's is spent existing in an excruciating state of tension. Neither one of us knows how to be. We speak very little, our communication reserved to the odd hello in the morning. It's awkward and stilted. There are no long conversations about how our days have been, or cuddles on the sofa. There is just Juliet and me: her lodger. Andrew and I had a fight a couple of days ago over his inability to close jars properly, and he whispered to me that I wouldn't be here for long, so what does it even matter? He stayed calm while I lost my shit, and Juliet obviously took his side, so since then I've only left my bedroom to get food or to wash. But today, when Juliet gets home from work, I want to meet her at the door with a teacup, sit and try to fix what's broken.

I really want to find the right moment to resolve things. I've been playing out possible scenarios in my mind, searching for the correct words; words that won't upset or offend her, but perhaps even lead us into a fresh start. I'm doing my best to suppress my feelings, but I know I want us to be more than friends. I hope that deep down she feels the same. And that she'll tell me.

I hear Juliet's key in the front door and give myself a quick once-over in the mirror. I look smart, like I've made an effort. I am wearing a large blue shirt that I feel good in.

But as I step out into the hallway, it becomes clear that she isn't alone. Again. I can hear Andrew's bellowing voice as I get closer to the front door and I immediately retreat back into my bedroom. They're both drunk and loud and they stumble straight to her bedroom, not bothering to close the door. I sit with my back pressed against my own bedroom door, my head on its hard, wooden surface. I hear Andrew laugh and after a couple of minutes, their conversation fizzles out and his grunts take over, eventually fusing with the sound of her moaning. It's disjointed and strangely rhythmic. I pull my head away from the door and cover my ears and close my eyes. I think about putting my headphones in and drowning out the noise, but instead, I just sit still. I take my hands from my ears and in the dark, sit staring at the ceiling, as I continue to listen to him enjoying her and to her enjoying him. I listen also to the stillness once they've finished, and I listen again as they go at it for a second time. I can't bring myself to stop. I can envisage them now too. It's as though I'm in the room with them, lingering like a spirit over her bed. Andrew is on top of her, her legs wrapped around him, their eyes locked as he pushes himself inside her. She takes a breath. My body recoils and my eyes fill with water. My vision is blurry. It goes on for ever. A new kind of pain.

When I come around, Andrew is snoring loudly, clearly fast asleep. I hear the sounds of quiet movement, of Juliet creeping out of her bedroom and making her way to the kitchen. I listen to her shake a jar of herbs and put the kettle on. I sit still in my room and wait for the sound of the kettle whistling. I picture her pouring the boiling water, sitting there and allowing the herbs to steep, something she insists is an integral part of the tea-making process. I lie down on the bedroom floor, listening to her potter around the kitchen, my heart beating faster and faster. There's a rush of adrenaline in my body as I gear myself to get up. Then I'm standing. I decide to head in under the pretence of needing a glass of water.

I make my way to the kitchen without turning on the hall light, tiptoeing so as not to wake Andrew but making enough noise to let her know I'm coming. When I walk in, she smiles, which is the most affection she's shown me in the last fortnight.

'Sorry, did I wake you?'

'Nah, I'm just really thirsty,' I lie, hoping she won't see the pain burning up inside of me. 'That tea looks good though.'

'There's hot water still and there should be enough herbs in there for you to get another cup out of it.' She gestures to the kettle. 'Just make sure to let it sit for a while.'

I smile back at her, happy that my best friend is letting me in, even just for a moment.

'Spliff?' I ask tentatively.

To my surprise, she replies, 'Why not?'

I roll us a joint and follow her into the sitting room. I sit down next to her on the sofa but am careful not to get too close. Careful too not to smell the scent of Andrew on her.

'I don't bite,' she says.

'I know, I'm just trying to respect your space.'

She doesn't say anything, and I hand her the joint.

'I'm getting the first instalment from my book deal next month, so I've been looking at places.'

'Elsie, you know you can stay as long as you want.' Her tone has less conviction than it usually does. And in any case, this line is starting to sound like a tired sales pitch that even she doesn't buy.

'It's okay, J. We don't have to pretend things aren't mad awkward between us. I get it. I was a dickhead. I can't ever explain how I feel and that's not fair on you. I fucked it. None of this is your fault. You try to fix it and I just keep breaking things.'

She doesn't say anything, just looks at me and takes a deep inhale, letting the smoke blow out of her mouth.

'Besides, from the sounds of things tonight, you and Andrew are getting on just fine. I wouldn't want to stand in the way of that.'

Her face fills with embarrassment, acknowledging then that I'd heard them, seeing in my face the self-destruction, that I had listened, been part of it somehow.

'It's fine, we all have sex.' I shift my body, searching for a more comfortable position on the sofa and avoiding her eyes.

'I mean, it's true, but it would have been better if you hadn't heard it.' Juliet inhales even more deeply this time then passes the spliff to me.

I want to ask her: why did you leave the door open then? But instead, I whisper:

'I'm glad you're happy with him.'

'Mmm . . .'

'He's your boyfriend and this is your house, and you shouldn't be worried that if you moan a little loudly that your best friend, who is also in love with you, might hear. That doesn't work, does it?'

'Don't say that.' I look at the shadows under her eyes and I can see that she's sad and exhausted. So am I.

'Don't say what?' I ask.

She tugs at the frayed sleeve of the purple jumper she's wearing.

'Don't say that you're in love with me. And say it so flippantly. Take it back.' She gets up off the sofa and sits further away on the bright Berber rug she bought a few years ago in Morocco. It's stained with memories from our past.

'I thought you wanted me to be honest about my feelings?' I move slowly and join her on the ground, so that we're sitting cross-legged opposite each other.

'Els, do you ever really listen when I speak?' She commandeers the spliff from my hand and a sharp, stinging pain surges through my body. I can't tell if she means it or she's just upset; either way it doesn't feel good to hear.

'I do. But you know I'm always late to things,' I say with a soft smile, reminding her of who I am. She doesn't like the joke. 'I'm not expecting you to do anything with it. It just came out, that's all. I'm high, you're high . . . we don't need to talk about it again.'

'God, you're so fucking selfish. Do you realise that? It's not so easy for me to just move on from you saying you love me. And after the conversation we had the other week? When I specifically asked you to respect my relationship with Andrew?' She shakes her head and stands up like she's going to leave the room. I swivel my body in her direction, standing in a plea for her to stay.

'Look, I'm not trying to fight with you, but why is it cool for you to tell me months ago that you're in love with me but not for it to happen the other way around?' I say in an urgent whisper, trying not to wake the beast sleeping in my place next door.

'Because that was then. And also because when I told you, I really told you. I didn't make passing comments, I didn't threaten an existing relationship.'

I feel myself getting mad again.

'Do you know what I think, J? I don't think you're really annoyed at me or this situation. I think you're upset because you're scared and feel like you're settling.' I wince, unsure of whether this will tip her over the edge.

'Settling?' She's exasperated.

'Yeah.' I refuse to back down. Juliet's angry.

'The person asleep in my bed right now loves me. Adores me. And he doesn't just say it. He *does* it,' she snaps back.

I can tell I'm losing her. I change tack and try to salvage the conversation. 'J, please try to see it from my point of view. I've been thrust into living with my best friend – my favourite person in the whole world – only to realise that I love her, months after she confessed she loved me and I cut her out. And everyone around us can see it. Even my seventy-eight-year-old nan! I've been dealing with a lot of stress – losing my home, my job, ya know? I'm sorry I didn't immediately realise. I've had other shit I've needed to process before I've had any room or capacity for us. I've only just stopped having those nightmares. And I'm sick of everyone else telling me that choosing to love is so simple because it isn't! Not for me. You've been showered in love all your life and I'm still figuring that shit out. And then, just when I thought I could maybe get over you, we have sex! And then you immediately change your mind! What do you want me to say? How am I supposed to be feeling?'

'I get all of that. And I've already said sorry for the other night. But I can't just jump when you suddenly decide you want me to.' Her tone has softened.

'I know, I really do. But I want you to recognise that we are two different people with *very* different ways of processing how we think and feel. We don't approach things in the same way, or even at the same speed.'

'You make it sound like I've been rushing you to make a decision, Elsie. I've given you months, *years* even.' She moves into the kitchen now so that we're separated by the hatch in the middle of the wall.

'J, I've had a lot of time to sit and think, and there are lots of things I would have said or done differently had I been able to. But I wasn't able to. And a lot of that is to do with the space I've been in, having no home or any stability or whatever. You have no concept of what that feels like, how that can fuck with a person.'

She looks at me then with a sadness that consumes her whole being. She goes to reach through the gap in the wall, searching for a finger, grasping for a palm to comfort me, when Andrew calls out from the bedroom:

'Babe! Are you coming back to bed?'

Juliet pulls back her hand. 'Yeah,' her voice cracks, 'I'll be there in a second.' Then she picks up her tea from the counter and makes her way back to him.

27

I wait for Juliet to head to school the next morning before leaving my room. I find Andrew also on his way out the door as I wander into the kitchen. He turns to look at me and sneers as he continues outside. Still half asleep, I prepare a cup of strong instant coffee. An email pops up with cover options for the book and just as I'm enjoying this moment of peace in the empty flat, about to get stuck in, there is a steady stream of knocks at the door. I'm not expecting anyone and for a moment I panic, before remembering that it must be one of Juliet's standing orders of eco products or vegan food supplies. But when I open the front door, my dad is standing there with one of my little brothers, Michael – who isn't so little anymore. I'm wondering what could be so important that Dad has brought them both all the way to London. He's always hated the city.

I can't believe that my brother is now taller than me with a fresh fade and tiny stud in his right ear lobe. His features have changed too. When he was little, his ears seemed too big for his face, but now they are just the right size. He's grown up since I last saw him. I push away the guilt that suddenly floods my body.

'Dad, Michael! What are you both doing here?' I can't hide my surprise.

'I'm sorry to just show up like this, but we really need to talk.'

My little brother is plugged into a tablet and barely smiles back at his older sister. It's been so long, perhaps he doesn't know what to say to me.

'Can we come in?' Dad says with a hint of desperation.

'Of course.' I'm still shocked to see them but I lead them into the sitting room. 'Everything okay?' I start to fuss around, plumping up scatter cushions and picking bits off the rug as I offer him a hot drink.

'Don't worry about all of that, Elsie.'

I stop my fidgeting and turn to face him.

'Dad, you're scaring me now. What is it?'

'I just wanted to tell you in person ... Me and your mum, well we're ...'

'They're getting divorced,' Michael says as he takes out his earphones. 'Mum and Dad are getting divorced, and to be honest, I don't know why they think it's such surprising news.'

'Right, okay.' I frown, confused. 'Is that true, Dad?'

He nods his head sadly.

'Yes, it is true. I wanted you to hear it from me first.'

I note then that his shirt is crumpled. Previously, he wouldn't even wear a pair of jeans that hadn't been ironed for him. And he has never ever shown up to visit unannounced before.

'Dad, are you okay?'

'I don't know, Elsie. I think it's been a long time coming. You know your mother and I met when we were children, and we haven't ever known anything else. It hasn't always been easy.'

'I'm so sorry.' Dad's walking around the room aimlessly

and my instinct is to comfort him, but for some reason I hold back. There's something else he's not saying.

'Dad, is something going on?'

'I don't want to go into too much detail. I just . . . I wanted to tell you face to face. That's all.' He looks nervously towards my brother as he says this. I take control of the situation.

'Okay well since you're here Dad, I actually have something I need a hand with outside. Michael, we'll be back in a minute. There's food in the fridge if you want anything, okay? Help yourself.'

'Yeah, yeah, yeah.' He lies down on the sofa and puts his earphones back in.

Dad and I head out of the flat and I lead us over to a bench on the Rye. Out of earshot of my brother, I try again.

'Are you sure you're okay?'

Dad looks fragile.

'Well, no. I feel like I'm missing a part of myself. And as much as your mother drives me mad sometimes, I wouldn't have her any other way.'

'So, what actually happened?'

He hangs his head and I sense shame.

'Dad, what did she do?' I suddenly feel defensive of him.

'She didn't do anything and your brothers don't know this so please don't make a scene when we go back inside.' My heart clenches in anticipation.

'I had an indiscretion and your mother found out.' Dad says this very quickly and I wait a few seconds for it to settle in.

'Poor Mum,' I whisper to myself, feeling guilty for always assuming she was the bad guy. The questions come flooding in.

'One or several indiscretions? And for how long?'

'Elsie, I don't think it's appropriate to get into the details of it . . .'

'I don't think that it's appropriate to cheat on your wife, Dad!' A woman walking by stops and stares as I raise my voice.

'I'm still your father, remember that,' he says in a hushed tone. He's embarrassed that I'm drawing attention to us.

'I want to know. I deserve to know.'

He sighs. 'Yes, it happened more than once.' He says this so quietly that I practically have to lip-read.

'With how many people?' My head is whizzing. I don't know who this person in front of me is. He was always the quiet, reserved, passive parent.

'More than just a couple. I don't want to go into it any more than I have already, okay? Please.'

'And Mum just found this all out?'

'Yes. We don't really speak about things openly.'

It's true. This is the most honest conversation I've had with my dad in years.

'How did this all come up?'

He won't look at me.

'After lunch at yours, she cottoned on to the fact that something had gone on with Helen and I. It was a long time ago though, Elsie. You and Juliet were very little. I stopped as soon as I realised how much it would hurt you all.'

I'm completely stunned. I say nothing.

'She confronted me about it for the first time last week. She'd never made a fuss about the others but this time, she decided she'd had enough.'

'So, you fucked my best friend's mum?' I stare ahead across the Rye in total disbelief.

'Language,' Dad says with bass in his chest. This used to scare me, but I'm not a little girl for whom a change of voice could induce unease. I don't flinch.

'You slept with my best friend's mum?!'

'It was a long time ago, Elsie. You don't understand grown folks' business. It was complicated.'

Rage rises in my chest. The audacity of him, the man who forced me to grow up when I was young, who doesn't know what I've been through these past few months, telling me that I don't know about life.

'It doesn't seem that bloody complicated to me. And you've shown up on my doorstep at the crack of dawn to tell me this ... why? You can't be for real.'

'I thought you deserved to know. I thought telling you was the right thing to do. It's important that we as a family move past this. We all make mistakes.'

Every time I think my parents and I are moving in a better direction, they manage to disappoint me again. I'm sad and angry and it suddenly hits me. All I can think is *fuck*. I don't want to be like this man in twenty years' time, emotionally distant and selfish and pushing the people I love away. I hope these traits aren't genetic predispositions.

'You're so selfish. The only reason you're here is to make yourself feel better. You literally don't give a shit about me or my life. You never reach out. I could literally be dying and you wouldn't know about it. I could also be having the best time ever, killing it in my career and guess what? You still wouldn't know.' I'm so angry, I could explode. Out of everyone, Dad had to choose Juliet's mum.

'I'm sorry to you, to Juliet and of course to your mother. But she's left me now. She's gone and left me to look after the boys. I can't get through to her. I . . . I thought you might be able to help.'

'So, you came here because you can't cope without Mum and now you don't know where she is? I'm not taking on the twins again, Dad.'

He looks down at the floor, guilty.

'I lost enough of my childhood taking care of them. They're my brothers but they're your responsibility, your kids.'

'Oh, please Elsie.' Dad clasps my arms and he looks desperate. 'Would you just call her for me? Tell her I'm sorry?'

I don't know why he thinks I'll be able to persuade her to hear him out. It's not like she's ever really listened to me before. But I want him to leave.

'If I call her, will you go?'

'Elsie!'

'I mean it. If I call her, you have to then leave me alone.'

'If that's what you want.'

I get out my phone and reluctantly dial Mum. I stand up and wander across the green so I can speak to her without him listening in. I hope that she won't answer but she does.

'Elsie?' She's surprised. Two calls from me in one month is a lot.

'Hi Mum. Look . . . I heard about what happened with Dad, and well, I'm so sorry. Dad's just shown up at Juliet's place and he wants me to find out where you are, but if you don't want to tell me, I completely understand.'

She sighs heavily down the phone. 'Tell him I need some time to think. I haven't left the country and he can manage without me for a couple of days. The boys aren't babies and I can't pretend not to see certain things anymore.'

'Okay, I'll handle him.' I look back at him sitting pityingly on the end of the wooden bench. 'Take the time you need, Mum. Don't you worry.' In this moment, I understand my mum in a way I didn't think possible. Maggie did call it.

I walk back across the park and relay this information to Dad, who appears relieved at the revelation that she hasn't moved to a tropical island. We wander back to the flat in silence. When we get back, my brother hasn't moved an inch on the sofa. He's lying there with his headphones on, still engrossed in his tablet. He doesn't look up when we walk into the room. I turn to Dad, who hasn't asked a single question about me since barging into our space, and say, 'Please take your son and leave.'

28

I arrive at the cinema to meet a girl I've been chatting to online. She's scrolling through her phone at the entrance of the Ritzy Cinema in Brixton. She looks exactly like she does in her profile, so we're off to a good start.

'Hey, Amanda?'

'Oh hi!' She hugs me and then straightens out the corset-style top she's wearing. 'So, I've been looking at the schedule. What do you fancy watching?'

'Anything,' I say.

'Something scary, maybe?' I've been on enough dates to know this means close contact is on the menu. And after everything with Juliet and my dad, this doesn't sound so bad.

'Sure! Why not.'

We make our way over to the counter to get our tickets, and just as I'm about to use my phone to pay, an email notification pops up.

Dear Elsie,

It was such a pleasure to speak to you over the phone. Apologies that it has taken me a little while to get back to you.

As you know, we have ambitions for this to be more than just a shop. We want this to be a home, a family and a safe space that community members feel they can make theirs. I particularly loved your ideas on the sort of events we can throw and thought a poetry night would be a fabulous idea! You were incredibly conscientious and I'm sure will help us make the shop a success.

We'd love to have you start work next week as we prepare for the opening. I'll just need a copy of your passport and NI number for now and I will share a rota with you shortly.

Speak soon!

Sandra x

Fucking finally. I have a job with sick pay and holiday and regular hours. And a book deal. I can now get myself a flat. I suppose this is a type of freedom.

'We'll take popcorn, some of that pick 'n' mix, nachos, a couple of glasses of wine, and two tickets to *Us*, please.' I'm grinning like an idiot and the person working on the till is less than interested in my good news as she gestures to the person behind me that they'll be just a minute.

'Anything else you fancy, other than me?' I ask my date.

'What's all of this for?' She laughs.

'Well, I just got offered a job! I know we're at the cinema, but we might as well celebrate.'

Amanda beams back at me, throws a box of Maltesers on the pile and asks me all about it.

After the film, we head out of the cinema and upstairs to the bar where I order us a bottle of prosecco. It feels good to know there will be regular money coming in.

'What do you do again?' I ask her, struggling to make conversation. She didn't 'get' the film. I thought it was pure mastery, but she doesn't seem like she wants to discuss it. I'm finding it hard to connect.

'I'm a teacher.'

'My best friend is a teacher.' I wonder what Juliet is doing right now. If it's even accurate to call her my best friend anymore. 'I bet you could teach me a thing or two.'

'That's cool.' Amanda doesn't even pretend to laugh at my dad-level joke.

'Do you fancy some shots?' I say, knowing it will make the encounter less strained.

'Sure.' She's much more serious than when we were speaking in the app. Quite blunt. I do most of the talking and she doesn't interrupt me, just lets me go on and on about the things happening in my life. We are sitting on opposite ends of the table and there isn't even a slight attempt being made on either side for us to get closer. She didn't even come near me during the movie.

'Juliet is like that though, ya know? Just kind and compassionate,' I ramble drunkenly.

'Who is this Juliet again?'

'My friend. She's amaaaaazing. You'd probably love her. Most people do.' I hear myself slur.

'Right.' She looks at me like she's confused and then at her phone as if she's waiting for someone to call or maybe rescue her.

'So, do you want to come back to mine?' I figure I might as well ask. There's nothing to lose. I lean forward in an attempt to eye fuck her.

This is the last time I'll take a girl back to the flat, I tell myself. I probably shouldn't, but it's late and Juliet will be sleeping now anyway. Bea's been airing my messages too, so tonight, Amanda is the best alternative.

'Where's your place?' she asks, tilting her head at me.

'Just down the road. It's the place I share with my friend.'

'The one you haven't stopped talking about all night? Look ...' She starts putting her coat on. 'This was nice and everything, but I think I'm going to head home. I've got an early start.'

I'm a little surprised she doesn't give in, but we exchange niceties, and when she leaves, I order one more drink. I still deserve to celebrate my new job. I don't remember leaving the cinema, but I practically run home when I'm finished. I feel giddy as I stumble back into the house, like I'm back to being a semi-normal human again. I'm excited to tell Juliet. Maybe it will even break the ice. She'll be gassed for me.

I get into the flat and switch on all the lights, making little effort to be quiet. But Juliet is nowhere to be seen. Usually, she's in bed at this time or curled up on the sofa with a cup of tea and a book about the moon or magic. But she's not here. I drop my bag and coat on the arm of the sofa and kick my Reebok Classics to one side before grabbing a glass from the kitchen and filling it with water. I bounce down the hallway in the direction of her bedroom. I part the door gently, just wide enough to see if she's in there.

The room is dark except for a fluorescent glow. It looks as

though she's lying on her side, under a blanket, completely immersed in her phone. Maybe she's watching porn. I whisper into the bedroom playfully.

'J, what are you doing under there?'

There's no answer as I prance into the bedroom. It's the first time in weeks I've been in here.

'I have some great news, J! I got a job and I'm going to get my own place. It's all coming together, just like you said it would ...' She doesn't respond, doesn't even stir. 'Juliet? Are you listening to me?'

I edge over to her bed and peel back the covers to reveal her face. She's staring at her inbox. Her eyes are red and puffy, and her face is pale. The salt lamp next to her bed lights up the right side of her face. It looks like she's been lying there for some time. I notice she's sniffling.

'Oh no, what is it, J? What's wrong? What happened?'

Tears stream down her face and it's as though her sadness is causing deep physical pain. She squeezes her eyes together tightly, her entire face crumpling in on itself. I suddenly feel terrified seeing her like this, and it sobers me.

'You can tell me what's happened, you know? You can tell me anything. J, you're scaring me. Please, tell me what it is.'

I position myself on the floor by the side of her bed, willing her to let me in again.

In between laboured breaths, she starts to speak.

'I ... I ... Emails ... They're threatening me ...'

She's crying heavily and I can barely understand her.

'Okay, J, breathe in for five and out for five, as deep as you can from your belly. Okay?'

I position her to sit upright in bed, breathing in and out. I ask her to repeat this a couple more times until her breathing slows down. She tries speaking again.

'I've been getting these, um ... these emails ... about my cam work.'

'Oh God. What sort of emails, J? Who the hell are they from?'

'They ... umm ... they just ... They were threatening to tell the school. They're screenshots of my profile. And I don't know how they found out my real name and where I work. What if they know where I live? Maybe I was stupid for thinking I could keep my two worlds separate.' She's alternates between sniffling and speaking as she tries to recount what's going on.

'We're going to get to the bottom of it, don't worry.' I feel so protective of her.

'No, it's too late. Whoever it is has already made it known to the school. When I walked into the classroom today, the way that Tom looked at me, it was obvious. Before he told me, I already knew that he knew.'

I could scream.

'I'm so sorry, J. It isn't illegal for you to get paid for shit men expect women to do for free. They can't discriminate against you.'

'They've said that if I go quietly, they'll write me a reference. The headteacher was pretty nice about the whole thing, if not a little awkward. But it's the staff, their judgemental eyes ... There's no point trying to stay now. It would drive me to madness having to look at them all every day. In their minds, I'm the world's biggest slut. The mums will probably think I'm secretly plotting to fuck their husbands.' She starts to whine softly, and the tears continue to stream down her face.

'Fuck what they say. Those children love you and you love your job. Don't make any rash decisions, okay? You're stronger than you think you are.'

She moans, pushing me away. 'I should have dealt with it earlier on. I just thought it would go away, like it was some sort of prank.'

'How long have they been messaging you? You know, if we find out it's that dickhead at work, that's harassment. I just need to look at him once and I'll know if he did it.'

'It's been about a month.' I can't hide my surprise.

'Why didn't you say anything to me, J? I'm here to ride for you.'

'I know, I just, I don't know ... We've had so much going on, and you know me, I'm not even on my phone that much. It was just a couple of messages. I didn't think it was anything serious, anything to worry about.'

She wipes the remnants of the last few tears from her eyes, and I feel a wave of guilt at not being there for her. After our blow-out I know that is how she feels too, like I don't see her, not all of her anyway. Even though I didn't know what she's been dealing with, I still feel so bad.

'I don't know what I'll do now. It could happen again at the next school I go to ... I like to do things on my own terms but I'm not sure I can continue with camming right now. The thought of it is overwhelming. And I feel weird, unsafe, like there's someone watching and wanting to hurt me.'

'Fuck them. And you don't need to figure it all out now. Remember what you told me the night I lost my flat? That I needed to give myself a minute.'

She moves over in her bed and gestures for me to join her. I crawl in and place my arm around her, holding her tight. It's warm under the covers because she's clutching a hot water bottle, which I assume is there to soothe her cramps – and the situation.

'I'm so tired, Els.'

'Just rest. Shhhh . . . rest.'

I try my best to remain measured. It's hard, though, seeing her in this state. I feel her body begin to tremble again, reliving the events of today. She battles through more tears to tell me something.

'You know, it was the way everyone was looking at me today, as though I was a stranger who didn't belong, some filthy outsider.'

I wipe tears from under her eyes and hold her tightly.

'You deserve so much more, J.' She folds in so that she's facing me. I trace my fingers over her forehead and then down to her cheeks.

'I love you, Juliet. I love you so much.'

She nuzzles into my chest, and within minutes, I feel the tension from her body begin to dissipate, as she falls softly to sleep.

29

It's 11 a.m. and Juliet still hasn't surfaced. She hasn't left the flat all week, not since she got exposed at school. She's decided to go back and finish the term though, before deciding what she will do next. She said she just needed some time to wrap her head around things. Over the past seven days, Andrew and I have established a rota, and we're both doing the best we can to ensure she has everything she needs. I work most days and he gigs at night, so he's around in the afternoons while I take the evening shifts. We barely speak but are able to tolerate each other for the sake of Juliet. Tomorrow she's due to be back at school. They won't give her any more time off.

Because Andrew has spent so much time in the flat, the space is starting to feel crowded. Every time I see his boxers on the drying rack, his guitar resting on the sofa or his long, black hairs in the plughole of the tub, I'm reminded that this isn't sustainable. I wonder if he's deliberately taking up as much space as possible. So, between shifts at the new job, I've been viewing flats. I didn't realise how much these viewings would feel like interviews. Every room has at least three people vying for it. But this morning, I heard back from a house-share with a bunch of freelancers in Brockley. Due to a last-minute dropout, they need someone to move in at lightning speed, so they don't get stung with covering the missing rent. The house is spacious, which means that I can keep to myself, and the fact that I don't have to give notice and can move in right away gave me an edge over the other candidates. I've not said anything to Juliet yet though, for fear of rocking this equilibrium we've found. A part of me feels guilty knowing that I'm leaving when she's going through such a hard time, but I know I have to tell her.

I knock gently on her bedroom door and deliver a pot of steaming-hot tea, placing it on her bedside table. She looks sleepy when I enter but shuffles upright.

'Listen, we need to talk. I haven't mentioned it but I've being looking at flats this past week. Andrew's here a lot, which is really great,' I quickly follow up, 'but you know, it feels like it might be time for me to move on.'

She shifts the weight of her body against her pillow and frowns down into the sheets.

'I've found a place with an empty room, and they want me to move in as soon as possible. They need someone to cover the rent . . . and well . . . it's in Brockley, so not that far I suppose. And well, what I'm trying to say is . . . would that be okay?'

'You were being serious about all that?' she sounds confused.

'Why wouldn't I be?'

'It's just that you've said you're moving out ever since you moved in, and you're still here.'

I laugh. It's true.

'I didn't know it would be so soon. It feels a bit sudden, is all.' She coughs gently into her fist.

I realise then that she's disappointed, and I am too.

'But it's for the best,' I say, trying to remain upbeat. 'You need your space, and you're in a relationship. You can't have me hanging around all the time. I can't be your creepy room-mate for ever.' I perch on the end of her bed, taking in the cluttered paintings on her wall.

'I'll be sad not to have you here anymore.' She ignores my ill attempt at injecting some humour.

'I'm only going down the road, J. I can visit, and you can visit.'

'I know.' Juliet doesn't hide the sadness in her voice.

'Hey.' I touch her arm. 'I appreciate you. If I didn't have you, I would never have been able to get back on my feet. Things have been a lot lately but you'll always be my favourite person on the planet.'

She smiles at me and I pour out a miniature cup of tea. She inhales and then sips on it, her hands engulfing the cup.

'It's really good news, Els. You deserve a home to call your own.'

I breathe out a sigh of relief. Having her approval means everything. It means I can let the group know today and start moving my things over tomorrow. I change the topic.

'So, what do you need ahead of your first day back tomorrow?'

'A new face?' She laughs a little. 'All I've been doing in here is thinking about how I should act or what I can do to make it not so bad. But I think the reality of the situation is that tomorrow will be what it will be, you know? The only thing I can do is go in there with my head held high and get on with it, not letting Tom or the rest of them throw me off from the job I'm there to do.'

I'm not sure if she's trying to convince me or herself.

'That is all very well-reasoned.'

'The reality is that running away now probably won't feel better in the long run.'

I know this too well.

'Well, you know who to ask if you want a Tom-shaped voodoo doll . . .'

'God. I still have no proof that it was him. I actually have this niggling feeling that it could be someone I know.'

'Fuck, really? That would be dark if it was. Who would snake you like that though, J? And why?'

'That's the thing. I don't know. Something just doesn't feel right. They knew more about me than what I make available online. But I could be overthinking it. Overthinking everything.' Juliet looks knackered and I'm not sure how to console her.

'Why don't we binge some TV when I'm back from work tonight? We can binge-watch an old series, take your mind off things?'

I'm offering this up for me, as much as for her.

'I'd love that.'

The next morning, Juliet leaves for work, and I feel sneaky not telling her that I won't be here when she gets back. But it will be easier this way. There will be no weepy, dramatic goodbyes. No long hugs full of words we can't say.

I've booked the day off. I take one last skim of the flat we've been sharing for months. It's calmly chaotic. The sofa remains draped in blankets to disguise how old it is, and the faint stains of spilt red wine remain in place on the rug. A couple of bunches of flowers have dried out, and the smell of herbal teas and weed lingers. I'll miss being here. It's not easy for me to feel at home but this flat quickly became familiar. Somewhere safe and full of love and laughter – and also tears, arguments and silence. I line up boxes of my belongings in the driveway to avoid any drama with the cab driver. My phone buzzes to let me know that he's arrived.

'You want all of this to go in there?' He says, shaking his head and gesturing from my things to his seven-seater, which has more than enough space.

'I think it should fit.'

'This isn't a courier service. And I have a bad back.'

'You don't have to help then,' I snap.

After a small amount of reluctance, the driver helps me pile up my things in the back of his people carrier and I get into the back seat. His car smells like Lynx. He drives me over to my new place and when we arrive, it doesn't take me long to lug my boxes up to my new bedroom, which is on the top floor, so I'm quickly out of breath. The house is spread over three floors and has a charming exterior of exposed brick and perfectly lined window boxes on every floor. Unfortunately, everyone's busy working, so no one offers to help me settle in. My room is beautiful though. There are natural wood floors, a skylight that thoroughly drenches the space in sunshine and a bathroom of its own. It's not cheap, but I can just about afford to be here. It feels like the home of an adult, something I've not felt like for the longest.

Not wanting to waste any time, I begin to unpack, deter-mined to make this place feel cosy. The room feels a little bare, and I envision the furniture I want to fill it with. A rug and an armchair would be a good fit. I unpack my final box and a crisp twenty-pound note falls out of a book sleeve. I smile.

'Hey, Elsie, can I come in?' It's Ben, the graphic designer who has the room just below mine. He's wearing circular frames, a pair of jeans and a plain blue T-shirt.

'Yes, hey, come in, come in. I'm all good here. I've got pretty much everything in now.'

'It's such a nice place, isn't it? I've been here for three years, and I never plan on leaving. The landlady never puts up the rent.' He laughs.

'I was sort of waiting for there to be a catch, you know? A leaky roof or something.'

'Ha! Yeah. Hey, I know it's the middle of the day but do you wanna go for a drink? There's a nice place at the bottom of the road. I can show you the area?'

'The perks of being self-employed,' I say, because I think that's the sort of small talk he's after.

'Exactly.' Ben nods virulently.

'Yeah, why not.'

We head out of the house, and he points out each shop and what it's good for. I've not spent much time in Brockley, but it seems nice enough. We sit outside the pub that's on our street and Ben gets us both a pint of cider.

Where did you go?

A text from Juliet pops up on my phone. I realise it's 4 p.m. and she will have just got home. I head to the toilet and phone her.

'Hi,' she answers. 'Where are you?'

'Listen, J, I thought it would be less awkward this way, if we didn't have a long and dramatic goodbye, I mean. I've hardly moved across the country ...'

'Oh ... I wanted to give you a proper send-off, but I get it ...' She tries to mask her disappointment and fails. 'How's the new flat then?'

'Oh, it's beautiful. Hang on, let me send you some pictures.' I ping a couple through.

'You really upgraded, hey? I'm happy for you.'

'At least now you don't have to worry that I'm going to kill you with my Dettol obsession.' I've been let off easily for leaving before she got home. I know that will have hurt her. 'Anyway, how was your first day back?'

'It could have been worse. Some of the teachers managed to hide their disgust, but it was plastered all over the faces of the others. Mainly the older ones. And Tom was as smug as he always is.'

'That bastard,' I say, and she's silent for a moment, probably contemplating the memories that point to him being the snake.

Neither one of us knows what to say to break the silence.

'Well ... I suppose I better go then. I should probably crack on and start writing this book,' I lie. 'It's not going to write itself.'

'Good luck, Els.'

'Thanks, J.'

'Oh, and Elsie?'

'Yep?'

'This is the start of something incredible for you, I can feel it.'

'Me too.' I smile into the receiver and she hangs up the phone. I head back to Ben.

30

Everything in my life suddenly feels new and full of potential. New home, new job! As far as bosses go, Sandra is actually all right. She's a laugh, if not a little neurotic. But I've enjoyed helping her with the build-up to the shop's official opening, which is tonight.

There is a lengthy list of last-minute touch-ups to be completed before people start trickling in. Under Sandra's instruction, I arrange a couple of bunches of flowers in colourful glass jars around the shop and put out the last of the cured meats as she nervously reorganises the same spots over and over again. She puts one bottle of wine down, tilts her head to the side and moves it again, unsure of which bottle looks best where. We talk through plans for the evening ahead and Sandra seems impressed with me, leaving me in charge of the logistics so that she can focus on welcoming customers.

Once the doors open, there's a steady stream of people, mainly locals who are curious at what the latest shop to pop up is all about. A couple of hours in, a man with a thick grey beard asks me if I knew that this shop had been a greengrocer for the past decade. I smile sympathetically as he proudly delivers the history of the street. It feels like one of Maggie's old stories. Lots of mothers with screaming children in tow come in and purchase multiple bottles. Sandra and I both work flat out, and she offers to cover me while I go outside for a roll-up. I take a little stroll down the street and sit on Goose Green. I worry about being gone for longer than I should be and head back to the shop. As I walk in, I spot a familiar-shaped person browsing in the snack section. Bea turns around.

'Elsie, what are you doing here?' She looks just as sexy as ever. In the weeks since I've seen her, she's filled out a bit and it suits her. Her signature jumbo twists are piled up in a bun at the top of her head and her skin is glowing.

'I work here! And hi stranger.'

'Hi.' She elongates her greeting and smiles at me. 'I've been craving these,' she continues, pointing to a jar of anchovies.

'Where have you been? I—' Just as I'm about to update her on my life and probe into the reason she's aired my last few texts, a man pokes his head into the shop and I recognise him from the photos dotted around Bea's flat.

'Everything all right, babe? I only have ten minutes left on the parking meter.'

Bea looks between us. 'Elsie, this is Karma. And babe, this is my friend Elsie.'

I try not to roll my eyes at the idea of me and Bea being just friends. Karma gives me a little smile and waves. 'And I think we'll just take this, Els, if you don't mind ringing it up,' Bea continues. We walk over to the till, which is nestled between a bookshelf and a large snake plant.

'That will be four ninety-nine please,' I say, running the salty snack through the till. 'I've never seen you eat anchovies before, Bea?!'

'Bea, didn't you tell her?' Karma walks towards her and clutches her stomach. 'Ever since we found out, she's been guzzling these down non-stop. We were driving past and she thought this looked like somewhere that might have them. She basically sniffs them out wherever we go.' Karma says this with real fondness and it takes me a second to catch up.

Bea doesn't look me in the eye. 'It's early days yet. Don't want to jinx it.' She laughs awkwardly and shifts around on her feet.

'Oh my God, congrats baby mama!' I instantly regret my choice of words but this interaction is excruciating and honestly it's hard to know what the hell to say.

'Thanks,' she says, as Karma makes a point of kissing her on the cheek.

I busy myself, packaging up her order in a paper bag.

'Well, here you go.'

'Babe,' Bea says, turning to Karma. 'Why don't you pull the car round and I'll meet you out front? I'm gonna grab one of those non-alcoholic wines too.' She points to the fridge next to the coffee machine. He senses she wants a minute to catch up with me alone, says his goodbyes and leaves us to it as I offer to walk Bea through the selection.

'Makes sense now . . . why you ghosted me.' I turn down my bottom lip and raise my eyebrows.

'I've just been busy . . .'

'Are you happy about it?'

'Of course, why wouldn't I be? I just didn't know how to tell you.'

'Now you and Karma are officially bonded for life. I was thinking that your boobs looked especially juicy.'

'Don't do that.' She pushes me playfully.

'I'm just kidding, you're off limits now. You, somebody's mum!'

'Somebody's mum,' she repeats, still trying to digest the information.

'He seems excited though.' I nod in the direction of the door.

'He would've got me pregnant ages ago if I'd let him.'

I don't quite know what to say in response.

I notice a queue forming at the till and a petite woman with three different types of orange wine in her hand growing visibly impatient.

'Well, I better go,' says Bea. She gives me one last shy smile before turning around and leaving the shop. I'm happy for her, but also feel like I've just lost another person I care about.

The rest of the shift goes well. I find my flow, telling customers about the benefits of natural wine and trying to make as many sales as possible. We sold out of orange wine which Sandra thought was a disaster, and a homeless man came in asking where Eddie was, much to her distress, but I gently redirected him to his friend sitting outside on a nearby bench.

'Do you want to have a glass with me?' Sandra asks at the end of the shift. 'You've worked so hard today. We ought to enjoy this moment. We've earned it.'

She pours a glass of white wine for us both and we catch up, getting to know each other a little better.

After my shift, I meet up with Leonie. Seeing pregnant Bea threw me a little bit and there is familiarity between Leonie and me. They aren't that bad. The shows she recommends are actually pretty decent and we debrief sometimes. We have a couple of drinks and I listen to her wang on about her life and her friends and her family that I doubt we'll ever get to the stage of meeting. Some things in my life are the same, others seem to be on permanent rotation. I fill her in.

'What are you doing after this?' On account of not having had sex with someone other than myself in ages, I lean into them and whisper in their ear. I notice that as my breath touches her collar bone, goosebumps appear.

'Whatever you're doing.'

We down our drinks and head out.

When we get back to my new place, Leonie is notably more impressed than the last time she was in my room.

'This is nice!' she says as we step into the hallway.

'Yeah, it's not bad.' I pull out a half-drunk bottle of rosé from my mini fridge – the first thing I treated myself to after I moved in. We drink a glass and then without hesitation, I pull Leonie onto the bed so that she's lying next to me. As I unbutton her trousers, I notice that she's wearing lacy red underwear this time.

'Someone is clearly prepared,' I say, looping my finger around the trim of her knickers.

'Well, I couldn't have you thinking that the only underwear I own is from the children's section in M&S.'

'Well, these certainly don't disappoint.'

Just as I'm guiding their knickers down their thighs, my phone buzzes. I ignore it once but as it rings a second time, Leonie can tell I'm distracted.

'Maybe you should answer it? Or turn it off?' she says, a little irritated.

I roll over and grab my phone, which is on the floor next to the bed. It's Juliet. She never usually calls at this time, so I pick up immediately.

'J, can I call you back?' I step outside of the bedroom and pause at the top of the stairs, out of Leonie's earshot.

There is nothing but sniffling on the other end.

'Are you all right?'

'No, I'm not all right. I'm fucking livid and I don't feel good. Andrew, he . . .'

'What has that little fucker done now? I swear to God . . .'

She starts to cry. I can't understand what she's saying and my concern grows.

'J, where are you?'

'Andrew's birthday.'

I put the phone on speaker and turn up the volume in the hope that I'll be better able to hear what's going on. Someone approaches Juliet and says:

'Babe, I'm so sorry. I was just jealous of all the guys you speak to day in day out. Do you know what that does to a person? It makes them crazy. You can forgive me, can't you?' It's Andrew. He sounds fucked too.

'You prick!' Juliet screams, but it gets caught in a gulp.

'Don't cause a scene, Juliet. Let's just forget this ever happened.'

'You're supposed to love me!'

'I do love you. But you're the one who did this. You and your flirtatious fucking ways.'

His voice changes and poison envelops every word he's saying. I try asking Juliet if she's okay but she can't hear me. They're screaming in the street so loudly that even though she's no longer holding the phone next to her I can still hear everything that is going on.

'I can't believe it was you all this time.' She pauses, and it sounds like she's too wobbly to gather her thoughts.

'How many guys do you think will actually want to date you? You're fucking loose.' Andrew then lowers his voice, presumably so that the people around him don't hear him. His voice becomes muffled on my side of the phone but I've gathered everything I need to know. Of course, he was the one blackmailing Juliet. She starts sobbing again and I want to reach through the phone and punch Andrew in the face.

'Fuck. You,' Juliet says between stilted breaths.

'You'll get over it once you realise that there's no one else who can give you what I can.'

I've had enough.

'J, hello?' She doesn't answer me so I shout this time. 'JULIET?'

Her sniffles sound closer now so I keep talking. I assume that Andrew has walked away.

'Where are you, J? What is the pub called? You need to tell me where you are now,' I say with urgency.

She finally replies, 'I'm in the Hope and Anchor.' She sounds completely deflated.

'Okay I'm coming. Just stay where you are.'

I go back into my room and explain to Leonie that I need to leave. She gets dressed quickly, clearly unhappy that I'm bailing on yet another date.

I order a cab and it feels like the longest drive ever. When I pull up outside the pub, I ask the driver to wait for me and switch the drop-off location to Juliet's.

I immediately spot her. She's sitting outside on a bench with her head hanging sloppily. She's the most drunk I've ever seen her, worse than what I imagined from the call. I prop her up and give her the bottle of water I took from the cab. I see Andrew in the distance smoking with a group of boys. I walk over to where they're standing.

'You piece of shit!' I can't contain my anger. 'You're gonna pay for what you've done to her, I swear to fucking God. I might even kill you myself.' Andrew says nothing, just stares me directly in the eyes. This makes me even angrier. 'And why the fuck is she this out of it? What did you give to her?'

When he finally speaks, Andrew is as cocky as ever. 'I don't know what you're talking about. She's had too much to drink, that's all. I mean, look at her. She's hardly making any sense.'

'You're fucking lucky I need to get her home right now because otherwise . . .' For a minute I think of executing the ultimate revenge and ruining his fucking life – showing his little fan club what he's really like. His attitude and subsequent treatment of Juliet isn't very punk. But in this moment, getting Juliet home is more important.

For once, Andrew looks a little scared. Fucking pussy.

I glare at him. His friends jeer stupidly behind him and his arrogance returns.

'I don't know why you think you can talk to me like this. You're the bad influence. Selfish day in and day out,' he says, clearly wanting to appear big to his friends.

I'm so angry but he isn't worth it.

'Move out my face,' I say, brushing him off.

I walk back over to Juliet and help her up and into the car, trying to maintain her modesty as her dress has been wedged into an unflattering position.

'I don't know what she thinks she saw, but I've told her it isn't true,' Andrew shouts over to me then. The distance between us emboldens him. 'It's my birthday, and she ruined it. She's being a shit girlfriend.' His pupils are huge and he's practically chewing out the side of his jaw. He points to Juliet like she's a broken, useless toy.

'You're a fucking mess,' I shout before slamming the car door shut.

31

I load Juliet into the back of the cab and try to prop her up. I
ask her if she's taken anything and give her the water the cab
driver hands me, but she's completely incoherent.

'What did you take, J?' I ask again, sure now that this isn't
just alcohol and she just looks back at me helplessly. I consider
taking her to the hospital, but I feel sure that whatever it is will
wear off in a couple of hours. It really isn't like her to get this
mashed up but she's rarely as upset as she was on the phone.

Juliet's restless and tries to get up out of her seat. I struggle to get her to keep her seatbelt on. The driver is growing
increasingly impatient, fearing that she's going to hurt herself
or throw up.

'You'll have to pay for any damage. Get your friend to sit
down or I'm pulling over and you'll have to get out of the car.
We have a long way to go.' His eyes are half-focused on the
road, half-focused on what is happening in the back of the car.

'Are you really going to kick two girls out of your car in the
middle of the night?' I plead with him. He says nothing, just
drives as fast as he can.

I check the app and we still have twenty-three minutes to
go until we are back at hers. Juliet, whose head is currently

folded in her lap, suddenly jolts upwards, agitated and not saying much. I've never seen her like this. With the squeezy water bottle in my hand, I try and re-negotiate our position in the back of the car so that she can take a sip, but she dodges my advances. I whisper to her, asking again what she's taken, but she doesn't respond and the driver turns to tell her to sit down as she continues to wriggle around. I try to pull her close to me and keep her still, but Juliet has always been deceptively strong, and she pushes me away. We're all gesturing, shouting, pleading, and then the driver loses control of the wheel, and we're spinning. Within seconds, the car veers into something hard. The driver is shouting, 'Fuck. Fuck. Fuuuck', and Juliet screams. Despite my best efforts to cradle her, Juliet is thrust from my arms with the impact as we continue rotating and crash into another hard surface. I hear glass smashing. It happens so fast and all I can smell is burning rubber. The driver is no longer shouting. Everything is still.

My head is throbbing. When I open my eyes, it's dark and I can't see anything. I pat around in the back of the car, feeling for Juliet but touching nothing but glass. The leather seats are sticky, I hope not with blood. There is a shard of glass wedged in my arm and it's oozing. I know it should hurt, but I can't feel anything. I stick my free arm into my back pocket and grab my phone, turning on the torch so that I can investigate for myself. The driver is in a bad way, though alive – an airbag props up his head. I can hear him groaning.

'Are you okay?' I ask, panicked. 'J, where are you?' I ask the air. No answer. Even though my vision is blurry and my head is pounding, I manage to dial 999.

'Hello! I, um, I don't know where I am, but we've been an

accident and I don't know where my friend is. She was here and now she isn't.' The operator tries to keep me calm and tells me not to move or under any circumstances leave the vehicle. She says someone is on the way to help us.

Desperate to find her, I unbuckle my seatbelt and continue to shine my phone light around the vehicle. My battery is low and the light from my phone is growing fainter. Between the airbags, I finally see a shoe. It's Juliet's – the right brown lace-up boot. The torchlight turns off as my phone hits five per cent and once again, I am in total darkness.

'Juliet, where are you?' I scream this time, loud enough so that she's guaranteed to hear me if she's awake. I wait for a response but hear nothing. She doesn't answer. Panic floods my body.

Not heeding the operator's instructions, I try to get out of the car. I need to find Juliet. The car door is jammed, so I force it open with my feet, which takes several attempts. I'm surprised I have any strength left. My limbs are heavy and sore and I'm now fully aware of the glass wedged into my arm. I'm standing and dizzy and once I've made it out, I can see that the hood of the car is crumpled and smoking. It smells like oil and burnt plastic, and there is metal and debris everywhere. The car has crashed halfway into a metal fence. As I crawl around the scene, everything is blurry. But then I spot a body lying limp across the car's front, its long, elegant limbs halfway through the window. There are limbs bent out of place.

It can't be.

Just as I'm edging closer to the front of the car, I hear a rush of sirens as ambulances and a police car appear. Two men approach me, torches in hand. 'Are you all right, miss?'

When I don't answer, one of them continues, 'We need to move you away from here, okay?' I don't move until he places his hands on my shoulders and gently turns me away from the car. There is a flurry of people moving around the vehicle, like flies swarming a dead animal. I can barely make them all out. A stretcher emerges and they're placing the driver on it. He is still groaning loudly. One of the paramedics puts an oxygen mask over his face and they take him into the back of their truck. Another stretcher is brought over to the scene towards Juliet.

I manage a few words as I'm led into an ambulance. 'I need to be with my friend. Where is she?'

'Your friend is being taken care of. They're doing everything they can for her,' a paramedic replies. 'You've been in an accident, and right now you're in shock.' I start to cry. 'That arm looks painful. Let me take a look.' Gently, he rests my forearm in his palm.

'I'm fine. I'm fine!' I say, pulling away. 'I just need to know where she is.'

'My colleagues are doing everything they can for her. What I need for you to do right now is look at me, okay?'

'Okay, okay, sorry.' I'm crying harder.

'How many fingers am I holding up?'

'Three.'

'Very good,' he says, wrapping a cape of silver foil around me.

'This is going to sting a little,' he says as he removes the largest piece of protruding glass from my arm and then a couple of smaller ones. I wince.

'I'm going to clean this and wrap it for now, but they will

probably give you some stitches when we get to the hospital to make sure it doesn't get infected. And the police will want to ask you some questions about what happened.'

I hear the words but my mind is elsewhere. I'm just thinking about her.

Once my arm is cleaned up, I stay sitting in the ambulance. No one says anything to me, so I try to stand up and move back outside to look for Juliet.

'No, you're going to need to stay where you are while they help your friend,' the paramedic says. He looks at me with a degree of sympathy that I can't quite comprehend.

I then see her being carried into another ambulance on a stretcher with breathing apparatus and lots of strange things attached. Her body is limp and lifeless, and looks nothing like Juliet.

'No! No! No!' I scream in hysterics.

'We're taking her to the hospital so that she can get the help she needs,' says the paramedic, checking my injuries a final time.

'I'm going with her,' I demand. 'I'm her family.'

'Are you her next of kin?' The paramedic asks.

'Yes, I am. I am her next of kin,' I lie. 'You need to let me in with her. She's my girlfriend.'

'Okay, you can sit in the back with her. But come now. We don't have much time.'

I'm rushed into the back of Juliet's ambulance. Her eyes are closed. I hold her hand, which is bloody and bruised.

'It'll be okay, I promise. You stay right here with me, J. You're not allowed to go anywhere,' I whisper into her ear, hoping that wherever she is, she can hear me.

'Do you know if she took anything tonight?' A medic asks me. I turn to face them.

'Um, I think someone did give her something. I don't know what it was, but she wasn't in a good state when I went to pick her up.'

The medic scribbles this information down, checks her pulse.

'Why? Will she be okay? Is she going to be okay?'

'We've stabilised her breathing, but it was a pretty nasty accident. We'll be at the hospital soon. Please try to stay calm.'

I ignore the medic's ridiculous request. Instead, I focus my attention back on Juliet, holding her hand and telling her that I love her.

'Please be fine, J.' Tiny pieces of shrapnel are piercing my heart. The pain is sharp and suddenly the thought of life without her is unbearable.

'You aren't allowed to leave me.' I sob as the image of her skipping through the front door, roses in hand, flits through my mind. I look down at her and I'm terrified.

Whatever is happening in the outside world feels distant. We're floating through the city like ghosts.

Eventually the ambulance stops moving, the doors open and several medics rush in. They begin to wheel Juliet out and I lose my grip on her hand.

One medic speaks quickly to me. 'We're taking her straight into the ER. You won't be able to come. You'll have to stay in the waiting room. I'm going to put a dressing on your arm and once we get to urgent care, they will take you in for an X-ray, and possibly give you some stitches to close the wound. Can you please contact any other family members or people who will need to know what's happened?' The information is overwhelming.

I somehow make my way into the waiting room. I sit in one of the plastic chairs and realise I need to call Helen. What do I say? I almost hope she doesn't answer, not straight away anyway, but the phone rings just twice and there she is.

'Hi darling, how are you? Is everything all right? It's a little late to be calling?' her voice is croaky.

'Helen, there's been an accident and . . . she's in the hospital. I'm with her, we're at King's College. How quickly can you get here?'

'Elsie, I don't understand . . . What do you mean?'

'Helen, I'm so sorry but Juliet's in the ER. She needs you.'

32

When I return from reluctantly having my X-ray and stitches done, I rush over to the counter to find out what's happening. The man on the front desk looks away as he spots me coming over.

'Madam, I've already told you, she is with the doctors, and I promise to tell you as soon as they have an update.'

'Are you sure there isn't anything you can tell me now?'

He puts down his pen, stopping what he is doing, and looks me in the eye. 'I know that you're scared, but as I said, they are doing everything they can, and I know exactly where you are sitting. I'll come to get you the moment there is any information.'

'What if you go on a break or to the toilet and something happens and they don't know I'm here?' I'm anxious and can't stop speaking.

'Then I'll make sure my colleagues are aware, okay? Now please, take a seat.' He looks tired and nods as he encourages me to step back.

Every minute that passes feels like an hour. There's an old coffee dispenser that I've given all the change I have to. There aren't many people in the waiting area, but there's a woman with a tiny, crying baby in the corner. She does her best to appease her child with her bosom, a little embarrassed that the small thing she is cradling is causing such a scene. An older man sits with his hands clasped together a couple of chairs down from me and I wonder if he's waiting to find out if his wife of a million years is going to pull through. Occasionally we exchange a sympathetic smile, but I'm terrified of going any further, of being pulled any deeper into a whirlpool of pre-emptive grief.

Helen bursts through the doors of the ER. I'm glad to see her but am also suddenly reminded of my dad's infidelities. I haven't seen her since I learnt this news. I hope I'll be able to act normally, for Juliet's sake. She's wearing a huge leopard-print coat and is completely flustered. She has blue silk pyjamas on underneath her coat and is on the phone to someone. Even though I'm sitting ahead of her at the back of the room, she doesn't notice me. My stomach drops. I will have to fill Helen in on everything that happened. I'm worried she'll be upset at me for failing to protect her daughter. When I was younger, she would shower me with love and affection. She'd do her very best to make me feel as welcomed and loved as her own flesh and blood ... but I grow fearful that this foundation is slipping away. She'll be wishing it was me in there rather than her child.

I hear her say, 'I'll call you when I know more, okay? I have to go.' She hangs up the phone and approaches the front desk. 'I'm looking for my daughter, Juliet Campbell. She's been in an accident. I need to know where she is immediately.' She speaks slowly, fully enunciating each word.

I make my way over to her and she immediately folds me into her arms as everyone in the waiting room pretends not to look.

The receptionist gives her the same spiel. 'We don't have any updates just yet. She's currently in surgery but I promise we will update you as soon as we can.'

'I should be in there with her.'

'I'm really sorry, Mrs Campbell, but we aren't able to let anyone in there with her. As soon as we are, you'll be the first to know.'

I take Helen by the hands and guide her in the direction of the plastic chairs.

'What happened, Elsie? What happened to my baby?'

I feel tears prickling the corners of my eyes again. 'I went to pick her up from Andrew's birthday. She was pretty out of it. I put her in a cab and, well, she was really agitated and wouldn't put on her seatbelt ... the driver turned around and ... we crashed. It all happened so fast.'

Helen covers her mouth as I speak. She's in total disbelief and I feel an immense amount of guilt for the part I have played in Juliet being here in hospital.

'I should have made her wear her seatbelt but I couldn't get her to sit still and I needed to get her home because she couldn't stand and her and Andrew had this huge fight because he'd been ...' I run out of breath, realising I can't finish that sentence.

'Elsie, this isn't your fault. Are you all right?' Helen asks, squeezing me close.

'I don't know,' I say quietly.

'Who was she with when you found her? You did the right thing to try and take her home, and you mustn't blame yourself for the fact that she didn't have her seatbelt on. This didn't happen because of you.'

'She would never usually get like that though. It's not like her.'

'It doesn't sound like her . . . I'm going to get to the bottom of it. Oh my darling Juliet, my darling, darling girl . . .' Her voice trails off. I don't think now is the right moment to tell her what Andrew did. 'And the fact that they won't let us in, the fact that I can't see her . . .' Helen starts sobbing and we switch places so that I'm the one holding her to my chest. I hadn't realised before but she smells exactly the same as Juliet, like rosewater. We sit united in our fear.

We take it in turns to go up to the counter hour after hour, only to be told repeatedly by the various receptionists that they sympathise but aren't able to let anyone into the operating theatre. But with every trip to the front desk, I expect, hope for, a new response. Knots grow inside my stomach, forming a lattice of sorrow and fear and I want to be sick. All I can see in my mind is her body and the car and the crash.

'Are you Juliet Campbell's mother and girlfriend?' A doctor finally approaches us as the sun rises outside. Helen doesn't respond to the fact that I've just been referred to as Juliet's girlfriend.

'Yes, that's us. Don't tell me it's bad news, please. I can't bear it,' Helen pleads.

'She's stable, although we've had to induce her into a coma. She's suffered some very severe injuries including several broken joints and some swelling on the brain. It was a bad accident. It's a miracle she's alive, Mrs Campbell. You have an incredibly strong daughter and she's certainly putting up a fight. We've done everything we can for now, and will just need to see how the next forty-eight hours go. We can't say a lot at this stage. The machines are helping to stabilise her respiratory system but we need her to come around to see how responsive she's been to the treatment. I can take you both through to see her now. Would you like to come first?' she says, speaking to Helen.

'She can come too.' Helen squeezes my hand tightly and pulls me along with her.

As I walk into the room, I close my eyes and hope that when I open them, Juliet will be back to looking her beautiful, bright self. But little has changed since we were in the back of the ambulance. There's less blood now that they've cleaned her up a bit, but Juliet still looks limp and lifeless in the bed, even though I can see her chest rising and falling through all the heavy machinery she's hooked up to. The room smells bitter, like antiseptic, and there is the hum of machines in the background. Helen virtually collapses on top of her daughter, kissing her and telling her that it will all be okay. I hold back, not wanting to encroach on them. I feel like an interloper, even though I desperately want to hold Juliet and do the same. Finally, after five minutes of Helen inspecting her daughter, she says:

'Elsie, have you called Andrew to tell him what has happened? One of us should. It's probably best he doesn't come down here just yet, even though I'm sure he'll want to. I can't believe he let her leave the party in such a state. If I see him now, I might strangle him. Thank God she's alive.'

I only say, 'Of course', not wanting to say anything more and upset Helen any further. She's ingested enough earth-shattering information for one day.

'Can you stay with her for a moment, Elsie? I'm going to head outside for a second to grab a cup of coffee. I need to be a hundred per cent alert for my baby. You heard what the doctor said: these next few hours are crucial.'

Helen leaves and I shuffle closer to Juliet's bedside to hold her hand, breathing in her scent and hoping that this will overpower the hospital's smell. There's nothing for me to say, so I just watch her. She has a perfect cupid's bow and her hair is contained in four large cornrows. I watch her chest to make sure it continues to rise and fall under the blue hospital robe she's wearing. She just has to keep breathing. If she keeps breathing, it'll be okay.

Juliet's flat is freezing. A window has been left open in the kitchen. It is eerily still, like a time capsule. I stare at her trinkets and feel overwhelming sadness. I can't believe that this has happened to my person.

I scan the room, pick up a ceramic elephant and place it back at the exact angle it sat previously. As much as I want to transfer some of Juliet into me, I also don't want to disrupt anything in her space. She's in every little thing in this flat and I need everything to remain as it was, just the way she liked it. Grief is starting to take over, and the pain is so palpable and profound that I feel it in my chest. It's crushing and I constantly feel like I'm having a panic attack. As I think back to our conversations over cups of herbs that would last until the early hours, I bury my head into my hands and shake from side to side in an attempt to soothe myself. I sit on the sofa, picturing us here together, smoking and laughing uncontrollably. I let out a faint chuckle as tears stream steadily down my face. The thought of never seeing her again is excruciating and I do my best at instructing my mind to build a collage of our best bits. This is how I want to remember us together.

I make my way into her bedroom and sort through her drawers, attempting to decipher which items will bring her the most amount of joy when – if – she wakes up. I told Helen I'd come back here and pack a bag for Juliet. I still have my keys. I take out a pair of red and white cotton pyjamas and hold them close to me. I drink in their smell. I can barely stop my eyelids from drooping, even with the number of coffees I've backed off. I decide to lie down just for a second. I sit on her bed and then find myself under the duvet with my head resting on her pillow. There are strands of Juliet's hair everywhere. I nuzzle into them.

But being in her bed isn't enough. I get undressed and put on her favourite jumper before hopping back in. I start to warm up, tucking every part of my body in carefully so that no heat can escape. I breathe deeply and try to block out the image of Juliet's limbs sprawled out over the front of the car – the newest nightmare I'm having to fend off. I try to conjure up instead the image of the girl who would lie in bed with me on Saturday mornings, drinking endless cups of tea. This could have been our bed, the place where we kissed and hugged and fucked. I shiver at the thought of these being the sheets that she and Andrew have laid down on, but I can't move. I don't want to be rid of her smell. I don't want to be out of her room.

Next to her bed, there is a notebook I've never seen before. It's purple and has her initials embossed on it: J.C. It must be her diary. I'm tempted to look, just to get a little bit more of her, but before I properly entertain the thought of invading her privacy, my phone starts to ring. It's Andrew. He doesn't bother to greet me.

'Have you heard from Juliet? She's not answering her phone and I vaguely remember *you* coming to take her off somewhere last night.' He says this in an accusatory tone.

I want to punish Andrew for not looking after the person he was supposed to protect but I bite my tongue. I know that once I allow myself to unravel, I can't be held responsible for what will leave my mouth.

'She's in the hospital, Andrew. It's not looking good.'

There's a pause as he takes in what I've just said.

'What! Where is she? Will she be okay? Oh my God, I need to see her.' He whines, clearly distressed.

'Listen, I know what you did and you're not welcome anywhere near her. If there are any updates, I'll text you, but that's all I'm going to offer.'

He snaps.

'She's mine, not yours. Not that you seem to get it,' he spits down the phone. I say nothing.

As he repeats 'I need to see her', I hang up. He's not worth it.

33

The hospital corridors are filled with worried parents clutching snotty and bruised children and elderly patients who appear to be a permanent fixture of the building. In Juliet's wing, it smells stale and like bleach. No one is smiling.

I walk in and the man at the desk remembers me. He gives me a sympathetic smile. I wonder if he ever sleeps.

'Your friend's boyfriend is in there with her now.' The receptionist looks bemused as he shares this information, looking at me, Juliet's 'girlfriend', to see how I'll react. I look down at the floor. I'm seething at the fact that Andrew figured out where Juliet was. He must have messaged Helen. I should have told her what he'd done yesterday.

'You know where you're going.' He gives me a little smile. I don't return it.

As I enter Juliet's room, I see Andrew sitting close to her bedside. He looks like he hasn't slept all night. He is visibly anxious and looks wild with his wet, wide eyes. I wonder how long he's been sitting there, in his unbuttoned shirt with those dirty Adidas trainers. I don't know when the right moment is to tell Helen what he's done so I sit in the corner of the room and unpack the clothes I've brought back for Juliet. Helen tells me there haven't been any updates but that Juliet remains stable, which they're saying is a good thing.

'We should chant for her together, Elsie. I've been chanting for her all morning,' Helen offers.

I remember the first time I went to Juliet's house and her mum was hosting a Buddhist ceremony in the sitting room. She'd insisted on me sitting and joining in. She was friendly with it. I was just eight at the time. I watched everyone keenly, joining in whilst Juliet sat in the corner of the room drawing.

'Sure, I'd like that,' I reply. I would do anything that might increase the chances of her making it through. 'Maybe after he's left, though.' I nod towards Andrew. I need to get him out. I do my best to avoid looking directly at him as he sits next to Juliet, but I can't help it. He plants a gentle kiss on her lips, and when she doesn't respond, I see a wave of sadness overtake him. She's more submissive now than he ever intended. He speaks gently into her ear, and I consider whether or not Helen would appreciate me dragging him away from her hospital bed once she'd found out the truth. A sniffly Andrew turns to Helen and before I can finish playing out multiple scenarios in my mind, Helen speaks. She can tell something's up.

'What did happen to my daughter last night, Andrew?' She's calm and I'm grateful she's the one doing the questioning.

'Well, we were out for my birthday and . . .' Before Andrew can finish his sentence, Helen interjects.

'I don't need to know why you were out. I'm asking about what happened once you were out. If my daughter chose to take drugs or if she was spiked. From the sounds of things, Andrew, whatever she had, she took a lot of it. Too much.'

Andrew hangs his head. 'Well, I, um . . . I found this stuff, sort of like LSD, off the dark web . . . but I was fine. Everyone else was fine. Not *fine* fine, but nobody went like Juliet did. I didn't know what to do.' Helen recoils, searching for the right follow-up question.

'If I hadn't have come, what would have happened?' I can't help but speak up. 'She was barely conscious when I got there, Andrew. And we both know why she took so much of that stuff in the first place, don't we? It was because she was upset. Don't pretend.' I look at him with the intent to spill his secret if he won't own up.

He doesn't answer me, just looks back at Juliet, trying to figure out what to say or do.

'Anything could have happened last night. And look at her now!' I shout at him. 'This is all your fault!'

Helen looks shocked, and she gets up and leaves the room. I should go after her and apologise. The last thing she needs right now is us battling it out. But I can't let Andrew sit here and pretend that he played no part in this.

'Look at what you've done. Poor Helen. She can't stand to sit here and listen to you speak with such vulgarity while her daughter is metres away in a fucking coma,' Andrew practically hisses, as he cocks his head and folds his arms. His hair is so laden with grease that it doesn't move as the rest of his body does. I feel genuinely disgusted.

'I've bitten my tongue for too long—'

'You cannot seriously be trying to blame me for the fact that she had one bad reaction?' Andrew cuts me off. 'Maybe if she'd been wearing a seatbelt, this could have been avoided. You're the one who put her in the cab while she was completely out of it.'

'How dare you—'

'She's an adult, Elsie. Not some fragile thing. She decided to take those drugs. That was her choice, not mine. I know you think you own her, but you don't.'

I'm seeing red now. I'm so angry that the possibility of killing him has gone from fantasy to a very real possibility. His eyes widen with shock as I roar. My whole body is hot as I scream vitriol at him. The shocked expression of a nurse passing by reminds me where I am and I reduce to a whisper-shout.

'Juliet can do so much better than you. I don't know why she's even your friend. I mean, honestly, look at you. You're a loose cannon. I tried to tell her. She's way too good for you.'

'So you think that because I didn't go to Oxford and I'm not posh AND I'm a big old dyke that I'm not good enough for her? The difference between me and you, Andrew, is that regardless of where I've come from, I know right from wrong. A distinction you clearly know nothing about. You were blackmailing your own fucking girlfriend!'

He flinches.

'You don't know what it was like for me, dating someone who does what she does! Having everyone knowing that if they search the internet, they'll find her there. That she's up for grabs to anyone who'll have her! It was fucking embarrassing!' He's out of breath, panicking.

There are so many things I could say to him, so many things I've been waiting months to say to him, but before I can, Helen's voice comes from behind me.

'You need to leave. Get out now, Andrew. And never come anywhere near my daughter ever again.'

34

Maggie is sitting on one of the stools in the wine shop next to a display of plain and sea-salt-flavoured breadsticks and an array of dips and tapenades. Sandra set this up to encourage people to buy the obscure range of accompaniments she continues to order despite them having a ridiculously short shelf life. Maggie looks fresh as usual, today in an all-black hoodie, tracksuit bottoms and black Air Forces. Since the accident, she's been making a point of visiting me every day, even though the wine shop is nowhere near where she lives. This is her way of checking in. One of Juliet's friends had organised a coordinated 'silence' for her last week – something about lots of energies being directed to her all at once. Bea had seen something about it online and told Maggie.

'Maggie, you don't have to come here every day. I'm all right,' I say, tracing my fingers across the stitches in my arm.

'You know me, I love the, um . . . artichoke and green tapenade,' she says, squinting at the label as she lifts one of the small pots up. 'So, where else would I be?'

'You're a bad liar but it's nice having you here.' I finish making us coffee behind the bar.

'You should probably slow down on those,' she says.

She doesn't know that I've not been able to sleep for more than a couple of hours a night. I've moved myself back into Juliet's and am sleeping in her bed. And every time, just as I'm dozing off, I wake up in a panic. The bad dreams are back.

'Evergreen' by Yebba echoes gracefully through the shop. I've made this the official track to my current heartbreak. I'm completely addicted to the devotion and pain she carries in her voice. When Yebba sings about standing at the water's edge and holding someone's current in her hands, I want to crumble. And as her plea for her evergreen grows more urgent and high-pitched as the song progresses, I want to become part of the melody. I must have played this particular song at least fifty times in the shop since the accident.

Sandra surfaces from the stockroom before I'm able to entirely lose myself. 'Everything all right, Elsie?' She smiles at Maggie. 'Hello, welcome. I hope Elsie here is taking good care of you?'

'She's taking great care of me, actually. As always.' Maggie smiles back.

'Great, that's really great.' Sandra pauses. 'So, Elsie, I know I said you could play whatever you like in here, but please opt for something a little more upbeat. And literally any other song. It's all about the experience, remember ...' She starts fluffing up some cushions and folding and refolding blankets. 'See, like this.'

I promise Sandra I'll get the folding right next time and wave her goodbye as it's my turn to lock up today.

'Does she know what's going on with you?' Maggie nods at the door as Sandra closes it behind her.

'Sort of. I didn't go into much detail.'

'Maybe you should tell her the truth. It might be good for you to take some time off.'

'I'm sick of people looking at me like I'm broken. And besides, I just started here. I can't risk losing my job. It was hard to find one in the first place.'

A guy holding the hand of a small kid places his shopping on the counter.

'Darcie, say thank you to the lady,' he says. I don't pretend to find her adorable, and when he realises I'm uninterested in his little girl's performance, he stops.

Maggie hangs around for an hour more, sitting in the corner of the shop, buying more drinks in an excuse to just be there with me. She's traded in her coffee for a small glass of red wine, though I know she wishes it was a Sol. She tells me about a date she has lined up this evening with someone from her past. Only now do I understand why her cologne is more pungent than usual.

'I didn't know you were still dating?' I immediately regret how clunky those words sound.

'Still?! The cheek. I'm not dead yet.' Maggie takes a large sip from her glass.

'I didn't mean it like that. I just meant . . .'

Maggie raises her eyebrows wittingly, and I decide to change tack.

'Where did you meet her?' I ask innocently.

'She's one of your lot, actually. A poet. I've known her for . . . what? Almost thirty years. We met at one of those Black women's parties in Peckham. We've been on and off, you know, casual for a long time.'

'A thirty-year booty call?' Involuntarily a laugh comes out.

'I guess you could call it that,' says Maggie matter-of-factly, her smile revealing a shining silver tooth.

The conversation provides respite between me checking my phone for updates. But as soon as 5 p.m. arrives, I lock up with haste and get a cab over to the hospital. My body is too weak to carry me by foot. I haven't managed to eat more than a packet of crisps today, which explains why I'm starting to feel faint.

Helen is in her usual position, flicking through magazines in the chair next to Juliet's bed. She welcomes me into the room with a smile. Juliet doesn't move, but her machines keep beeping. I walk over to her and kiss her on the cheek. I've brought a stack of books to read to her. The doctors have said there is no harm in it and that she may well be aware of the things going on around her.

'I brought some leftovers from the shop in case you're hungry.' I hand Helen some breadsticks and a hummus dip.

'You're a good girl,' she says as she cornrows Juliet's hair. She's done a remarkable job of keeping it looking fresh throughout her stay in hospital.

'Elsie . . .' I can feel that something is on her mind.

'Yes?' I respond nervously.

'I've been meaning to speak to you about what happened between your dad and I. He told me that you found out.'

I'm shocked they're in contact but try not to let that show. I've been thinking about bringing it up with Helen, but my mind has mostly been elsewhere.

'It was a long time ago but it doesn't change the fact that it wasn't the right thing to do.' She takes my hand and forces me to look at her in the eye.

'Did J know all this time?' I whimper.

'No, I never told her.'

I look down at the floor sadly. 'I haven't told her either. I didn't get the chance.'

'Listen, my sweet. I know it's upset you. I understand if you're angry at your dad, at both of us. And I'm truly sorry. But I want you to know that your father loves you. So do I. And so does Juliet,' she says, looking back to the bed where she's resting. My whole body sighs.

'I love her too.'

35

I grab a cup of tea, a spliff, and because I know I should eat, some toast. I'm wobbly and my feet struggle to carry me back to the bedroom. It's 5.30 a.m., so too early to visit Juliet at the hospital. On my way back to Juliet's room, I catch sight of myself in the mirror. My hair has grown – not that anyone will notice – but it looks out of control to me. My eyes are red, a combination of being slightly high and stressed out. I've been neglecting my usual oiling routine and my skin is beginning to dry out. I can barely remember to wash. I say *Nam Myōhō Renge Kyō* three times (Helen is starting to influence me) and open up my laptop, hoping that this time I'll finally know where to begin this book and what to write.

After fifteen minutes of rearranging my seating position and re-reading the original poem over and over again, I've barely written a sentence. Every time I try, I delete everything and start again. All of the words feel too small. I think of me and Juliet, together in bed. Her in my arms and me reading to her. She sings whilst watering her plant babies, and I think about the amount of time it takes her to twist her hair, and about her pink toenails. I think about all of the things that I should have said while she was still here.

It's been ten days since the ambulance ferried Juliet into the hospital. My routine now varies between shifts at work, heading to the hospital to read to her and returning to her flat where I stare blankly at my computer screen and type out approximately three words of my book each evening. I've ignored the last email from my editor asking me for an update. I consider informing them of what's happened but decide against it. I don't want any special treatment. Everyone is constantly checking in on me. They're all unsure as to what to say.

> Ben: Everything okay? I haven't seen you around the flat for some time.
> Bea: Els, I heard about Juliet. Is there anything I can do? You can always call me.
> Leonie: Want to go for a drink sometime soon? L xx
> Maggie: Remember to breathe, kid.

And then there's a voicemail from Nan:

> Your nan is worried about you. Give me a ring and bring me up to date. Okay then . . . bye bye.

All I want to do is scream. I don't know where to put all this grief, all this pain. I google: *Where can I go to smash stuff?* And it turns out it's really a thing. There's a place in Highbury where you can smash things for either thirty minutes or an hour at a time. It's called The Rage Room. I click on 'Book your appointment' and the form I fill in asks me how I found out about them. I consider typing: *My best friend is dying and I'm full of rage.* Instead, I say 'through a friend'. But at the checkout, it says it costs £250! A fee of £250 just to break things they probably found in a skip. So I close the browser and decide to go to Epping

Forest in the dead of night on my next day off instead, where I can scream into the night for free.

I've been having what I call mini panic attacks. They aren't the full-blown kind, but I usually still end up in a pile on the floor. They happen whenever I think about the fact that Juliet is probably never going to wake up. Or when I've been searching online to see how many people survive comas after being asleep for more than two hundred hours. The odds don't look very good and the doctors have stopped being reassuring. They keep saying they are doing everything they can, but I'd prefer it if they were more upfront.

I stand up and stick my head out of the bedroom window in an attempt to ground myself before the anxiety takes hold. My phone is now synced to the Bluetooth speaker in Juliet's room so I can always hear it. Juliet and I have shared a Spotify account for the past couple of years and she's only ever made one playlist: it's the least seamless amalgamation of her favourite songs. I press 'shuffle' and India Arie's 'Video' plays. It's a song you can't not dance or sing along to. It's cheesy but in a good way. I belt every word at the top of my lungs. I dance from one end of the room to the other, tears streaming down my face, and I let them. As they grow, so do my movements. My sobbing gets louder with every shift.

I jump as my ringtone floods through the speaker and into the room. It's Helen.

'Helen, what is it? Is she okay?'

'Elsie, my darling girl is going to make it. She's going to make it! I can't believe it.' My body feels light suddenly, as if I'm floating into the air. My grief turns into joy.

'The swelling on her brain has gone down significantly and they are going to bring her out of the coma, likely in the next hour or so. I know she'll want to see you when she wakes up. Can you come?'

'I'm already on my way.'

There is a sudden rush of blood to my head and I feel as though I could topple over. I slip my feet into a pair of Vans, grab the first thing I see – a long black duffle coat – and leave the house. When I'm halfway down the street, I realise that I'm grinning like a sociopath, tears still streaming down my face. The breeze is refreshing. I don't care that people are staring at me and my mania. She's awake!

I walk to the hospital so that I can plan what I'll say when she wakes up. Distracted and walking at such a speed, I bump into multiple people. They're all annoyed, but when they see me, they don't say anything. It's like I'm floating. I practically run up Denmark Hill, managing somehow to avoid turning into a sweaty pile on the pavement.

'Juliet, my Juliet!' Helen says at a volume so loud that it seems like the words themselves wake her up. Juliet's eyes open slowly, like a newborn baby entering the world for the first time. She doesn't speak, just takes in her surroundings and does her classic half-smile, though I'm not sure it's deliberate. She looks spaced out. Helen kisses every part of her face over and over again like a mother hen furiously pecking at one of her chicks. For a moment, they look like the perfect picture of family life. Afterwards the doctors are fussing around Juliet, checking the machines and making notes. Eventually one of them says:

'We'll leave you to it. There is a button there for emergencies and one of the nurses will be back in soon to check on her again.'

'Thank you,' says Helen. 'Thank you for bringing her back to me.'

I approach Juliet's bed slowly, large syrupy tears clutching at my cheeks.

'I thought … I thought …' I pause. 'I'm just so happy you're awake.'

Her warm brown eyes are droopy. She's visibly exhausted and her face is gaunt. She doesn't say anything but she doesn't need to.

'You were in an accident, Juliet, but we're going to get you back to your old self,' says Helen. 'I've got a diet and homeopathic recovery planned. You'll be back and strong before you know it.'

She smiles down at her child.

Helen turns to look at me and then she says, 'I need to make some calls. I have to tell my sister that her niece is going to be all right. So many people have been chanting for her and look!'

She doesn't leave the room entirely, just makes her way into a corner and with much theatrics, begins recounting Juliet's wake up to a long list of family and friends.

I take over her seat, holding Juliet's skinny fingers. I watch her eyes open and close until she's out for good, and Helen and I sit with her for the rest of the night, watching her sleep, thankful that in the morning she will wake up again.

The next day I decide to respond to my mountain of text messages, informing each person that Juliet is awake, letting them know that she hasn't been taken from us. Instantly, prayer emojis and smiley faces flood in. I take a short break from watching Juliet to go and get some coffee from the machine, and when I come back, she is sitting upright in bed. I've not seen her in any position other than lying down for weeks. My lips tremble as I hold back tears. I'm equal parts delighted and shocked to see her like this. She's put on her brightly coloured stripy T-shirt, and she is now easily the most colourful thing in this sterile hospital room, maybe even the whole wing.

'Elsie . . .' Her voice is quiet and strained, but her face lights up when she sees me.

'Hi, you!' My hand covers my mouth in total disbelief. She's really here.

In a second, I'm by her side and I scoop her up in my arms without thinking. I hope she isn't sore but I don't let go. I haven't done this in such a long time. Both of us are reluctant to break our embrace though I am mindful that her body is delicate.

'It's okay, I won't break.' She smiles into me.

I laugh and she lets out a gentle giggle before coughing. I let go of her and reach for a glass of water on the table in front. I hold the straw to her mouth and she takes a small sip.

'How are you feeling?' I sit on the edge of her bed. I'm lost in her eyes and the freckles around her nose. Her face has regained its colour. It's more beautiful than ever before.

'Well, like someone who has been in a coma for a while, I feel completely fucked. But I'm glad you're here.' Her movements are slow as she twists her body and lies back down on the bed.

'What a stupid question.' I shake my head.

'It's okay, Els. It's not like we've been here before.'

'Yesterday, you were properly dozy. I swear when you opened your eyes, it was like you were taking everything in for the very first time.'

'For a moment, I thought I had forgotten how to speak, but thank God I just had a severely dry throat.' It takes some effort but she swallows before continuing to talk. 'I was so happy to see you.'

My heart bursts wide open as she says this.

'I'm here, J. I've been here every moment I could. You know, reading to you most days and trying to buss jokes so that you might laugh and wake up.' Tears pour from my eyes and she reaches out for my hand. I lean in so I can be even closer to her.

'I'm supposed to be the one who cries all the time,' she jests, as a single tear rolls down her cheek. 'You know, I think I could hear your voice while I was out of it.'

'That's mad. Like you were trapped inside yourself?'

'Not quite. It's hard to explain.' She pauses. 'It felt like I was dreaming.'

'God, you really are a witch. How many people can say they've had an out-of-body experience and seen the other side?'

She giggles.

'Juliet?' I say cautiously.

'Yes?'

'I'm so sorry for what happened, you know, with Andrew. I want to kill him.'

'Oh, I don't want to think about him, not now. Or ever.'

'Of course. Whatever you need.' I search her face, wanting to know how she's feeling. 'The most important thing now is that we focus on getting you better.'

'Well, I have one idea ...'

'Oh yeah ... ? What's that?'

She holds my gaze for a second too long and my heart starts to beat wildly. Softly and without hesitation she says the words I've been waiting months to hear.

'I think that if you come here, kiss me and tell me how you absolutely can't live without me, that would make me feel—'

I lean into her before she's had a chance to finish her sentence. My Juliet. My best friend.

We melt away.

ACKNOWLEDGEMENTS

During the writing and editing of this book, my father, Harry Little, was diagnosed with and died from motor neurone disease. And even as his illness had rendered him bed-bound, he watched and read every interview I had given. In fact, he told anyone who would listen how proud he was of his daughter, Liv, the writer. Even though he isn't physically with me, he is permanently etched into my heart, and I know he would be brimming with pride to see this book making its way into the world. Dad, I love and miss you. And to Charlie, my stepfather, who passed away five years ago, I know you are with me too.

I have to begin by thanking my gorgeous, fiercely intelligent little sister Iona – the first person I shared a version of this book with. You give the best notes, and even though you've only been alive for seventeen years (fifteen at the time of writing this book), you are incredibly wise and will no doubt continue to be the person with whom I sense check all of my creative ideas. Thank you for being unapologetically yourself.

Mum, my love for you runs deep, and I couldn't be more fortunate that you chose me to be your daughter. You made sure that I knew the power of my voice from day one and continue to inspire me through your love, strength and resilience. Aunty

Monica, I won the lottery by having a parent with the most beautiful twin sister (inside and out). The energy, support and love you both show me is endless. Lucky me, I have the best hype women in my corner.

To my love, Suhaiyla, thank you for always believing in and encouraging me when I've been in my messiest and most unsure states of being. You spark joy and creativity and the depths of your intuition continue to inspire me. To love you is to know magic.

Nan, you're the source. It's no secret that the love you've shown me through food and stories is woven into these pages. Thank you for creating a legacy of women who are unafraid to exist loudly.

I must also thank my friends, especially Charlie; you are a sister at this point. I appreciate you reading versions of this book and offering me your thoughts and feedback. How fortunate am I to have the most incredible editor as one of my best friends and favourite people in the world? Roisin, we have come a bloody long way from sipping cans of K Cider on Peckham Rye, and I cannot believe that we are both writers (it still feels funny to say). Thank you for being the most gorgeous friend with an unwavering belief in me. You continue to show up for me through joy and pain. I absolutely adore you and cannot wait to be holding your book in my hands.

And Efe who read parts of this book and fell in love with the characters as much as I did writing them (and by this, I really mean fancying Bea). Nikesh (you have always been a huge source of encouragement and your writing classes got this novel going). Rashida, Iman, Tia, Dom, Fenn, Nadia, Dre, Khloe, Neela, Kit, thank you for encouraging me throughout the various stages of this book. I am so appreciative of you all for holding space for me when your lives are already SO full and for having unwavering belief that this book would be a success. I could name many more people who have loved, supported and opened doors for me over the years. I am full of gratitude.

Sharmaine, you have been the most wonderful friend, confidant, mentor and editor. Who knew that we would become lifelong friends after meeting you on a train in South London all those years ago. My love for you extends beyond our working relationship. I am so grateful for the way you have been a fierce defender of my peace and continue to remind me to choose happiness. I'm also so glad that you hammered home the importance of studying. Going back to school has made me an infinitely better writer. You are a legend.

And my agent Abi! It's been such a long time and your endless support, belief and excitement for *Rosewater* from day one has carried me through. You are not only the coolest person in the business, but your brain continues to blow me away. The taste! The artistry! Thank you for believing in me and pushing my writing to be the best it can be.

I would also like to thank the rest of the team at Dialogue Books, especially Amy, Millie and Emily. And to the wonderful Caolinn from Zando – you encouraged me to go deeper than I thought possible with my writing. And to the incredible team at Get Lifted. I had so much fun working on this with you. And to my lovely long-standing agent at Storm, Paula, you've been calling me a writer and creative before I had the confidence to name myself as those things.

To my dearest Kai, thank you for bringing Elsie's poetry

to life. I had the most fun going back and forth with you over voice notes to capture the energy and essence of this book. I knew your artistry and tone of voice would make the poetry housed within these pages sing. Thank you, friend.

And finally, thank *you* (especially to those of you who gassed me up from the second my book announcement dropped). I have poured my entire heart into this book, and I hope you have felt it.

Bringing a book from manuscript to what you are reading is a team effort.

Dialogue Books would like to thank everyone who helped to publish *Rosewater* in the UK:

Editorial
Sharmaine Lovegrove
Caolinn Douglas
Amy Mae Baxter
Adriano Noble

Contracts
Megan Phillips
Bryony Hall
Amy Patrick
Sasha Duszynska Lewis
Anne Goddard

Sales
Caitriona Row
Dominic Smith
Frances Doyle
Hannah Methuen
Lucy Hine
Toluwalope Ayo-Ajala

Design
Nico Taylor
Charlotte Stroomer

Production
Narges Nojoumi

Publicity
Millie Seaward

Marketing
Emily Moran

Copy Editor
Ruth Patrick

Proofreader
David Bamford

Operations
Kellie Barnfield
Millie Gibson
Sanjeev Braich

Finance
Andrew Smith
Ellie Barry

Rights
Kate Hibbert

Audio
Dominic Gribben
Alana Gaglio
Liam Wheatley
Suhaiyla Hippolyte